"Love never fails!"
1 Cor 13:8

A SACRED
SILENCE

A SACRED
SILENCE

A NOVEL

ASHLEE S. KINSEL

Deep River
BOOKS

A Sacred Silence
© 2016 by Ashlee Kinsel

Published by Deep River Books
Sisters, Oregon
www.deepriverbooks.com

ISBN: 9781940269801
Library of Congress: 2016931979

Printed in the USA

Cover design by Robin Black, Inspirio Design

This book is dedicated to
my Heavenly Father
whose creativity, passion, and extravagant love gave me the heart
to courageously write this story.

ACKNOWLEDGMENTS

THERE IS NEVER "ONE" PERSON behind any achievement, but rather a team of many who encourage and support. This book is a reflection of the "team of many" who cheered me on, prayed for me, and read and reread the manuscript for *A Sacred Silence.*

I am deeply grateful to Deep River Books for giving me the opportunity to publish and to work with such a great team of designers, editors, and professionals.

Also my gratitude to Barbara Scott, my editor, who reined me in more than once and helped me continually refine and stretch the heart of this story. Thank you, Barbara, for your wisdom and patience.

And to my community of "many," thank you! I am touched by your steadfast friendship and support.

Finally, with great love and thanks to my family: Garrison, Georgia, and Richard, our three amazing and inspiring children who have always cheered me on, and to my husband, Karl, who years ago said "yes" to my dream of writing. I love you all very much.

CHAPTER ONE

SAN ANTONIO, TEXAS

February
1964

"SWING ME HIGHER, DADDY!" Eliza's voice cut through the crisp, winter day. "I wanna touch the clouds." She stretched her feet as the swing lifted her higher and her cotton dress flew up toward her face briefly covering her eyes.

"My tummy is giggling, Daddy! My tummy likes it." She could feel the strength of her father's hands pushing against her small frame, and her heart begged for more.

"Daddy, are you having fun? As much fun as me?" She waited for his response, her heart fluttering in her stomach. She could no longer feel his hands on her back, and the swing began to slow. Worried, she kicked her legs to try to touch the ground.

"More, Daddy. It's too slow. I need a push." With every second of silence, panic and confusion began to fill her chest. She strained to turn her head and see his tall figure behind her, but her eyes blurred the objects around her instead.

The sky above her suddenly turned gray and the clouds obscured the park. She opened her mouth to cry out, but she couldn't make a sound. No longer protected by her father's presence, she was forsaken, alone, terrified. She clung to the cold chains holding the swing, her eyes frantic and her pulse racing.

"Daddy!!!!"

The sound of her own voice startled her from her sleep, and she sat up abruptly in the chair. Looking around, she recognized the familiar layout of her mother's home, but she was still groggy and stunned. She reached across the arm of the chair and touched the soft hand of her mother, who rested beside her peacefully in the matching chintz recliner.

"I must have dozed off. What time is it?" she said to herself as she searched the side table for the clock. The face read 4:00. She slumped back not wanting to disturb her mother, but still undone by the hauntingly real nightmare. She put her hand to her chest to calm her heart and reassure herself.

Gently, she slipped out of her chair and walked toward the glass doors framing the backyard. The afternoon had brought in rain clouds and small droplets clung to the windows. She rubbed her eyes and tried to study the landscape before her, but the dream was all too real.

Why would I dream about him now?

The last memory she had of her father was their trip to the park by the springs, his hands pushing her ever so gently, yet firmly, as happiness filled her. After that he was gone. She labored now to picture his face as she stood facing the oak trees in her mother's backyard. Her mind only brought him up in a blur.

"Eliza."

She quickly turned and smoothed her hair before answering. Leaning over the arm of the chair, she took her mother's hand and bent down until their eyes met.

"Yes, Mama. I'm right here."

"Can you get me some water? My throat is so dry."

"Yes." Eliza lifted the water glass off the side table and bent the straw toward her mother's mouth. Ever so slowly, her mother parted her lips to let the cool water quell the continual dryness in her throat.

"Thank you, darling. It tastes so good."

Eliza smiled. Although cancer had robbed her mother of her natural beauty in the last several months, Eliza could still see the same determination and strength in her face.

"You look worried. I can see it in your eyes." Her mother's statement penetrated the uneasiness she was working to hide since her dream.

"I must have fallen asleep for a bit and had a strange dream, that's all."

"About what?" Hope struggled to adjust herself in the chair while waiting for Eliza to respond.

"It's nothing, Mama. Really. How are you feeling?"

"I know you and I know that look on your face. I may be sick, but I am still your mother and I still care when I see that concerned frown on your face."

Eliza smiled and conceded to her plea. "I dreamed about Dad. He was pushing me on the swings, and then all of a sudden he vanished. I was left at the park, terrified. I woke up shouting his name. It's a little creepy, that's all."

"I'm sorry. That is disturbing."

"I am just not sure why I would dream about him now, after all these years."

"Well," her mother's voice was tender and cautious, "I don't want to tear at old wounds that have long been buried, but I'm sure my being sick has a lot to do with it."

Eliza nodded her head.

"You realize, Eliza, his leaving us had nothing to do with you, but at five years old I'm sure it didn't seem that way to you. He just didn't like being tied down and he didn't like the demands. Your father wanted the world to be swept up in his dream and it just wasn't possible with a wife and child."

She reached for Eliza's hand. "He was at war within himself."

As her mother's words settled around her, she said, "In my head I know that, Mama. I guess my heart still doesn't understand. I'm probably just tired that's all. I'll be fine. Let me get your wrap and help you put your feet up."

Eliza tucked the edges of the wool shawl around her mother and lifted her legs to stretch them out on the ottoman.

The doorbell rang and Eliza rose. Her mother touched her arm before she walked away. "Promise me you will say all you need to say to me. Don't let my frailty stop you from being truthful with me. I need to know you've said all you want to say."

"I will, I promise."

The night nurse arrived and Eliza knew Harold, her stepfather, would soon be home.

"Would you like to stay here tonight?" her mother asked.

"No, I'll go back to Grandmother's in a little bit. I'm sure Ada has something waiting for me."

"It seems like you would get lonely there, Eliza. The house is so big and empty. With Mother gone, I can't imagine it feels the same."

"It does to me. I feel safe there and I definitely don't get lonely. Ada is there just about every day, and Uncle Henry and Auntie Amelia next door are always checking in on me. Mama, I'm fine, really."

"You haven't had a break in caring for me for months. I'd like to see you do something with your friends. What about Claire and Tommy's wedding this Saturday evening? Are you planning to go?"

"I declined."

"Why? You need to get out from under taking care of me and go enjoy yourself."

"I just didn't feel up to it. Besides I'd rather be here with you."

Harold walked through the door and Eliza could hear him greet the nurse in the kitchen as she prepared her mother's dinner. His footsteps echoed off the wooden floors as he made his way toward the living room. Pulling off his doctor's coat, he laid it on the back of the sofa before greeting her mother.

"Darling," he whispered as he leaned in to kiss her cheek. Eliza watched as her mother reached to cradle his face with her weak hands and return his kiss. "How is everyone today?" he asked while reaching out to give Eliza a hug.

"Fine, sweetheart. Come sit with us. How was your day?"

"My day was the usual—lots of patients and not enough time. Eliza, Drew's dad was in today for his yearly checkup and asked how you and your mother were."

His words caught Eliza's interest, and she could feel the tiny tug in her heart.

"He said to tell you both hello and said they miss seeing you. I told him I'd be sure to give you the message." He loosened his tie, and Eliza adjusted her gaze to her skirt. She flattened the pleat with her fingers and pretended to pick lint threads off the fabric. She hoped her silence wouldn't give her away.

"Have you seen Drew lately, Eliza? You two were practically inseparable last summer," her mother gently asked as Harold pulled her closer and ran his fingers through her hair.

"Not really. He and I decided to cool things off when I made up my mind to return to Dallas last fall to pursue my master's degree. From what I hear he's doing quite well and building a pretty big name for himself in his legal firm."

"But why wouldn't you all connect since you've been home? You were only gone for four weeks when we discovered I had cancer and you came back." Her mother continued to press.

"I really haven't gotten out much. Besides, I didn't want to involve anyone else in all that we have going on. Do we really need to talk about this right now?" Eliza's voice was ribbed with irritation, and she knew it was time for her to go home. Bringing up Drew had only upset her. She could feel a wave of regret building in her thoughts. Gathering her things, she bade Harold and her mother good night.

As she walked out into the evening, the smell of the coming spring was unmistakable. The mountain laurels had already blossomed and their purple blooms draped the branches. She made her way to the Buick and started the car. She cranked the windows down allowing the brisk air to flood her face, her mind, and her heart.

Watching her mother deteriorate day after day had aged Eliza. She had abandoned her dream of obtaining a master's degree in journalism. It had been the right decision, but the days and nights had begun to wear on her. Sadness and heaviness seemed to be her constant companions.

Her grandmother's big, white house greeted her as she pulled in the driveway. She could see the light from the kitchen casting a glow from the sash windows. Walking to the door, her ears picked up the humming of Ada's melodic voice and her heart began to lift.

Pausing, Eliza looked up at the giant balcony surrounding the front of the house. Memories of tea parties and reading books on the porch swing with her grandmother flooded her thoughts. She would wait perched by the railing for her mother to come home at the end of the day. She'd tear down the stairs as her mother came through the back door. Now she walked alone through that same door. Only one familiar, sweet voice remained . . . Ada's. From the sidewalk she could feel the warmth of Ada's big, dark arms wrapping her up in a hug. As always, Ada was the anchor that Eliza clung to, and her loving words gave her the comfort she craved.

"Hi Suga'," Ada's deep, joyful voice greeted her as she came through the back door. "How's your mama doing?"

"She's trying to stay strong, but I can see her strength slipping away. She seems to sleep more, and I can tell it's getting harder for her to move around. I know she really hurts, too, but she doesn't want me to know. I'm stronger than she thinks, Ada."

Ada chuckled as she reached into the oven to pull out the roast. "That you is, Miss Eliza. That you is . . . strong much like your mama and your grandmamma."

CHAPTER TWO

DREW HILLSON PACED the floor of his office after spending an exasperating day with two stubborn and prideful clients. He adjusted his tie and sorted the papers scattered across his desk.

His latest case was exactly what he had dreamed about in law school, but, ironically, it seemed to be a growing storm with insurmountable difficulties. Who would have imagined two of San Antonio's most prominent oilmen fighting over drilling rights to an insignificant piece of property in east Texas that belonged to a crippled widow would cause such statewide attention. The opposing counsel was causing all kinds of trouble by dragging up past history that was bordering on slander and begging to start a fight to further his reputation as a "bulldog."

"Drew." The sound of his boss' voice jolted him from his frustration, and he turned to see him standing in the doorway. "I need the documents organized by the morning before we file. I want the notes from today typed and numbered so we can reference our position and put the squeeze on Seymour. He's making a mockery of all of this and he's gonna get trampled if he's not careful."

"Yes, sir. I'll get on it right now and see you in the morning at eight o'clock sharp."

"Attaboy," John Peters replied as he slapped the doorframe. "Don't let Seymour rattle you. He's just strutting his stuff. We'll have this thing shut down by the end of the week."

"I don't doubt it, sir."

"The Hunt brothers like you. I can tell. At the pace you're going, you'll move up faster than anybody this firm has ever hired."

"I appreciate the confidence, sir."

"Good night and make sure you lock up when you leave."

"Will do. Good night."

Drew reviewed the monumental task set before him and remembered Tommy's bachelor party coming up at the end of the week. He had promised to help organize the festivities along with Mitch. He decided to plow through the paperwork and skip dinner with the wedding party tonight. There would be plenty of time to celebrate later in the week, especially if they could nail this pest of an attorney running up legal bills and digging up mud.

After an hour of sorting, typing, and recording, an incoming phone call jerked him from his focus.

"Hello, Drew Hillson here."

"Drew, it's Becky. Are you going to the dinner tonight? I was hoping I could get a ride with you."

"I think I'm gonna have to miss. I'm overloaded with a big case right now, and my boss is expecting me to be ready to file in the morning."

"Such a shame. We were all looking forward to being together to kick off the big week." Becky's voice was like honey over the phone, and Drew smiled at her innocent, yet targeted, request.

"I know. I'm sorry. I was hoping to be there as well. I'll make it up to everyone . . . I promise."

"You'll be missed," she responded. Hearing her voice tempted Drew to leave his office and join the dinner party.

He smiled to himself at her genuine reply. She was sweet, confident, and alluring, but as much as he was around her, he still held back. It was an invisible wall he couldn't quite touch or understand, although he felt it often in her presence.

"I'll miss being there too. Tell everyone hello and to save some of the fun for me."

"Sure," she said, giggling.

"Night, Becky. I'll call you tomorrow. I want to know what I missed."

"Perfect. Talk to you soon. Bye."

He hung up the receiver and let his hand linger as well as his thoughts. She was all around perfect in every way but one . . . she wasn't Eliza. He wished Eliza would at least talk to him so he could get a gauge on her heart, but she had pretty much shut herself up taking care of her mother.

They hadn't talked in more than two months. He had called her when he heard the news about Hope. The cancer was fairly advanced and he had offered to help in whatever way he could, but the coolness in Eliza's voice led him to conclude she wasn't open to visiting with him.

His heart ached for her, and yet, she resisted him. He couldn't tell if she was angry, scared, or depressed. All he knew was that she had shut out most every one of their friends except for casual visits and occasional run-ins at the corner store. She was acting impossibly, he thought. But then who wouldn't? Losing her grandmother suddenly three years ago and now her mother—these were the two women who had raised her and esteemed her. They were all she had.

Eliza would be alone after Hope passed, and he wondered what she would do then or where she would be. Why couldn't she see that she needed him and her friends? Why was she making this harder by shutting out the support of their community?

He shook his head to free it of the disconcerting thoughts that only seemed to leave him more perplexed. He never believed in isolation. He always determined to lean on those you trust when you hit the bumpy roads. He didn't agree with the way Eliza was handling all of this, but who was he to judge?

The loud ring of the phone once again cut through the stale silence of his office.

"Drew Hillson."

"Drew, I need you to bring the files by my house when you finish tonight. I decided I want to get a jumpstart on the case before I walk into the office tomorrow. I have a feeling Seymour is going to call me first thing and try to catch me before I head to the courthouse. He'll want to negotiate, and I want to corner him quickly."

"Yes, Mr. Peters. I can have it there by 9:00. Will that work?"

"Perfect, I'll be waiting." The other end of the phone went dead, and Drew began to work expeditiously to make the nine o'clock deadline.

As soon as the clock hit 8:45, he gathered the files into his briefcase, reached for his jacket, and headed out the door. The parking lot was still and his new, red Chevy pickup was the only vehicle remaining. He climbed in and started the engine. He turned north on McCullough Street and headed for John Peters' home in Monte Vista where generations of wealthy oilmen, big brand cattlemen, and astute bankers lived among its tree-lined avenues.

The dark streets made the names difficult to read, but Drew found King's Highway and took a left. He was all too familiar with this particular street. Eliza had lived here with her grandmother and mother in the "big, white house" (as so many fondly called it).

He could see its silhouette in the night sky as he parked his truck directly across the street in front of Mr. Peters' home. The Peters were Eliza's neighbors and social friends with her family.

Drew removed the key from his truck and stepped out onto the pavement with the files tucked under his arm. Standing in the dark, he turned to look at Eliza's house. The lights were on and he could see through to the living room and inside the kitchen. Peering toward the upper balcony, he could make out the porch swing. Suddenly, his eyes stopped on the form nestled in the middle of the swing. He knew it was Eliza. She was the only one living there now, and he was sure Ada had already caught the 6:30 bus home.

He wondered if he should call out or walk over and knock on the front door. It was dark, and his new truck was not familiar to her so he was certain she hadn't recognized him. Before he could make up his mind, he saw her rise and go inside. One by one he watched the downstairs' lights go dark, and he knew there was no chance of talking with her tonight.

Disappointed, he remained frozen. Why did he care so much about someone who had made it seemingly impossible for him to help? Passing the bar paled in comparison to figuring out Eliza Cullen.

CHAPTER THREE

ELIZA COLLECTED HER PURSE and books before heading over to her mother's house. It was already Thursday morning, and Claire had called her last night begging her to reconsider and come to her wedding on Saturday. It would be a shame for Eliza not to be there as she and Claire had been friends since the eighth grade.

However, she felt uneasy about leaving her mother while she attended a social function, even if it was Claire's wedding. Eliza could tell the end of Hope's time on earth was drawing near. Her mother's conversations were more labored, and her stamina was all but gone. Harold seemed anxious too. He came home earlier each day and had canceled all his appointments on Friday. He wanted to soak in as much time as possible before she passed.

"Good morning," the familiar voice of her godfather called through the back door. Eliza recognized Henry's voice and walked toward the kitchen to answer him.

"Hi, Uncle Henry, come on in. I'm here."

"Eliza," he said as he hugged her and gave her a kiss on the cheek. "I wanted to catch you before you left. Amelia made pancakes. Will you come eat with us?"

Looking at the clock, Eliza paused before answering, "Harold is still at home with mother so, yes. Pancakes sounds delicious, thank you."

They walked out the screen door and crossed the drive to Henry and Amelia's house next door. The smell of maple syrup already greeted them as they walked up the stairs.

"Sweet girl." Amelia placed the tray of bacon on the table and hurried to hug Eliza. "You look as beautiful as ever, always . . . just like your grandmother. You have her hair color too. How's your mother? Henry and I were thinking of coming by today if you think that would be all right?"

"She'd like that. I can tell she's fading." Eliza's eyes pooled with tears and she clenched her teeth, straining to hold back the wave of grief that rose on the inside.

"My goodness, you have been so strong for her . . . for all of us." Amelia reached to wipe away Eliza's tears. "My sweet girl, come and let's sit together."

Henry held out a chair for Eliza, and they gathered around the kitchen table. Amelia served the pancakes with bacon while Henry poured the orange juice and coffee.

"I want you to come to Claire and Tommy's wedding with us this weekend," Henry spoke over his coffee mug. "And before you answer, please hear me out.

"You've been with your mother almost every day these last several months and honored her and loved her, but she doesn't want you locked away, distressed, and alone because of her. She's concerned you've forgotten how to live."

Eliza's eyes darted back and forth between Henry and Amelia, hoping one of them would cave and give her a way out. Both held their ground firmly, but compassionately, and continued to push her to go with them on Saturday.

"I don't have anything to wear," she said, pleased with her legitimate reason and hopeful it would dissuade them.

"I've already taken care of that. Karen at Julian Gold's is sending over several dresses for you to try. Your mother is insistent you go." Amelia smiled and reached to touch Eliza's arm. "She loves you and thinks this would be good for you. Please go."

"It doesn't seem like there's a way to get out of this, so I guess I'll go, but I don't think I'll be up for attending the reception." Eliza could feel the desperation of wanting to run well up inside her. How could she celebrate when her mother was slipping away? What were they all thinking?

"I agree, let's just plan on going to the wedding. Thank you for hearing us. When Harold called last night, he said your mother kept bringing it up and he was beginning to get worried. It's important to her that she sees you learning how to live again." Henry cleared his throat when he finished. "I promised her we would take care of you now and always."

Eliza managed a smile as she could hear the concern and sincerity in Henry's voice. They meant well and she knew their hearts were in the right place, but she still would rather not go.

Mustering a response, she said, "I guess I didn't realize how much time has gone by since I saw my friends. Most of the time it seems hard to relate to any of them, and I don't want people to feel sorry for me. I see it in their eyes—the looks of pity."

"They want to support you. As young as you and many of your friends are, they've not had to go through the difficulty you're going through now. They may not know the right things to say, but I think their hearts mean well. You are much loved, my dear. So why don't you let this community surround you."

Eliza nodded, appreciating the loving nudge from Henry and Amelia. She didn't want to burden her friends with her dreary circumstances and keeping herself apart had seemed like the easiest way to protect her friendships. It would be hard to celebrate with others when she was losing so much, but she was willing to give it a try—if that's what her mother wanted.

She arrived at her mother's just as Harold was slipping off to work. He had meticulously lined up Hope's medications as he had done every day since the battle with cancer began. Eliza admired his courage. She couldn't imagine finally finding the love of his life after all these years only to be married for three short years before cancer robbed them both of what they longed for—true love. It was cruel, and cancer had no respect for their dreams. It seemed to ravage all their lives, like a typhoon holding them hostage to its destruction.

She leaned against the counter, feeling the anger in her mounting. Where was God in all of this? Where was the God of love her grandmother had so often spoken of and relied on? The condolences, the casseroles, the visits all were thoughtful, but none of it healed her heart. She needed more. She had no idea where to find her answers, but she knew she needed more.

She rinsed her hands under the cold water in the sink and splashed her face before going to sit with her mother.

"Mama." She leaned in to kiss her on the forehead. "How was your night?"

"Restful, I think," her mother said, smiling wearily. "Yours?"

"Good, but my breakfast was more interesting. I ate with Uncle Henry and Auntie Amelia this morning, and they were gracious enough to ask me to go to Claire's wedding with them." Eliza could feel her mother's stare, and she paused before continuing. "So, I think I'll go. Just to the wedding, but only if that's all right with you?"

Her mother gave her a weak smile. "Yes, I'm so glad you're going. I want to see you happy. I want you to have fun, and Claire will be so honored you are there." She took a deep breath and seemed to rally the strength to continue.

"Don't be afraid for me. I'm not afraid to die. I've made my peace with God. I want you to promise me . . ." She reached for Eliza's hand and held it with all the strength she could gather; her hands were cold and delicate. "Promise me you won't live life the way I did. I spent too much time striving; it wore me out. Look at me now."

Eliza could barely hear her mother as she breathlessly formed each word, taking her time to enunciate each one. Eliza leaned in toward her mother's face, straining to catch all that she said. She knew her time was short, very short.

"You've been my light . . . all these years," she said with tenderness. "You kept me going, and you made me smile even when I wanted to weep. The gift of you was life for me. I don't want to leave this earth before giving you permission to love the gifts of life that you have been given."

Eliza watched as her mother slowly reached to try and fold the edges of the cream-colored wrap around her shoulders. She was struck by her mother's dry, brittle fingers, now sapped of any strength. The fingers that once stroked her hair, rubbed her arm, and held her face were now shriveled.

Her mother's voice was weak, and Eliza watched as damp tears slipped down her cheeks.

"Mama, rest. You're working too hard."

"Don't build walls like I did because I was too afraid. You can't save yourself. It doesn't work. I tried for so long and it makes for such a tough fight. I built walls to protect myself, but it just shut others out." Her voice rattled as she continued striving to finish.

"I couldn't accept that your father's leaving was his choice and it was not because I wasn't good enough. I put a lot of stress on myself trying to prove I was worthy." She licked her dry lips. Eliza rubbed ointment on them.

"Rest, Mama. You're wearing yourself out."

"Cancer has a way of putting your life into one, long scene. I see so much I could have done differently. I just didn't know how. I pushed my own mother away even though we lived in her home. I didn't want her advice or wisdom because I didn't think she understood loss."

"This is not the time to dig up regrets," Eliza said, hoping to ease her mother's anxiety and quiet her.

She could see her mother's chest struggling to rise as she formed the words on her lips. Every time Eliza thought she had finished speaking, her mother pushed to say more.

"My only regret is that I waited so long to trust love. Do you remember how my mother used to say 'that the one thing you can count on in life is change'? I wish I had learned sooner how to love and trust through the changes. I resisted and it created misery. She was right—change happens.

"Don't wait to learn how to love, Eliza. Trust more of God and less of yourself. He will take care of you. I never saw it until now. Though I am dying, I am finally living."

Her mother's eyes closed as she drifted off again. Her small frame relaxed into her bed, and Eliza sat staring at her features.

Still visible were the creases of strain and time, but beneath it all she was still the beauty she had always been. Eliza stroked her thin hair and listened to her soft breathing.

"I hear you," she whispered close to her mother's face, tears flowing down her cheeks.

CHAPTER FOUR

DREW ADJUSTED TOMMY'S TIE and gave him one last hug before he became a married man.

"Always thought you'd be heading down the aisle before me," Tommy joked. Drew smiled at Tommy and the nervous tone in his friend's voice.

"All in due time, my man. You're the forerunner. I'll learn from your mistakes." Drew chuckled and placed the boutonniere in the buttonhole on Tommy's lapel. The soft, cream-colored rose let out a sweet fragrance as he adjusted its stem and secured it. "Let's get you all pretty before you take that one last walk as a single man."

"You make it sound so final." Tommy tugged at his shirt sleeve to adjust it under his coat.

"It is."

"Tommy!" Cheers of excitement and chaos erupted as the rest of his groomsmen joined them in the vestibule. The photographer rushed in behind them and hurried to capture the moments of celebration and ribbing. After high fives and a few slugs in the arm, the photographer settled the party and convinced them to pose before the organ music began to play.

"Say good-bye to freedom," a deep voice heckled from the back row, instigating another roll of laughter.

"Only you would know," Tommy shouted back.

"It's time." the wedding planner said, rushing through the doors to adjust the groomsmen's collars and brush their coats. She gave them one last inspection before escorting them to the front of the church to usher in the guests.

"See you in the big moment, buddy," Drew said before walking toward the chapel entrance.

The doors opened and the organ music filled the church as the groomsmen graciously ushered guests to their seats. Drew walked down the side aisle after seating several friends of the bride. Peering toward the front, a figure in a green, silk dress caught his eye as she stood at the entrance and took Mitch's arm. Her physique was unmistakable, flawless. Her honey-brown hair was carefully styled in an elegant uplift. He felt his knees almost give way as his attention remained fixated on Eliza.

Even mixed among the many attendants, she still captured his heart. Her perfect, slim features seemed to glow in the light of the church's stained glass windows. He slowed his pace and watched as she and Mitch walked up the aisle. His eyes never left her. He could see her endearing smile as she looked up at Mitch after he seated her with Henry and Amelia. Even now as Drew stood in the back, her silhouette was illuminated and everyone else faded into the background.

The last few guests trickled in, and the groomsmen began to gather and line up in the foyer when Mitch found him.

"I just walked Eliza in. Thought you'd want to know." Mitch leaned in as he spoke to Drew.

Drew nodded. He reached up to loosen his collar.

"How'd she seem?" Drew was still in shock that Eliza had showed up tonight. This was the last place he expected to see her. He wanted to speak with her. He wanted to know how she was.

"Places everyone. Line up quietly." The wedding planner interrupted his thoughts, and he took his place between Tommy and Mitch.

"Show time, boys!" Tommy shouted from the back of the line.

One after the other the groomsmen walked to their places at the front of the church.

Drew's gaze was on Eliza. If there was a chance to penetrate the silence between them, he was ready to take it. He knew she had heard snippets about him and Becky. Becky had a tendency to exaggerate their relationship to most of their friends, and Drew wanted a chance to tell Eliza the truth. He still loved her. He still hoped that through all of this she would realize she loved him too.

As he stood at the front, he had a direct view of her sitting in the sixth row in shimmering emerald. The fitted bodice accented the slender shape of her body. The passion he held for her rose readily within him. He could see the way her lips formed whispers as she spoke to Henry next to her.

She lifted her chin and their eyes met.

He could see that stress had thinned her face, but the same glow and striking features were still there. The depth of her hazel eyes was still as intriguing and sensuous as ever. In one quick instant she still took his breath away, and it was all he could do to stop himself from walking straight to her. He refused to take his eyes off of her even when the trumpets blew, announcing the arrival of the bride.

He watched Eliza rise and stand as Claire made her way down the aisle on her father's arm. Oh, if she would just turn around and acknowledge him before being seated. Eliza's eyes followed Claire and her father down the aisle and to the altar. As the groomsmen began to shift their stance, Eliza's eyes locked with his once again.

He felt intensity building between them as, in a quick instance, they softly smiled at one another. The walls of isolation between them began to melt without a word spoken. He wanted to scoop her up and leave the church. He was desperate to hear all she had been going through and wanted her to know he hadn't given up on them.

He tapped his foot anxiously, wishing the ceremony would conclude so he could approach her. The sermon seemed endless, and he tightened his hands. Tension began to build inside of him, knowing he was going to walk down the aisle with Becky. What would Eliza think?

As the wedding party began to leave the church, dread overtook Drew's face as he hardened a smile and surrendered his arm to Becky before they walked down the aisle. Becky tucked her arm in his and her face seemed to warp into an exaggerated smile. When Drew peered down at her he realized his lenses for Becky had changed. She didn't look the same to him as she had.

He clenched his jaw as he felt Becky was working to make a spectacle of the two of them. It was the exact opposite message of what he wanted to send Eliza. Compelled to connect with her once more he tried to catch a glance from her, but Becky's endless chatter and tugging on him forced his eyes forward.

The guests filed out of the chapel behind him. The chatter of conversation flooded the church.

Eliza stopped and took a long look at the chapel and the people surrounding her. This was the church of her youth. Life-changing moments for so many took place here. Baptisms, burials, weddings. One day the community was celebrating, the next day mourning. *How quickly life changes.* She realized she would be back, too soon, to bury her mother.

"Ready?" Henry came alongside her, offering his arm. She nodded and fumbled with her stole as it slipped from her shoulders. She smoothed the bodice of her dress and reached for her clutch purse.

As they walked down the aisle, she could hear the wedding party outside lining up for pictures. Fear darkened her face. She didn't want to see Drew with Becky again. It pierced her and she couldn't handle another heartbreak even though she knew Becky was what Drew needed— someone who was invested in him, ready to dote on him, and build a life with him. She couldn't do that. Her life was stagnate right now, waiting on death to close yet another door and usher in another good-bye. Besides, she wasn't even sure if she would stay in San Antonio once her mother passed. Heading back to Dallas just might be the best remedy for her grief.

She had brushed Drew off soon after she had returned home, believing distance was the only coping mechanism she could rely on to keep her strong for the journey ahead—helping her mother die peacefully.

Don't wait to learn how to love. Her mother's words echoed in her mind as she walked down the aisle in silence. She wasn't sure if it was only "how" but also "when." She knew she loved Drew, but life always seemed to have other plans . . . changes. Changes that pushed them apart, and she was sure that after these past months of silence any hope of reuniting with him had been lost. He was moving on and she accepted it, even encouraged it the last time they talked in the fall. It was cruel to make any demands of him while she lived with such unpredictability. She didn't have the ability to love him in the way he deserved, and she had accepted that as painful and disheartening as the realization had been. It would be unfair to come back into Drew's life now when he had begged her not to shut him out.

Abruptly, Eliza cut to the corner of the stairs, telling Henry and Amelia she would meet them at the car. She felt her way down the dark stairway and was ready to bolt toward the parking lot when she felt someone grab her arm. Stunned, she spun around to see Drew standing behind her.

"Where are you going? I've been waiting outside the church hoping to catch you. I wanted to say hello and see how your mother is doing?"

She tried to form words out of the bubbling of confusion inside her, but nothing seemed to come out.

"Most of all I want to know how *you* are doing?" Drew continued to probe.

Straightening her skirt, she managed to collect herself enough to respond. "I'm fine, thank you. I'm sorry. You startled me a little bit." She couldn't think of what else to say. She could smell the familiar scent of him and stared as the backlighting from the church chiseled out his profile and his six-foot frame.

"I guess so, the way you were about to tear down the stairs. Are you coming to the reception?"

"I think not. I'm heading home with Uncle Henry and Amelia."

"I was hoping we could visit. I haven't seen you in months."

"Tonight would be a tough time to catch up. There's so much going on. Aren't you supposed to be boarding the trolley for the reception?"

"I had to bring my own ride because Tommy left his suit at the house. Let me at least walk you to the car. I'm going that way."

He offered his arm and Eliza took it. His touch melted her heart and her whole body seemed to go weak. She resisted the urge to put her head against him where she could bask in his warmth and sturdiness. She felt the ache of her heart as she denied herself the pleasure of him.

Why had she been so insistent they keep their distance from one another? Fear. The walls. Just like her mother had warned her, the walls offered her protection and she was letting fear do all the talking.

"How is your mother?" Drew's rich, deep voice caught her attention.

"Doing as best as she can. She's really struggled this past week. I'm not sure how much longer she has."

"I'm so sorry. I always liked your mom. Can I help in any way?"

"There's really nothing anyone can do. I just take as much time as I can to be with her, except for tonight. She was pretty insistent that I come."

"I'm glad you did. You're still the prettiest girl I know."

Her face went crimson at his compliment, and she squeezed his arm not knowing what else to say.

"I'd like to come by and see her if you think that would be all right. Would you be comfortable with that?"

"Sure." Caught off guard, she wasn't certain what to say. "I just need to warn you, she doesn't look the same. She's not the woman you remember."

"What about you? May I come to visit with you too?"

"Drew . . . I don't want either of us to get the wrong idea. You've moved on, and I'm still dealing with a lot. The last thing I want is to hurt you again. You are finally happy. I saw the way Becky looked at you tonight. She's in love with you. It's obvious. I'm not willing to get between you."

Eliza could see Henry and Amelia talking with another couple while waiting by the car.

"I want to explain something about Becky. You don't . . ."

Eliza cut him off. "I've got to run. Thank you for walking me to the car. Tell Claire and Tommy congratulations. The best time to come by tomorrow is probably around 1:00." Eliza hurried her words and waved good-bye before getting into her godparents' car. She watched as Drew's head dropped, and he put his hands in his pockets. She followed his figure as he strode toward the other side of the parking lot in the dim light. She wasn't ready to hear about Becky, and she wasn't ready to offer more than a thank you and a hello even though every part of her wanted to linger in his presence.

Eliza shut the door, hoping Drew hadn't noticed her voice shaking. She was eager to get home. Even if the walls were supposed to be crumbling, her fear of what was behind them held her back. The thought of coming undone in front of him petrified her. It was much easier to live in denial that nothing existed between the two of them anymore. It was much easier to focus on leaving San Antonio after her mother passed. Staying here and watching her friends go on with their lives was going to be impossible, especially watching Drew and Becky, and knowing she had driven him straight into her arms.

Stay safe, she reminded herself.

CHAPTER FIVE

ANXIOUS TO GET TO HER MOTHER'S HOUSE, Eliza scurried out the back door, the early morning air stinging her eyes. Harold had called at sunrise and told her to come as quickly as she could. He had seen a shift in Hope's breathing in the night and knew it wouldn't be long.

"Mama, just wait for me," she whispered in the car as she sat impatiently at an intersection.

Finally, her mother's house came into view, and Eliza parked the car and grabbed her things. She had left home so fast she had forgotten to put up her hair. Now a wave of amber locks obstructed her view of the sidewalk. As she fussed with her hair, Harold caught a glimpse of her arrival and opened the door.

"She's still asleep. I'm not sure if or when she will wake up." He hugged her as she came across the threshold.

Without saying a word, Eliza moved toward the guestroom and saw Mama lying peacefully in her bed by the windows. Her hair was combed, and she was dressed in her favorite nightgown, the yellow silk one Eliza and her grandmother had bought for her on their trip to New York.

"I'm here, Mama. Harold called me this morning early, so I got here as fast as I could. You look pretty in your yellow gown. Grandmother would be so pleased to know you're wearing the gown she picked out for you at Bergdorf's."

She saw her mother's eyelids flutter as she continued to speak.

"Keep resting. I'm staying right here. Harold and I won't leave your side."

They stepped into the hallway to speak.

"She's slipping away." Eliza's voice trembled with emotion, and Harold reached out to hold her.

"I'm so sorry. I know how much you love her and how much she loves you."

"Is she hurting? I just don't want her to hurt."

"No, she's very comfortable. I've made sure she is. I doubt she'll wake up again."

"Can she hear us?"

"I believe she can. We need to encourage her now and reassure her that all is well."

"I think so too. I need to call Ada and Uncle Henry and Auntie Amelia. They'll want to be here."

"Yes, and let's ask Father Wilton to come as well and pray with us."

"She'd like that." Eliza stepped into the guest bathroom to pull herself together before making her phone calls, but her lip trembled as she faced the mirror. Flustered and weak, she slumped to the bathroom floor, and the flood she had held back came rushing forward like a geyser. Sobbing, she lost any restraint she had and her chest heaved with every breath. She felt as if her very life was being sucked out of her.

"Why are you doing this to me? Why are you taking her away from me when I need her? You have no right!" She yelled her assaults at God, demanding answers from Him but hearing nothing in return.

"I hate your silence. I hate that when I cry out, you don't answer! I hate being alone. I have no one after you take her. Who else do you want? Me? Fine, take me too. I'm too tired to fight." She crumpled on the bathroom floor and buried her head in the rug, grabbing its corners with her hands. "And I already shut the door on Drew, afraid you would take him too! What else do you want from me?!!!"

Her sobs came faster now, from a place she didn't recognize. She didn't care. She was no longer holding anything back. She lay breathless on the floor, empty. The room around her sounded like a vacuum in her head. She could feel her veins throbbing on the side of her head, and she labored to concentrate on her breathing to calm herself.

Be still and know that I am God.

From the void of silence, she heard the words in her heart and strangely they quieted her. Not sure if she remembered them from Sunday school, or if someone spoke them over her—to her—in this very moment.

"Be still and know that I am God." She repeated the words out loud to remember and felt a gentle wave of comfort wash over her.

Grabbing hold of the counter, she pulled herself up to stand in front of the mirror. She began to splash water on her cheeks. Waiting for the blotchiness to recede, she repeated what she had heard over and over, letting the words seep into her heart.

Be . . .

Be still . . .

Being still was the last thing she wanted to do. She wanted to run. She knew how to scurry and rush and care for others and move quickly from one project to the next, but she realized she didn't know how to be still . . . to just be. It terrified her.

"Be still, emotions, be still, heart," she practiced telling herself, wanting the words to work at piecing her back together. She wouldn't allow herself to face the others like this . . . so frail and undone.

The nurse's footsteps in the hallway turned her attention back to her mother. She pulled her hair up and wiped her face once more before leaving the bathroom. Looking behind her she felt someone was watching her, but a quick glance over her shoulder confirmed no one was there.

She walked into the kitchen and made phone calls to Ada, Henry, Amelia, and a few of her mother's close family friends to let them know she was nearing her time. Father Wilton said he would come by today to pray. Harold had already called his sons in Houston to encourage them to come tomorrow.

Shortly after lunch, the doorbell rang and she heard Harold open the door. She could hear men's voices and realized it must be Drew. She had almost forgotten he was coming. She met him before he and Harold reached the guest room.

"Hey," she smiled as he rounded the corner.

Without saying a word, Drew wrapped his arms around her, pulling her in as close to his chest as he could. As he held her, Eliza felt her body relax at his touch.

"You all visit and I'll sit with your mother," Harold offered as he patted Eliza on the back and walked down the hallway.

Drew kissed the top of her head and nestled his face in her hair.

"Before you say another word, I have some things I want to say. Can we go somewhere to talk?"

Eliza moved back from his embrace and led the way to the study on the other side of the house. Sitting across from her, Drew pulled his chair close so their knees touched. Holding her hands in his, he began to speak.

"I would be lying to you if I let you believe it has been easy for me to move on. I felt as if I betrayed you at a time when you needed me the most. But you didn't want me here. You haven't wanted me around. I respect that and the last thing I want to be is a needy guy. That's never been me. And regardless of what you think, I'm not here to do that. I'm not here to ask you to reconsider and let me in. I'm here as a friend who cares deeply and who is brave enough to tell you that you can't do this alone. You can't keep isolating yourself.

"Eliza, you need your friends around you. You need more support than Ada and Henry and Amelia. People want to help. You've always been the first one to help others, to make a caring phone call, to gather friends together to support each other. We all want to be that for you now. You've changed, shutting us all out, and it isn't working no matter what you are telling yourself.

"People deal with tragedy and death all the time. You can choose to do it alone and afraid, or you can let people in to help. You can't control what's happening, but what you can control is what you choose to believe about what is happening and how you deal with it.

"I remember when Tommy's brother died in high school in a car accident and our church youth leader gathered me and Mitch and Tommy. He told Tommy that darkness festered in isolation and that we were to sharpen one another as iron sharpens iron. We made a pact with Tommy that from that day forward we would carry the light for him when he couldn't do it for himself. It was hard that first year, but Tommy persevered and we all were better for it."

Drew's words rang sharply in her ears, and she felt her heart turn. Tears filled her eyes, and she couldn't stop them from coming. She just let them fall, dampening her cheeks and her navy sweater.

"I guess I just don't know how. It's not that I want to be alone. It's . . . it's sometimes hard to know how to ask for help."

"I know, but picking up the phone and talking to those you trust could be a start. And it doesn't have to be me. Catherine, your best friend since as long as I can remember, has been so concerned about you, but you won't even allow her to come be with you."

The concern in his eyes made all he said real to her.

"You just don't understand," she managed, hoping another rush of sobs wouldn't erupt.

"You're wrong about that. We all understand more than you know. Pain makes people do funny things, Eliza. Don't let it take you prisoner and lie to you that nobody cares or can't help."

Drew's honesty stung. She knew what he was saying was right. Her heart agreed with each appeal of compassion. Only her mind still tried to blot out the truth and justify her brushing off her friends and him.

"Will you let me be your friend and help?"

Biting her lip, she replied softly, "You make a pretty good case." She leaned in and gave him a hug.

"By the way, I want to clear up anything you may have heard about Becky and me. It's not serious. She is fun to go out with and a nice distraction, but we aren't serious."

"As long as she's good to you that's all that matters. You deserve to be with someone who is as generous with her heart as you are with yours." Before she realized it, Eliza reached up to touch his face and felt the intensity of her feelings for him rise to the surface.

Drew reached up and caught her hand before she could pull it back. Ever so gently he kissed her palm and closed his eyes. She savored the feel of his lips, and she yearned to kiss his face, to fold back time and start again, but time was unyielding in its constant march forward.

His eyes reached for her, and she could feel the pull of his affection. "I'd like to stay and help if you'll let me."

Eliza nodded, the desire for him glistening in her hazel eyes. "Your honesty today has helped so much already." She paused before continuing, caught off guard by the swirl of emotions inside her. "Can I ask you something?"

"Anything."

"Earlier today when I got here I just broke down in the bathroom. I'm so angry. Angry toward God and what I feel He is taking from me. I don't even know where all that anger came from, and I didn't even know it was growing inside me. I'm embarrassed to say this, but I yelled and fought and challenged Him. I couldn't hold it back. I kind of scared myself. It was like listening to another person almost. Is that normal? Am I going crazy?"

Drew eased her tension with his understanding grin, the dimples in his cheeks highlighting his already handsome, well-defined face. "No, you're not crazy. I would guess that's pretty normal for what you're going through. You can't expect to handle this logically because none of it makes sense. It's one day at a time. Everybody wrestles with the man upstairs one time or another." The reassurance in his voice comforted her. "But I do believe this: keep asking the questions. You'll get your answers sooner or later."

She closed her eyes and smiled, grateful that his words affirmed in her heart that she was right where she needed to be and she was all that she could be in this moment.

The voices from the living room trickled down the hall, and Eliza felt pressed to join them even though she wished this time with Drew could last a few moments longer. He'd challenged her today in a much-needed way, and his honesty carved out a new path for her. She could feel her countenance lighten even though the days of sorrow hadn't lifted. She felt something that she'd long become accustomed to living without—hope. It was as if a tiny flame had been lit inside her, beckoning her forward.

CHAPTER SIX

THE SETTING SUN CAST LONG SHADOWS through the leaves of the oak trees that lined Harold and her mother's backyard. Eliza stood on the edge of the patio, leaning against the wooden railing. She watched as a cardinal bumped the glass of the bird feeder, urgently searching for more seeds. His bright red contrasted against a dark-green backdrop. She could hear the neighbors' children playing on the metal swing set in the yard caddy-corner to her mother's house.

Strange how life carries on, seemingly oblivious to the life that is ending behind me. Her thought left a harsh sting.

Most everyone had already gone home now except Henry, Amelia, and Ada. Sadly, Drew's urgent court case had caused him to leave to prepare for a morning deposition. She missed him more than she realized. It was so natural having him at her side this afternoon. His constant adoration and care, checking on her as they both moved in and out of the small crowd of longtime family friends. The house just felt warmer knowing he was there.

"Are you up for some company?" Henry asked as he opened the sliding glass doors.

"How's she doing?" Eliza turned and gestured for Henry to stand beside her.

He leaned over the railing next to her and clasped his hands. "I'm afraid it won't be long. Harold is with her now taking her vitals and overseeing the medications before the night nurse arrives. He's held up well having to be doctor and husband. It can't be easy."

"He's loved her the whole way through."

"As have you," Henry added to the delicacy of the moment.

"Yes, but his love is different. It's the vulnerable, risk-taking love that says I'm yours no matter what, no matter where, no matter how . . . I'm yours."

"That it is."

"How do you know?" Eliza turned to face Henry.

"What do you mean?"

"How do you know the person you think you might love is truly the person you're willing to love for the rest of your life?"

"I think you may have already answered your own question."

"How?" Eliza wasn't following him.

"Willing to love. You said it. Are you willing to love another, because it will be a choice you will make every single day? Yes, love is a feeling, but most importantly, love is a choice. You can take care of it and see that it grows, or you can let it stagnate, wither, and die."

"It sounds like work more than just a feeling."

"It is," he answered. "And it will be the most important work you will do while you live here on this earth—to love and to love well, especially the one you choose to marry."

"How did you figure all this out, Uncle Henry? How did you know?"

Henry sighed as he stepped back from the railing, the sting in his eyes evidence that tears were forming. He cleared his throat.

"Well, from the past—a place I haven't visited in a long time."

Eliza watched as he combed his graying black hair with his fingers and took a deep breath.

"I had the privilege at a young age," he began, trying to steady his voice, "of watching two people I loved very much learn to love each other well despite all they had to go through to be together and all they had to overcome when they were forced apart." He tried to turn his face away from Eliza but she could see him biting his lip.

He pressed on. "I understood from that time forward that love was a gift that I have the privilege of giving to my wife every day and receiving from her. I vowed to live each day loving her well, and I can say love has never failed me. It challenges me, stretches me, but has never failed me."

"Who were they—the people you were talking about?" Eliza asked carefully, knowing his heart was tender.

He patted her hand upon the railing, taking his time to respond. "It's not my story to tell right now, but one day I'll share more."

The sliding door quietly opened behind them.

"Henry, Eliza, come inside." Amelia bid them in to the house, motioning with her hand. "She's nearing the end."

Eliza hurried past Amelia straight to her mother's bedside and knelt down. She pulled her mother's limp hand to her lips wanting to feel her warmth one last time.

"No regrets, Mama. No walls. You're free to go, to love."

She could feel Ada come up behind her to hold her. "That's my brave girl," she whispered in Eliza's ear. "Time to go home, Miss Hope. I got yo' baby girl and the Lord's coming for you."

"Hope, I love you and . . ." Harold's voice broke as he struggled to finish and reached to kiss her on her forehead, "Thank you for marrying me. I'll see you soon, my darling."

Amelia reached to touch Hope's arm. "We love you, Hope. We'll take good care of Eliza. Be at peace now."

They stood vigil over her as her breathing slowed and finally stopped. Eliza could feel the warmth recede from her mother's hand and watched as her mouth remained frozen with her cracked lips slightly parted. Eliza stood up and held onto Ada. Ada's thick arms were strong enough for the both of them, and she smoothed Eliza's hair while she softly cried.

"Just let it out, baby girl. You ain't got to hold nothin' back. Ada's right here wit ya."

Henry handed Ada his handkerchief, and she cradled Eliza's face in her dark, protective hands and wiped her tears. "Let's get you home. You gotta get some rest now, Suga'."

"I think that's a good idea," Harold added, his face grim with pain. "We've all had a long day."

Picking her head up, Eliza said, "We need to call the funeral home first. They'll need to come pick her up. I'd rather wait until she has left first before I go."

"They're on the way now. I called them an hour ago, knowing she only had moments left," Harold said.

"Thank you." Eliza approached her mother one last time and touched her face.

"I'll see you again, Mama. In the meantime, tell Grandmother 'hi' for me."

"They're here," the nurse said as she ushered in the attendants from the funeral home.

Eliza stepped back, giving them space to prepare her mother's body. The room was heavy and silent. She watched as they carefully placed her mother's body in the black bag before moving her to the stretcher. The room was still as they wheeled her down the hallway.

Eliza's eyes followed them while the wheels rolled across the hardwood floor. Carefully, she saw them make the corner toward the front door and she sank onto the chair by the now empty bed.

"Ada, Eliza, let us give you a ride home. I want to make sure you get home safe and we can easily come back for your car in the morning," Henry said as he stood next to Eliza. He reached down to lay his hand on her back.

"That's a good thing. I'll stay wit Liza tonight so she not alone," Ada added as she reached for Eliza's hand.

Nodding, Eliza rose to her feet and walked over to Harold.

"Good night, Harold. Please get some rest. We'll need our strength." Eliza leaned up to kiss him on the cheek, his eyes sagging with the weight of despair. The heaviness was thick throughout the house, and Eliza needed fresh air. She was ready to be alone, ready to crawl into the sheets of her bed and sleep. It was 10:30 p.m. by the time she and Ada bid Henry and Amelia good night at the big, white house.

"You go on up and I'll clean up down here. Get you a hot soak in the tub."

"Thanks, Ada. Good night."

The long stairway seemed endless to Eliza as she dragged her feet up one step at a time. The exhaustion had finally hit her. The night made everything seem so final as she stared out the balcony window. A few stars dotted the night sky, and she could make out a sliver of the moon. The silence she once relished now felt like a cold, nameless echo. She thought about calling Drew to let him know her mother had passed, and mainly just to hear his voice, but it was too late. She decided against disturbing him, remembering he had a big day at his law office tomorrow.

She traced the words he said to her earlier one by one in her mind. The sincerity and depth of his voice remained fresh in her heart. It wasn't hard to choose to love him. She wanted to take it all—every generous, passionate piece of it, but something hidden inside her held her back. How was it possible to give love, but not be able to receive love? She let the question drift in and out of her thoughts, too tired to push herself to figure out the answer.

"What you still doin' standin' here. Thought you'd be in the bed by now," Ada said as she labored up the stairs, grabbing hold of the railing and pulling herself toward the top. "You gonna wear out. Nothin' gets solved in the late of the night, I can promise you that."

"Just lots to think about. That's all."

"Suga' you's got to get still and that don't mean stand still, it mean be still . . . in yo heart and yo mind."

Eliza whirled around at Ada's words, the same words she had heard earlier from somewhere outside herself.

"How did you know?"

"What you mean how do I know? The good Lord tell us to be still and know that He is God. How else can He take care of us if we buzzin' 'round and lettin' our minds do cartwheels all the time? You can't hear Him that way."

"I meant how did you know I heard that same thing earlier when I was at Mama's house? I went into the bathroom and had a complete meltdown, yelling and screaming at God. It was awful. I've never been like that before and then out of nowhere I heard, *Be still and know that I am God.*"

Ada chuckled. "That sound like the Lord all right. He done comfirmin' in yo heart what he tryin' to tell you. When he speaks twice, you best listen. He wantin' to help you, baby girl."

"I guess so. I'm just not sure what He's trying to say."

"I think you best start with 'Be Still.' Now get into bed and shut those eyes. Tomorrow don't wait. It shows up on time, every time."

"Love you."

"I love you too, suga'. See you in the mornin'." Ada smiled as she walked down the hall.

Eliza stood by her bedroom window and listened as Ada sang from down the hall, her soft, low melody filling the silence. Eliza shuddered at the stillness and wrapped her arms around herself.

CHAPTER SEVEN

DREW STRAIGHTENED HIS NECKTIE in the mirror and tugged at his navy coat. He was planning to leave the office by noon to get to the funeral. The week had been full of depositions, meetings, and overtime. He hadn't seen Eliza since Sunday and wasn't able to reach her by phone. He had left word with Ada that he was tied up at the office but was planning to be there Thursday. It felt like a cheap excuse after his big speech about letting people in to help. He hoped his words hadn't grown cold in her mind.

He sighed as he tugged at the black tie again, frustrated with the twisted notch at the top. Ripping it off he started again realizing it was almost 8:00 and his first meeting started at 8:30. His fingers fumbled, but finally he was able to get it straight. Rushing to grab his briefcase, the phone rang.

"Hello."

"Drew?"

"Yes . . . oh . . . hey, Becky." Irritation laced his greeting.

"Hi. I hadn't heard from you all week and I started to get worried. Where have you been?"

"I'm slammed at work, and I just haven't had a chance to call. Listen, I'm running out the door for a meeting right now as a matter of fact."

She cut him off before he could finish. "How about dinner later? It's Thursday. Certainly you could get a break by now?"

"Not tonight. I'm going to a funeral this afternoon, and I'm not sure about where I'll be afterward."

"You mean Eliza's mother's service?"

"Yes."

"I thought you hadn't even spoken to Eliza since last fall?"

Drew picked up on the jealous tone in Becky's voice and knew whatever he said it wasn't going to go over well. He didn't have time to get into any explanations with her so he scrambled to end the conversation. "Can I call you later? I can't be late today."

"Fine. Good-bye, Drew."

The line went silent before he could answer, and he could feel the ice building between the two of them. At one time she was the sweet distraction he needed, but now her edgy tone all but extinguished his interest. Perturbed he grabbed his briefcase and headed out the door.

In haste Drew parked his truck outside the church and hurried to the entrance as he could hear the organ music playing. His left pants' cuff hung on his leg, and he reached to pull it down almost tripping over the curb. He planned to get here earlier to check on Eliza, but his meeting with the Hunt brothers ran late and his boss was determined to tidy up the paperwork before they both left for the day.

He thought of Eliza and how poised she had been through all of this. Even in sorrow she still had that youthful grace about her he had always loved, the way she held her head with a slight tilt to the right and her back straight, elongating her frame.

Drew slipped in next to Mitch and Jeff who had saved him a seat in the back.

"Thanks," Drew whispered as he sat down.

"No problem." Mitch handed him a program.

"Have you talked to Eliza? How is she?"

Mitch bent closer toward Drew, trying not to disturb the people around him. "I went by last night, and she seemed to be holding up well. Catherine was there along with some of our old high school group. She looked better than I'd see her in a while . . . almost like her old self. I think she was glad we were there."

"Glad to hear it. Work has been a real beast this week, and I haven't gotten by since Sunday."

Eliza's black-wool dress hugged her slender body. She adjusted the magenta American Beauty rose pinned to her dress she had picked from her grandmother's garden that morning. She touched the strand of pearls belonging to her mother draped around her neck. Both were sweet reminders of the two women who had raised her and loved her so dearly.

Standing at the parlor window, she could see friends and acquaintances filing into the church to pay their respects. She fondled the plain, vanilla paper of the memory card, feeling its thickness between her fingers and read the calligraphy across the front once more: Hope Barksdale Cullen Gates 1910-1964.

Her eyes swam with tears. *Mama, no regrets. You're at peace now.*

"You 'bout ready now, Miss Liza? It's time." Ada's husband Theo's thick, heavy voice spoke from behind her as he carefully put his hand on her shoulder. Eliza turned to meet his dark, umber eyes moist with tears. As large as he was, his heart was even bigger. "We all gotta line up now."

She took his arm and walked toward the others.

"Let's get you a hanky, baby girl." Ada gestured as she approached Eliza and began to dab at her cheeks. She, too, wore a soft pink rose from the garden on her dress as a tribute to Dusky, her grandmother, the matriarch they all so dearly missed and the woman who blessed the generations that followed her. Eliza tried to find solace in knowing her mother and grandmother were together now, but the sting of loss was still too raw.

One last time they all held hands and prayed before entering the church, Eliza in front with Harold, then Henry and Amelia, Ada, Theo, and Harold's two sons. The smell of hydrangeas and fragrant lilies, all Hope's favorites, filled the church as they waited in the narthex.

Father Wilton's voice filled the church as he began to read the Scriptures. At the close of the last hymn, the crowd stood and moved slowly down the hallway toward the parlor, each guest waiting to give their condolences to the family. The crowd swelled and then filtered through the side entrance to the walkway. Outside the day was brilliant with the signs of spring pushing out the browns of winter.

Eliza lined up with Henry and Amelia, along with Harold and his sons, and greeted and thanked the many who came to offer their condolences. She noticed a group of her friends had gathered and were chatting by the finger sandwiches. She could see Drew's back as he talked with Catherine along with Mitch and several others.

Eliza was relieved the crowd was thinning and it would be time to go soon. The new heels she bought were squeezing her feet and she felt her arches cramping. Shifting from one leg to the next, she hoped no one would notice her unease.

"May I take the remaining flowers to the retirement home down the street, dear?" Ms. Gillian from the altar guild asked politely.

"Please. I'd hate to see them go to waste."

"They'll be much appreciated. Lovely service. Your mother was such a kind woman."

"Thank you."

"Eliza." Father Wilton walked up as he gave one last look around the room. "Please let us know what else we can do to help. I'd love to see you joining us regularly on Sundays. Mrs. Pimberly and Mrs. Funston are starting a Bible class on Sundays for some of our younger folks. Perhaps you'd like to join? I know they'd love to have you."

"Thank you for the invitation. I'll . . . I'll look into it," Eliza answered, hoping he couldn't pick up on the discomfort in her voice. Quickly, she shifted the topic. "I appreciate all you've done for my mother. Your kind words were very comforting today. You did a wonderful job."

"Well, that's what I'm here for . . . anytime."

"I appreciate it." She gave him a quick hug and began to walk over to Ada who was gathering their things. Suddenly, her heel caught on the carpet and she stopped to free her shoe by bracing herself against the stone column near the entrance of the parlor.

"Can I help?" She recognized his unmistakable voice, smooth and strong. Before she could turn to see his face she felt the familiar stirring in her heart.

"Thank you. Just in time." She smiled and held Drew's hand to steady herself as she slipped her foot back into her shoe. He placed his hand on the small of her back, and she could feel a rush of heat move through her body.

"Got it?" he asked with a tilt of his head. The light coming through the windows accentuated his strong features and the smile in his eyes.

"I think so."

"How was the burial this morning?"

"Tough . . . just so final. More difficult than I imagined, but grateful we buried her prior to this afternoon. I think it made the service more bearable."

"You 'bout ready to go, baby girl? Mr. Henry gonna drive us home," Ada said before she stopped to recognize Drew. "Mr. Drew, it's good to see you."

"Thank you. Good to see you too, Ada. I hear you've been taking good care of Eliza."

"Tryin'. She gotta get some rest. She been runnin' strong takin' care of her mama."

"I'm doing fine, Ada. I promise. There'll be plenty of time to rest." Eliza reached for Ada's hand and held it.

"Drew." Henry walked up and put out his hand to shake Drew's. "Good to see you. Thank you for coming. We're gathering at the house for ham and biscuits. We'd love it if you could join us?"

"Sure, that'd be nice. Eliza, can I give you a ride?"

Eliza hesitated and looked at Henry and Ada as if asking for permission.

"That'd be just fine, Mr. Drew. We got lots a platters an' such anyway. Doubt we'd all fit in Mr. Henry's car." Ada patted Eliza's arm. "We'll see ya'll at the house." She turned and wobbled her way toward the table in the back, her humming filling the empty spaces of the room.

Drew offered his arm to Eliza as they began to walk toward the parking lot.

"Hold on a minute." Eliza bent down and pulled off her shoes while hanging onto Drew. "Much better." The feel of the ground on her feet was soothing. She closed her eyes for an instant, allowing herself the pleasure of being on his arm with no restraints.

Drew chuckled. "Won't that rip your hose?"

"Probably, but I don't care. My feet have been screaming for the last hour. You have no idea how good this feels."

"Now that's the Eliza I remember . . . carefree, playful, and running around barefoot." He held open the door to his Chevy pickup, and Eliza climbed in.

"I like your new truck," she commented as he slid onto the seat next to her and behind the steering wheel. "When did you get it?"

"About a month ago."

"You've been saving up since high school."

"I know. It's exactly what I wanted." He turned the key and revved the engine. "Gotta love that sound."

Eliza couldn't help but laugh. She cupped her mouth as the sound of joy almost startled her. She couldn't remember the last time she heard herself laugh.

"What?" He laughed along with her. "What are you laughing at?"

"I don't know," she said, giggling. "It's so loud. I wasn't expecting that."

"Yep, that's what makes it so perfect."

"I'm sorry." Her face creased with laugh lines as she tried to stifle her giggles. "I think I'm delirious." She wiped her eyes and paused to catch a deep breath.

"It's good to see you laugh . . . even if it is about my engine." Drew shook his head and backed the truck out of its parking space.

They passed the familiar streets of the Laurel Heights neighborhood before entering Monte Vista. Eliza noticed the vibrant blooms on the bushes and the flowers peeking from the gardens. It was as if a veil had been lifted from her eyes. She was mesmerized at the signs of life popping up all over. If they had been there this morning, she hadn't noticed, but now, riding alongside Drew with bare feet, she saw them.

"You were really strong today," Drew offered as he glanced at her. Eliza's eyes were lit with a wonder that had been fogged over for the past several months. "I'm grateful to see life returning to you even though it's been a rough day."

He slowed the truck as they pulled up in front of her house, shut off the engine, and then walked around to open her door. She swung her legs over the seat and took his hand as he helped her out. Before they were able to walk on, Drew embraced her.

Eliza could hardly stand as the pull of her affections for him left her breathless. Caught off guard by her intensity, she closed her eyes and felt his body against hers. She could feel the pulse of electricity running through her, thawing out every cell within her, loosening every muscle. If not for the solid embrace of his arms, she was sure she would give way to the ground.

Tilting her chin up to his, she let the sincerity of his eyes linger in hers. With feather-like lips, he kissed her forehead and slowly took a step back. She felt like she was falling into him and hurried to balance herself on her tiptoes. He caught her with his hands as they slipped to her waist. Wishing to speak she tried to move her lips to form words, but they remained frozen, held captive by his presence. With a gentle move, he took her hand in his and walked her to the back door, while Eliza's head still reeled.

Ada was already in the kitchen preparing the ham and biscuits and setting the trays on the table in the garden room. The roses planted by her grandmother peered through the windows, showing off their palette of colors while the early evening light danced off the small fountain in the backyard as it splashed in the basin.

Eliza reached for a biscuit and walked with Drew onto the back porch. They sat together on the porch swing as they had done so many times before. Neither of them spoke. Eliza still wanted to savor the lingering touch of their embrace.

Finally, her voice broke the silence as she found the courage to speak. "I'm scared."

His face looked puzzled as he turned toward her.

"I'm scared I won't know how to go through life. I'm going to miss out on so much . . . so much I wanted to know, to learn. There are just a lot of questions I still want answered." She paused, letting her vulnerability ease its way to the surface.

Everyone always saw her as put together, focused, driven, but not anymore. She was done with the masks. If he wanted to love her and if she wanted to love him then her rawness needed to be uncovered.

"I'm not sure I understand," he said, stroking her arm.

"I didn't even have the chance to know who my family was—what they were like. I know it may sound silly, but the fact that the two women who came before me are silenced now is scary. It's like I'm facing life all alone."

"But you've got Ada and Henry and Amelia. Won't they be able to answer your questions?"

"Yes, and not really. It's not the same." Exasperated, she realized she wasn't making any sense and she so desperately wanted him to understand what she was trying to say. "It's hard to explain. It's things like, I don't even know who my dad was. Or how did my grandparents meet? How come my mom was an only child? It's questions you don't think about asking until everyone is gone. I think it's the silence that scares me the most. I'll never be able to hear my mother's voice again or my grandmother's. They were all I had."

"I'm so sorry. I wish there was a way I could help, especially with the fear. What can I do?" Drew rubbed Eliza's hand.

"I don't know. I think it's something I'll have to get used to. I have to learn how to live differently—without them." She turned to look at him, her eyes pleading for his encouragement and understanding.

He folded her in his arms. "If I know anything about you, Eliza, you'll find a way not only to live again, but to live well." He eased his face in front of hers.

She could feel his breath on her skin as he spoke. Watching his lips, she was more drawn to him now than ever. She could feel his restraint as he stopped himself from going any further. He was still the compassionate gentleman she remembered.

Softly she spoke as they remained face to face with only a sliver of air between them. "I have to believe you're right. How it will happen, I'm not sure."

Be still . . . Be still and know . . .

The faint whisper of the familiar words lingered in her ears once more.

And know . . . That's the part she needed to figure out.

CHAPTER EIGHT

THE LIGHT PEEKING THROUGH THE CURTAINS stirred Eliza from her deep sleep. Her eyes resisted opening, and her body ached. Slowly she stretched and stared at the ceiling. Laying her head back on the pillow, she remembered it was Monday and she had promised Harold she would come over to help go through a few of her mother's things.

The weekend had been a blur filled with visits from old friends and her first reluctant trip back to church. Catherine had convinced her to step back into life again amongst their community, but it almost made her feel weak. The best part of the whole day had been meeting Drew for lunch and having him help her at the house, sorting through legal papers she needed to get for Harold.

As she pulled back the covers and swung her legs over the bed, a familiar scent caught her attention. She smelled Ada's waffles and bacon drifting up the stairs. She smiled and began to get dressed.

Heading down the stairs, she greeted Ada with a hug.

"Good morning, Ada," she said as she breathed in the aromas of the kitchen. "Smells so good."

"Good mornin', Suga'. I figured you be needin' a good breakfast this mornin'. You get any sleep last night?"

"I did. In fact it was hard to get up this morning."

Eliza sat down with her plate and began to enjoy her breakfast when the phone rang. She and Ada exchanged glances, and Ada motioned for her to stay seated.

"Hello, Barksdale residence," she answered.

The voice on the other end responded coolly. "May I speak with Eliza Cullen, please?"

"May I tell her who's callin', please," Ada said in a protective tone.

"Yes, this is Allan Garrett calling."

Pausing, Ada slowly covered the mouthpiece of the phone and whispered to Eliza. "It's for you, a Mr. Allan Garrett?"

Puzzled, Eliza reached for the phone, ignoring the concerned look in Ada's eyes.

"This is Eliza," she said cautiously into the phone.

"Good morning, Eliza. My name is Allan Garrett. I am an attorney with Garrett, Smith, and Jones. I'd like to meet with you regarding some unfinished business with your grandmother, Mrs. Dusky Victoria Barksdale's estate."

Drawing a blank, Eliza scrambled to interpret what he was saying.

"I'm not sure I understand, Mr. Garrett. She died over three years ago, and I thought it had all been settled. I don't even remember your name or your company's name being involved," Eliza replied coldly into the phone.

"You are correct, Miss Cullen. Neither I nor my company was involved in that particular portion of her estate. I was, however, retained by your grandmother over fifty years ago, and I need to fulfill my end of the business arrangement she hired me to do. If you'd allow me to visit with you, I'd like to come by around 11:00 today. Will that work?"

"I guess that would be all right," she replied. "I'll look for you then. Do you know where the house is?"

"Yes, thank you. I'll see you promptly at 11:00." He hung up.

Confusion crossed her face as she placed the phone back into its cradle.

"What's wrong, baby girl?" Ada asked.

"I don't exactly know. This attorney claims he needs to meet with me regarding my grandmother and something she hired him to do. Do you know this man or why he would be coming to meet with me?"

"No." Ada stared out the kitchen window while wiping the counter with a dishrag. "I can't say I do, but I reckon yo grandmamma knew what she wuz doin' so don't be 'fraid. He's just a man an' he's just comin' to talk business."

Bewildered, Eliza finished her breakfast and decided to call Drew to find out what he knew about Mr. Allan Garrett. Surely, he would have some useful information.

"Drew Hillson, please."

He answered after the call was transferred. "This is Drew."

"Drew, it's me."

"Hey, how are you? I've been waiting to call this morning. I didn't want to wake you. Were you able to get some sleep?"

"I did, thanks. Something really strange has come up, and I need to ask you a question." Eliza spoke in a worried tone.

"Go ahead."

"Do you know a lawyer by the name of Allan Garrett with Garrett, Smith, and Jones?"

"Yeah. I mean I don't know him personally, but he's definitely one of the top dogs in the business. Why?"

"Well," she said, twisting the cord in her fingers, "he called this morning wanting to meet with me over an issue in my grandmother's estate. His timing couldn't be more terrible, but he says it can't wait."

"Do you need me to be there? I can get over there if you'd like. Or meet you later in the day?"

"I think I'd better meet with him alone. Maybe you could swing by after work?"

"Sure. I'll see you around 6:00. You sure you're all right?"

"I don't think I have a choice right now. I have to be. What more could there be?" Eliza rubbed her temples and traced the cracks in the wood floor with her eyes.

"Sure you don't want me there?"

"I want you here, but the way Mr. Garrett sounded he was pretty intimidating and serious."

"Then call me if you need to, I can be there pretty quick."

"Thanks. I'll fill you in tonight." Her hand lingered on the receiver grateful she could confide in him. Grateful the drama in her life hadn't completely shut him out, again.

She set out on a walk with curiosity and irritation swirling in her mind. Hoping she didn't run into anyone, she turned the corner that led down to San Pedro Springs. She dipped her toes in the cold water and watched as the water lapped over her feet. She picked up several rocks beside her and counted them in her hand. Five stones. A determination rose inside her as she was inspired to give each stone a name: fear, loneliness, isolation, regrets, grief.

One by one she tossed each rock into the water, calling out its name. She watched as they disappeared, sinking to the bottom. Turning, she picked up five more and rolled them in her hand. Naming each one, she tucked them into her pocket: hope, love, joy, trust, life.

"I'm keeping these. You can have the others." She looked at the sky to acknowledge God in the only way she knew how. Keeping her right hand in her pocket, touching the five, smooth stones, she walked back to the house.

"I'm back," she hollered to Ada as the screen door slammed behind her. She walked upstairs to change and placed the stones in a silver dish by her bed, naming each of them out loud again.

Before she knew it, the clock in the hallway struck 11:00, and she peered out the window anticipating her visitor.

Mr. Garrett arrived on time in a navy business suit complimented with a white shirt and yellow tie. She watched him make his way up the sidewalk. He was an older man, probably around seventy, with a kind face and glasses. His hair was graying, and his mannerisms revealed a man who had spent the better part of his life behind a desk. Eliza opened the door and asked him to come into the garden room and sit down.

He laid his briefcase on the table and began to speak with his hands folded.

"Miss Cullen, my sincere condolences, regarding the passing of your mother. I know the timing of all this seems confusing, but it is the way your grandmother Dusky wanted it and planned for it to be."

She continued to listen in bewilderment as he pressed on. Suddenly, realizing she must look skeptical, she softened her smile, encouraging him to continue.

"Your grandmother hired me roughly forty-five years ago. She had a private matter that she wanted to entrust only to one person, a stranger, someone outside the family and purely on a professional basis, so she hired me."

"Well, why didn't this come up then or before she died?" Eliza said. None of this made any sense.

"I understand your desire to have all these questions answered immediately and completely, but I must present this as your grandmother desired. Shall I continue?" He seemed genuine.

"Yes, go ahead. Please forgive me. I'm a little tired these days. It's been a long winter."

"Understandably so, Miss Cullen. No need to apologize. I was explaining that your grandmother asked for my complete secrecy and professional services.

"Please understand the information I am about to give you is all I know. I do not know how or why all this came to be. That part was never my business."

"I understand, or at least I'm trying to." She turned away from him and gazed toward the backyard. Her glance tripped over the rose bushes once more, almost as if she expected to see her grandmother in her large sun hat with her hair swept up in a graceful bun, tending the blooms.

His voice jerked her back to the present moment. "Upon your mother's death your grandmother requested I come visit you. She only wanted you and not your mother to know about this matter. I don't know why. It was not my place to know or ask. But I can say as long as I have known Dusky, I am sure she had good reason. Do you want to hear the rest?"

"Of course."

He proceeded carefully with his words. "Close to the headwaters of the Nueces River in Uvalde County up in the hill country, your grandmother owned a sizable piece of property. It was in her possession before I even met her. All financial matters regarding this property are current and will continue to be. I have a map to the property along with a letter from her addressed to you. She asked me to give it to you at this time." He pulled out several pieces of paper from his briefcase, laying the yellowed paper carefully on the table.

"Here is the map. The homestead is located off the main ranch road." As he talked he pointed with his finger, showing Eliza the old road she would need to follow.

"I must add, Miss Cullen, that I have never visited the property. I am only trustee of the ranch and look after the finances. Your grandmother took great care in going over the details of its location with me so you could find it easily."

"Did my grandfather, Timothy, know about this? Was he in on all this too?"

"Yes," Mr. Garrett said, nodding his head. "He knew about the property, but it belonged to your grandmother, and he made sure it was set up that way. He, as well, agreed it was to remain a secret until the next generation was of age."

"I'm not sure I'm getting any of this, Mr. Garrett. I never would've expected something like this." She felt confused and a tinge of annoyance. Her fingers nervously smoothed the folds in her plaid skirt, and she adjusted her posture wanting to catch his words as the pleading look on his face beckoned her to stay engaged.

"I understand. It does sound mysterious, but I urge you to please read your grandmother's letter before you make any judgments. She has taken much care to pass this on to you, and she requested I see her promise through. After you've read her letter, call me as soon as you can." He reached across the coffee table and handed her his card as well as the letter and then gathered his briefcase to leave.

Rising, he paused to address her one more time. "Thank you for your time, Miss Cullen. I know the circumstances are difficult. This is how Dusky wanted it, and I feel sure she knew you could handle it. Again, please call me as soon as you can." The formality in his voice left her heart dry.

Taking the sealed envelope from his hands, her eyes fell on the familiar writing across the front. She clutched the letter tightly in her hand while walking him to the door.

"Thank you, Mr. Garrett, for helping my grandmother. She was an amazing woman. I miss her terribly. Please accept my apology if I seemed short with you. It's not my intention."

"Thank you, and yes, she was," he replied flatly. "She truly was a dear woman. Good day, and I look forward to hearing from you." He turned and stepped onto the wide front porch, adjusting his coat. Then Eliza watched him walk down the sidewalk to his car, his heels clicking against the cement.

Taking a deep breath, she stared at the envelope in her hand once more. The only indication of its age was the yellowing edges. Eliza walked toward the kitchen, seeking Ada's voice of wisdom. She felt certain Ada knew about this and would help her understand all the secrecy and timing.

"Ada, are you in here?" She peeked through the doorway.

"In here by the laundry, Suga'."

"Did you hear all of that?" she called through the kitchen.

Ada walked around the pantry wall, folding a shirt as she answered.

"Honey, you know Ada better than that. If it somethin' I need to know, I know you tell me. If it somethin' I don't need to know then I don't know. Simple as that."

"Will you come sit with me for a second? I need your help figuring something out." Eliza pulled out two of the chairs from under the pine table.

"Sure, Suga'. Lemme set this down over here."

The chair creaked as Ada sat down next to Eliza. She leaned back and folded her arms across her middle, rubbing her hands that Eliza knew ached from arthritis.

"Apparently, my grandmother had some property up in the hill country in Uvalde County that she kept secret from my mother and me all these years." Eliza looked at Ada, waiting to see a surprise reaction on her face, but Ada stayed her steady gaze unmoved by the news.

"Go on," Ada bid her.

Prompted by Ada's reassurance, she began to explain all that Mr. Garrett had divulged. "Except for my grandfather and Mr. Garrett, it doesn't seem that anyone else knew about it, not even Mama. Did you know, Ada?"

"Nope, can't say I 'member nothin' about that."

"Mr. Garrett brought a map and a letter to me from my grandmother. He says this is how she wanted things done. My mother wasn't supposed to know about it—only me after Mama died. I just don't understand all this. Grandmother wasn't like that."

"An' we sure this gotta do with Miss Dusky?" Ada's skeptical eyes leaned forward to look at the letter. "Tha' be her writin' all right. Well, we can't go gettin' all worked up 'bout somethin' we don't know nothin' 'bout. Miss Dusky wuz a good woman with good ways. She gonna make it all straight. We best not go bakin' bread without first readin' the directions. Best read the letter, baby girl."

Eliza nodded and put her head in her hands. Tears pooled in her eyes and dripped onto her palms.

Ada scooted her chair closer to Eliza's side. Her great big arms surrounded her, and she rocked her slowly from side to side, humming her favorite hymn, *Old Rugged Cross*. Her pure, deep melody filled the kitchen, singing comfort into the lonely parts inside Eliza.

"You gonna be all right," Ada whispered, patting her back. "You gonna be just fine. You just hurtin', honey, and it's okay to let it hurt. 'Cause when we do, God comes to comfort us. Maybe this just one way He comin' to comfort you . . . through yo' grandmamma. Let it be, baby girl."

Through her tears, Eliza managed a soft whisper. "Ada, if the Lord loves me so much, why did He take them away from me? Doesn't He know I need them here with me? I don't know what I'm supposed to do. I'm scared. I need them."

Ada's roughened fingers wiped her face and tipped up her chin. "Baby girl, our Lord understand loss. He understand losin' those we love. He weep with those who weep. He mournin' wit you. We ain't never gonna know 'til we sittin' wit Him the whys. You gotta ax Him how to help you now, who He wanta be for you now. He got some mighty big love to give you.

"If all we doin' is countin' losses, then we can't get up. We ain't never gonna see His answer if we lookin' at what's gone. He's gonna do somethin' different now, Liza. Be still. He gonna answer you, an' you gonna know."

"But I don't know how," Eliza said, struggling to answer. "I don't see Him or feel Him like you do. I feel lost when it comes to God."

"Now, look at me, baby girl. Open your hand just like I'm handin' you a gift." Ada cupped Eliza's hands as she held them open. "Just like that, you waitin' to receive, and He's gonna give you somethin' you need. Now do the same wit yo' heart. You don't have to know it all—that His job. You stay like that in yo' heart, and He gonna fill you with life. Just ask Him. That's all you gotta do. That's what He's waitin' on."

"How did you learn to talk to God like that?"

Ada looked out the window and paused before responding.

"'Fore you wuz born, I wuz young an' my family was po'. My mama an' daddy worked pickin' cotton in the humid plantations of Louisiana, an' all the while life never changed for them. Day after day that cotton crop wuz the same, an' night after night they had the same bellies to feed.

"I wuz the youngest out of five. It wuzn't easy keepin' a home an' food for all of us, so my older brothers left to find work in Texas while my sista an' I stay with Mama. But in 1917, Daddy decided to move us to Rockport, Texas. He heard they wuz buildin' ships for the war an' the money wuz good. Mama didn't want to leave that oak-covered shack we called home, but she knew better than to argue. A good backslap from his hand is all it took for any of us to know we best keep our mouths shut 'round Daddy talkin'.

"We said good-bye to our little, wooden home sittin' in those big ole' oaks an' left on foot wit a small cart an' a donkey headin' for Texas an' Mama hummin' hymns the whole way. It wuzn't but ten days into our journey that trouble came on us in the late of night an' left its ugly mark on me. Daddy didn't have a chance against that gang of men who beat him to death as we watched hidin' in the trees. Mama jumped in, but the man's hands were too quick for her an' she went down. Sista had her hand over my mouth. I wanted to scream but couldn't. She grabbed my hand an' we ran tearin' through brush with a small bag we grabbed off the cart."

Eliza held Ada's hands tighter. "I had no idea. I'm so sorry. Please, you don't have to say anymore."

"Baby girl, you gotta know the redemption of it all. The Lord kept us safe in that small town of Rosenberg. A sweet doctor's wife saw us hidin' in the bushes by their backhouse like a couple of wild dogs. She took us in an' cleaned us up an' fed us. She treated us so nice. We stayed with her an' da doctor for three months an' help 'em. That's where I meet yo' grandfather, Mr. Barksdale. He wuz travelin' through on business and came to see da doctor. Doctor's wife knew one of my brothers wuz in San Antonio an ax if we could ride back wit him. He said yes, an' sista and I went not knowin' what to expect. He offered us work and tha's how I came here. I musta' been 'bout thirteen years old an' sista sixteen.

"We both worked for your grandmother until sista get married a year later an' gotta job at a beauty shop. Day after day the Lord teach me to look up, to look at Him. To ax him to help me cuz I had nobody. Since Mama an' Daddy wuz dead, I talked to the Lord. I didn't ax why. I just ax for help an' He answered. I wuz scared, but I learned I could trust the Lord.

"He know loss, baby girl," she said as she pushed Eliza's hair back behind my ears. Her touch was so gentle and gave Eliza comfort. "He know just what to do. Give Him a chance to help you."

She kissed Eliza's forehead and gave her one more squeeze before walking back to the laundry room. Her words hung in the air, and Eliza let the depth of her story settle over her own heart. Now she understood Ada's childlike faith and unwavering joy. She led by love and comforted with compassion. She truly was His arms and hands.

"Thanks Ada," she whispered, rising from her chair. "You are a gift." Gathering the yellowed envelope in her hand, Eliza went upstairs to her grandmother's sitting room to read her letter.

On the wooden stair landing, she stopped to admire the sunlight spilling through the windows. As she continued upward toward to her grandmother's room, she paused and smiled at all the family photographs along the wall.

Each photo was dear to her with its own story to share. She wanted to savor them all by turning back the clock even if only for a day. Quietly she walked into her grandmother's sitting room anxious to open her letter and still mulling over all that Ada had said.

She struggled with understanding how God could fill such loss. Looking down at her hands, she practiced cupping them together, waiting for them to be filled. She felt silly, but Ada's faith was so strong and so pure that it urged her forward. She could feel her lips trying to form a question, but she kept them pressed together not letting any sound escape. She wasn't sure if she was ready for His answers.

CHAPTER NINE

DREW WATCHED THE CLOCK in his office as the hands moved to 11:00. Rummaging through his mind, he was confounded by Mr. Garrett's phone call to Eliza. He had seen most of the estate documents Dusky and Hope had as he and Eliza spent the better part of yesterday organizing what she needed to take to Harold.

He remembered their conversation on Thursday night after the service and how frightened she admitted to feeling. Concern furrowed his brow as he imagined what another blow might do to her. How it might send her away from him.

Standing by his window, he watched the figures on Broadway below and saw the March winds blowing debris between the buildings. He watched as a young mother clutched the suspenders of her son and hurried him across the street while holding onto her hat with her gloved hand. Drew could tell the little boy was enthralled with the window display at Woolworth's and not eager to leave.

"Mr. Hillson." Glenda, his secretary, interrupted his wonderings.

"Yes," he replied, twisting at the waist to face her.

"There's a young lady here to see you." A surprised look shot across his face. "She says it's a private matter and would like to speak with you now. Is that all right?"

"Who is it?"

"Becky Tarabow."

Drew could hardly contain his exasperation. He had managed to avoid her the past week and knew she must be steaming at this point.

"Go ahead and send her in," he replied reluctantly, wishing he could figure out a way to avoid a confrontation with her, especially at his office.

He could hear her heels clicking on the tiles as she came down the hallway.

She stood in the doorway, her purse dangling from her arm as she took off her gloves. "Drew," she began without waiting for him to welcome her. Her voice sounded shrill in his ears. "We need to talk."

He could feel the stab of her glare. He motioned her to a seat at the small table in his office. He cleared away the stacks of files from the top and sat down, feverishly trying to figure out what to say.

"It's obvious you're avoiding me, and I don't like it." She pursed her lips together and stared at him. A muscle in his jaw jerked as he took her indignation like an icy slap.

He decided to downplay her accusation and resisted lashing back at her. "Work has been wild. I've hardly left the office."

"That's not true. Mary Grace said she saw you at lunch with Eliza yesterday."

"And our other friends too. Look, Eliza is a good friend and always will be. She's been through some pretty rough stuff lately, and I'm going to be there for her."

"When you and I started seeing each other in November, I asked you about her and you were pretty certain it was over. Plus, you all weren't even speaking. But now, all I hear all over town is you've become her knight in shining armor. How do you think that makes me feel?" Her lip trembled as she jerked her head toward the plate-glass windows.

A hint of compassion rose in Drew as he realized he had caused her pain because he wasn't sure what he wanted. Now that he and Eliza were talking again, it revived a hope in him that what they once had would be again. And that wasn't Becky's fault.

"I see your point." He reached over the table to take her hand. "I'm sorry. I'm not trying to hurt you or avoid you, but I'm not being fair to you either."

"What are you trying to say, Drew?" He could see the fury rising in her face at the anticipation of his next remark.

"It's not right that you feel . . . neglected." Confused by all that had been turned upside down in his heart, it was all he could manage. He knew he needed to be honest with Becky, but he feared she might cause a scene at his office and he had to placate her at the moment. Showing up here unannounced was enough of a scene. He just wanted her to leave.

"I agree, so what do you want to do about it?" He sensed the challenge in her response. Surprisingly, he was not moved to gloss over the truth he knew was welling up inside of him.

A strange look crossed her face that sent a shiver up his spine. The carefree, giddy sparkle in her eye that he had seen so many times before was gone. Her eyes were frosty and hard as she glowered at him.

"We'll grab dinner one night this week. I promise."

"You promise?" She stuck out her lower lip.

He recognized her pouty, seductive look and wondered why he had put up with her childishness all this time. He knew he needed her to leave, and he knew it was time to cut ties with her once and for all.

"Maybe Wednesday? I've gotta run now. I'm supposed to meet my boss at Club Giraud for lunch in fifteen minutes."

Hoping she was satisfied, he watched as she gathered her purse and stretched her hands through her kid leather gloves.

"Wednesday it is." She reached to wrap her arm around his neck as he stiffened at her touch. She brought her lips up to his and gave him a kiss, letting her touch linger on his face.

He peeled back from her and escorted her to his office door.

"Bye, Drew," she said as she slowly rounded the corner of his office.

He waited until he could hear the click of the hallway door before slumping into his desk chair. *What have I gotten myself into?* She had turned on him, and her distaste for Eliza was apparent.

Maybe his friends had been right. Maybe her immaturity was the cause for her lack of dignity today. Whatever it was, he was certain he needed to end his relationship with Becky. Regardless of what happened between him and Eliza, Becky had left a chill in him that he still couldn't shake.

CHAPTER TEN

SPOTTING HER GRANDMOTHER'S favorite sage-colored chair, Eliza decided it would be the perfect spot to read her letter. She nestled snuggly into its cushions with her legs tucked under her and pulled the gold cashmere throw still lying across the back of the adjacent small sofa over her body. Glancing to her left, she saw her grandmother's pens still sitting in the white porcelain cup next to the chair. Nothing was out of place.

Carefully, she opened the sealed envelope and pulled out her letter. Anxious to read her grandmother's words, she breathed deeply as her eyes began to soak in the words on the page:

My dearest Eliza,

Thank you. Thank you for having the courage to open my letter and read it. How I wished I could tell you all this in person, but I believe it's better this way. I think you will agree as you find out more. It will all make sense, I promise.

I have rewritten this letter to you many times throughout my life and yours because I did not know when you would read it and where life would have led you. I finally settled in my heart that this was the last time I would rewrite this first letter to you. Hard to imagine, but true, that I wrestled with my words for decades.

On November 10, 1955, I sealed this letter one last time and handed it to Mr. Garrett. You, my dear, were only fifteen, and if you remember, your favorite song that came over the radio that year was "The Yellow Rose of Texas." I'm sure you have a new favorite by now.

I do hope you weren't too hard on Mr. Garrett. He is only the "messenger" as they say, and I know how inquisitive you can sometimes be.

Smiling, Eliza caught herself giggling at her grandmother's tender humor even at such a time as this.

Sometime ago I asked Mr. Garrett to help me. I had property in the hill country that I wanted to put into a trust for my family. The only catch was I didn't want your mother to know about it, so I chose to wait until she passed to tell you. Life never seemed to let up for her, and I never could bring myself to upset her with all of this. I just couldn't bring this up with her for fear it would break her. As strong as she appeared to be on the outside, I knew her heart was tattered on the inside.

Time is funny in that way. You think you have so much of it and then, suddenly, it's gone. All that needed to be said is lost in the silence of those who pass away.

I am realizing as I write this and you are reading my letter that my precious Hope must have passed on. I am so sorry, Eliza. I know how much she loved you. Being an only child isn't easy . . . I know. There is so much pressure to be special and smart and seemingly so alone when your parents pass—in your case your mother and me.

But most importantly, take care of you. You have always been so darling and such a heart of sunshine. I so loved our little tea parties you hosted and would invite me to attend on our balcony. Or the walks we took to the springs.

I know I miss you. We had such delightful conversations you and me. I liked your mind: inquisitive, caring, passionate—all the wonderful qualities of a woman. You never shied from a question, and you knew at a young age how to offer a sincere compliment. A true mark of a polished diplomat, I might add.

That's why I am hoping you will try to understand me. Try to understand that I had to handle things this way. In time you will have your answers.

Now, allow me to explain more about the ranch. Do you remember all the times I went on vacation to the hill country, oftentimes with Uncle Henry and Amelia? Well, it was this place on the Nueces River. It was my retreat back to world I once had to tell good-bye, and the only way I could keep those memories alive was by keeping my private haven tucked into those rocky hills and nestled among the clear springs.

Now I'm leaving you this ranch, dear, that is if you would like to have it. Do not feel obligated. You may decide you'd rather not revisit my past, and Mr. Garrett can handle all that too. The decision is yours.

If you go, the ranch house is waiting for your first visit. It is filled with objects from another life, one I shared with only a few. Also, you will find a locked closet filled with my memoirs. The key to it is in Mr. Garrett's possession, although he doesn't know what it opens or what is in the closet. No need to worry. I've got instructions for all that too.

Do you remember all the mornings I sat and wrote? Well, most of those journals are yours now. In them you will find a true, historic account of my life and why I have kept my stories tucked in my heart all these years.

You may ask why I just didn't let the secrets die with me. Well, I couldn't. It is not my nature. When I died, I wanted to know at least one of my descendants would know the truth, and that someone is you. Now you can decide to bring the real story to life or let it stay buried with me.

You must decide before you go to the ranch though. It is an all or nothing agreement. I am sorry but this is the way I wanted it, and Mr. Garrett will not do otherwise.

This isn't about trickery or danger, dear, even though it all sounds a bit ridiculous, but what you discover will change your history and hopefully, your life to come.

Laying down the page in her lap, Eliza searched the room with her eyes. Not quite sure what to make of all this she continued reading, mystified by all the secrecy. Shaking her head, she finished the letter:

I am sure at this point you must be asking yourself what to make of it all. It is never an easy decision to decide if one wants to have their past rewritten per se, but that is what you will discover. I wasn't exactly truthful about my past nor was your grandfather.

No, we weren't criminals if you are even thinking that. We just chose to cover over painful truths that could hurt your mother. Silence seemed the better option and going forward in life versus backward was the right choice. She needed stability growing up and a firm family foundation. And I needed to keep my eyes forward.

Finally, in my own way and in my own time, I can tell my story. My desire is that what I share with you gives you courage to face whatever life may bring, as the one thing you can count on in life is change . . . which we all realize is beyond any of our control. But what I believe you can control is how you choose to handle change, how you allow it to form your own life.

Please let Mr. Garrett know your decision so he can proceed in whatever direction necessary. If you do decide to go, I hope you will go ahead and go sooner rather than waiting. I know you will love it as much as I did, dear, and I think you may stay awhile.

I love you. Raising you was a double blessing in my life. You kept my soul filled with life and love. God's plan was a good one for me, and you were definitely the treasure in it.

Give the big, white house a kiss from me.

Much love,

Grandmother

The corner of Eliza's eyes filled with tears upon reading the last words of the letter. Standing, she paced the room with her hands on her hips.

"I can do this," she whispered, encouraging herself while wiping the tears from her cheeks. "No more crying," she determined as she walked to her room and picked up the small, silver dish by her bedside with the stones nestled together. Touching each one she remembered the names she had given them: hope, love, joy, life, and trust. Her fingers lingered on trust. She opened her palms and placed trust in her hands.

"I will trust," she spoke out loud. "I will trust." As timid as she felt at the moment, the desire in her was stronger. The questions that she knew still remained might now be answered through her grandmother's memoirs. Her grandmother was about to break the silence, and Eliza knew the only way to truly sink her fear was to drown it out with trust.

She pictured her grandmother as a young woman caught between the real world and the one she felt she must hide. Her silence had haunted her until her death. Now, her true voice would be heard long after her footsteps had disappeared. Eliza wanted to hear what she had to say.

What could possibly cause such upheaval in her life now that she hadn't already been through? Trust. What better way to be still than to trust, and then she would know. Grief had lied to her, but trust ushered in a new voice—one she wanted to pull close to and listen to carefully. She made her decision as she laid the rock back in its place.

Rising, she walked back to her grandmother's room to pick up the letter she had left in the chair and heard Ada calling from downstairs.

"Suga', you be needin' anything else? I be leavin' here shortly."

"No, Ada," she called back as she descended the stairs wanting to meet her in the foyer and give her one last hug before she left. "I'm fine."

Ada offered a tender smile as she spoke. "I got some leftovers in the oven for you, so you get some meat on them bones."

"I will, thank you. And thank you for sharing your story with me today. You're so strong."

"And so are you, baby girl. You'll see." She cupped Eliza's face and patted her cheek. "But the even better news is, He's stronger."

"I think you may be right. I'm going to call Mr. Garrett tomorrow and tell him I want to go see the ranch. I owe it to her, and I owe it to myself. I couldn't go through life not knowing what she was trying to tell me. I'm going to trust."

"You doin' the right thing. It's easy to run; it ain't easy to stop and trust."

"So true." Eliza followed Ada out the back door before watching her walk down the sidewalk to catch the bus.

CHAPTER ELEVEN

ELIZA PAUSED BEFORE DECIDING to walk over to Uncle Henry's and Aunt Amelia's. She knew they would know more, and she wanted to find out what they knew prior to Drew's arrival. Rapping on the painted, wooden door, she heard Amelia's footsteps and anticipated her sweet face as the door swung open.

"Hi, darling," she said, leaning in to give Eliza a kiss on the cheek.

"Hi, is Uncle Henry here?"

"Sure, honey, he's in his study. Why don't you go on back?"

"Uncle Henry?" Eliza called out as she rounded the corner.

"Eliza, come on in, sweetheart. How are you today?"

"Confused."

"Confused? About what?" He put down his paper and offered her a seat.

"I got the strangest call and visit today. A lawyer named Allan Garrett phoned and then came by this afternoon. He had some business my grandmother wanted him to attend to after my mother passed. Apparently, my grandmother had a ranch near Uvalde that she kept secret all these years and now that Mom is gone she wants me to know about it and go visit. She said in her letter you all went there too. You know about all of this?"

Removing his glasses, he rubbed the lenses as he spoke. "Yes, I do," he responded as he kept his gaze downcast.

"You do?"

"Yes, but I, like Mr. Garrett, was not allowed to discuss it until the proper time. Dusky had a certain way she wanted this handled, and I respected that."

"Can you tell me more?"

"Not yet, Eliza. I can't talk about all of this until you come back from the ranch. Trust me, it will make sense."

"That seems to be the hot word of the day: trust. I can't say I under-stand the timing either."

"I hear what you're saying, but it truly is perfect timing. Trust her, Eliza. She knew what she was doing." He took her hand, and she nodded. "She wouldn't do anything to hurt you, you know that. She had a reason, a very good reason, why she decided to handle her affairs in this way. I know you'll realize that soon enough."

"Maybe you're right. I'm willing to go. I'm just not sure that what happened in the past has any benefit to my life now. I'm sure it's interest-ing—don't get me wrong—but why she waited and chose to speak now puzzles me."

"Truthfully, I think you're going to find a lot of freedom, not for her, but for you."

He leaned over to give Eliza a hug, and she could smell his Old Spice cologne, a scent she'd been familiar with since her youth.

"Why don't you eat with us tonight? I'm sure Amelia's got something delicious planned."

"I would but Drew is coming by at six to eat with me. Thank you though. I'll talk with you after I call Mr. Garrett."

"All right then. Good night. Try not to stay awake, giving it too much thought."

Six p.m. rolled around, and Eliza heard Drew's knock on the back door. She felt her stomach do a flip at the anticipation of seeing him.

"Hey, Liza," he said, giving her a big hug. His tall build practically filled the doorframe.

"Hi there." She squeezed him back.

"So how was the secret meeting with Mr. Garrett?"

"Interesting. Come and sit down in the kitchen. I'll warm up our plates. Can I fix you some tea?"

"Sure, sounds good," he answered as he struggled to loosen his tie. Re-moving his coat, he laid it on the chair next to him and rolled up his sleeves.

"So, what happened? My curiosity has been building all day. It was hard to concentrate on much else."

"A lot. It's sort of a strange deal. Grandmother has some property in the hill country. She didn't want my mom to know about it, so Mr. Garrett had to wait until Mom died before he could tell me. Even more bizarre is that Uncle Henry knows about it, but won't disclose anything until after I go to the ranch."

"That's bizarre." Drew looked bewildered. "I wonder what the big secret is? It's just a piece of property. Lots of people have ranches in the hill country."

"I know. I have no idea what this is all about. Mr. Garrett showed me the location on the map and then handed me a letter from her, asking me to either go to the ranch or pass."

"What are you going to do?"

"I'm gonna go, of course. I'm much too curious. Wouldn't you go? Don't you think I should?"

He hesitated. "I guess . . . It just depends."

"On what?"

"On a lot of things. What's at the ranch? Who's there? You don't just take off on a wild goose chase alone. I'm kind of surprised Henry is in agreement with all this. Haven't you been through enough?" Drew's voice grew agitated. She could tell he was getting stirred up as he shifted his weight and put his hands in his pockets. "I don't mean to be curt or disrespectful to your grandmother, but I'd rather you have more information before you set out, that's all."

"She did say she had some old journals she wanted me to read. I don't think she or Uncle Henry would ask me to do something dangerous." She stopped herself before she went any further, seeing the disconcerted look on his face.

Eliza could see that Drew was puzzled and frustrated, but was trying to get that across to her without offending her. After a few moments, he offered his opinion.

"I think I should go with you. At least make sure you get there safely and everything is as she described or hoped it would be."

"You don't have to do that. I'll be fine. From what I can already tell I'm pretty certain she's got it all planned out. I think I need to do this by

myself—if that makes sense. It's what she asked me to do, and I really
need to have courage right now . . . the courage to trust. It's the only way
I know to overcome grief. I'm sick of the silence, the loneliness, the sadness." She leaned against the counter and faced him, her arms crossed
protectively over her chest. "I want to know. I want to know what she felt
she had to guard all these years."

He faced the windows, standing with his back to her, his right hand
rubbing his jaw.

Eliza gently approached him from behind and put her hand on
his shoulder, hoping to stir him from his obvious disappointment. He
reached up and held her hand while still gazing out at the evening sky.
Eliza knew they had been stretched to the limits of the impossible in their
relationship. The snaps and twists of life had all but broken them completely, and now, here they were again. And she always seemed to be the
one pulling at them the most.

"I haven't been fair to you," she said still standing at his back. "You
have always been there for me no matter what, and I realize I haven't always been there for you." He turned to face her, taking her hand into his.
She leaped onto the tiny ripple of courage inside her and for once let her
heart speak. "I love you, Drew, but I don't think I know how to love well,
and it's selfish of me not to love you well. I've seen lately how I've thrown
so much of what you gave me away, dismissing it because of my own false
pride. It's me. It's my lack that's the stumbling block, not you."

His eyes softened as he fixed his gaze upon her face. She could feel
her heart swirling with his unspoken tender gestures. He didn't have to
speak. His soft, brown eyes said everything.

"I love you, and I've never doubted that you loved me well. I've seen what
you had to face as an only child, and that has been heartbreaking to watch,
but I had to step back and let you walk through it the way you wanted. When
I saw you at the wedding, I knew by the look in your eyes, even after all these
months of silence and absence between us, you still loved me."

"How could you tell?"

"I know you too well. Your eyes have never lied to me. Your mouth
maybe, but not your eyes."

Touched by his words as well as amused, Eliza grinned and felt a weight of regret lift off her shoulders. He brought his lips to touch hers, slowly and sweetly.

Pulling away gently, he leaned to whisper in her ear and with every word she felt his lips brush against her skin.

"Go. I'll be here when you get back."

"As much as I love you, it would be cruel of me to make a promise to you right now. I don't want to break either of our hearts again."

"Please, let me in," he begged, cupping her face with his hands. "You won't regret it."

Her mind turned to the stones she kept in her room: love, trust, life, hope . . . joy. They were the promises she made to herself and the promises she was holding out to be fulfilled.

"I'm not sure of myself yet. I need to know I can love without regrets, without fear. Whatever is behind me, I want to put it behind me so I can move forward."

"Then I'll wait," he said, letting his hands linger on the small of her back.

She agreed with a nod of her head, moved by the gentleman he continued to be. How effortlessly it seemed for him to love her. That's what she wanted . . . effortless love . . . no reservations, no regrets.

The image of Drew and Becky at the wedding rose up in her mind surprising her. He hadn't mentioned Becky or their relationship, but Eliza needed to know where he stood with her. As difficult as it was, she couldn't leave the conversation without testing his words.

"What about Becky?" she asked, breaking the beautiful moment between them.

"Yeah. I've been needing to talk to her, but just haven't found the time. I don't know. I'm not in love with her, but . . ." Eliza could tell Drew was stumbling over his words, and she felt she needed to ask the hard questions. Otherwise, what was this between them if it wasn't challenged? Easy to say in three words, but perhaps, even harder to choose minute by minute. "She's not the one I'm standing here with. She's not the one I love."

"Does she know that?"

"No, she doesn't. I'd planned to tell her this week regardless of what transpired between us that she and I were over. But I haven't."

"I see . . ." Eliza's voice faded, and that sick feeling in her stomach the night she saw them together returned. She heard what he said and what he wanted to say to Becky, but the aversion to their relationship still caused a reaction on the inside. They both had much to sort out, and confessing how much they loved each other may have been premature. She wondered.

Love never seemed to have an easy answer.

CHAPTER TWELVE

FIRST THING IN THE MORNING, Eliza picked up the phone and dialed Mr. Garrett's number. A voice on the other end answered, "Garrett, Smith, and Jones."

"Good morning," she said firmly even though her hand was starting to shake. "May I please speak with Mr. Allan Garrett?"

"One moment, please."

"Mr. Garrett's office."

"Hi, this is Eliza Cullen. May I please speak with Mr. Garrett?"

"Let me check and see if he is available. One moment."

She heard a click as she was put on hold. Her hand started to sweat, and she could feel anxiety climbing in her chest. *Why am I so scared,* she asked herself, and before she could answer, Mr. Garrett's voice came through on the other end of the phone.

"Good morning, Miss Cullen. How are you today?"

"Please call me Eliza, and I am doing well, thank you. I read the letter and I'd like to go and see Grandmother's ranch in the hill country."

"Very well, I'll need give you her precise instructions and go over some details. Would you be available this afternoon or tomorrow?"

"This afternoon would be fine if that works for you?" she replied eagerly.

"How about 4:00? May I come by your home then?"

"That will work perfectly. Thank you."

"Ada," she called out as she walked down the back stairs into the kitchen. "Mr. Garrett's coming again today at four to give me directions to the ranch and go over a few details. I'm thinking of leaving Thursday morning. Do you mind looking after the house while I'm gone? I plan to be back in a week, but I truly don't know."

Ada looked up from her ironing. "Yes, Suga', you go on an' don't worry 'bout a thing here. If I need you, I'll call you, but you be sure to give yourself the time you need. Time to hear the answers."

"What would I do without you? You're the only family I've got. Thank you for letting me lean on you. I love you, you know."

Ada took Eliza in her arms and held her close. "You are God's child, baby girl. You are a child of love . . . yo' mama's, yo' grandmamma's, mine an' His. You nothin' but love, Suga', nothin' but love. God didn't give you fear, but peace an' love an' strength. You gots to remember that, ya hear?"

"Yes, ma'am." Eliza felt a lightness in her chest she hadn't felt before. There was a taste of freedom in the air. What kind she wasn't sure, but she was ready for it.

Ada had set out brownies and some mint tea prior to Mr. Garrett's arrival, and Eliza cleaned off the table in the garden room, setting the magazines on the credenza by the window. She could feel a faint twinge of excitement percolating inside her. It seemed like forever since she had dropped those five stones into the springs and kept what she wanted. One by one she was being filled with hope and joy and love and trust and life.

As soon as she made a final walk-through of the room, she heard Ada calling her from the front hallway. "Telephone, Liza. It be yo' friend, Miss Catherine."

"Thank you," she said as she took the receiver from Ada's hand. "Hi, Catherine."

"Hey, I was wondering if you want to catch an early dinner tomorrow night with a few girls who are getting together at the country club."

"I don't think so. I've got some things that have come up with my grandmother's estate and I'm leaving town Thursday."

"Like what?" Catherine sounded confused.

"It's sort of complicated right now, but I'll fill you in later . . . maybe next week?" Eliza was hoping to derail Catherine's questions. She wasn't ready to share about the ranch with anyone except Drew and Ada—the two people she knew she could trust the most.

"Then all the better to come be with us tomorrow night."

"What time?"

"5:30-ish?"

"I'll try. Just don't bring up anything about today. Sometimes the girls can be so nosey."

"I promise. If anything it'll be a good distraction."

"True. I'll see you tomorrow. I've got to run." Eliza hung up with a sinking feeling. She felt uneasy about going to the country club tomorrow night. Why did she agree to do that? Hopefully, it would only be a harmless distraction. It might do her some good after all.

Mr. Garrett arrived on time, and Eliza was eager to hear what he had to say. After serving him some tea, she sat down beside him as he rummaged through the contents of his briefcase.

"Let's see. This packet contains two keys—one to the house itself and the other to a closet in the house. Each one is marked," Mr. Garrett said.

Eliza nodded, acknowledging his directions.

"When you arrive you will meet an older, Mexican couple that has looked after the ranch for decades. His name is Juan Carlos and her name is Carmen. I've notified them that you are coming in the next few days. They will be ready for you. Carmen does all the cooking so no need to worry with provisions. All that is being handled by them. They have had a longtime relationship with your grandmother as well as the ranch. You're in good hands with them.

"Here's the phone number to the ranch in case you need to leave it with anyone."

He passed Eliza a white card with the phone number written on it. She recognized her grandmother's penmanship once again. He laid out a Texas state map across the table and began to give her directions to the ranch.

"When you leave here, you'll want to head west toward Uvalde on Highway 90. From there you'll turn northward on Highway 55 to Camp Wood. Camp Wood is a very small town and will probably be your last chance for gas. It'll be about one hour before you arrive at the headquarters from there.

"Remember, even though we are going over this right now, it's all written down in precise detail by your grandmother so you shouldn't have any problem finding it.

"As you continue from Camp Wood, after about twenty-five more miles begin to look for a poorly marked dirt road with a small wooden sign that reads Dry Creek Road. After about five miles look for an old metal barrel on your left with a red bandana tied to it. Turn left there and you'll have a rough, rocky road for the remainder of your trip. You'll cross over a stream and then two cattle guards. When you pass the second cattle guard, look for an old gate with the words Rancho Perdido—the Lost Ranch. Turn in there and stay on the main road. You'll know it is the right road by the flat-rock stream that follows along its side. After about a mile you'll cross the river and see the house."

"It does seem pretty well laid out. May I ask you a question?" Eliza's mind had already run ahead to the "what ifs," and she was curious to know a bit more, especially if things didn't go according to plan.

"Certainly."

"What would have happened if you died before my mother? I mean how would I have ever known all of this?"

He smiled. "We had a plan for that too. One of my contemporaries in the office who is thirty years younger than I am knew I had a client t he would need to take over if I should pass. At my office, I kept a detailed file for him should the need arise."

"She simply thought of everything, didn't she?"

"Absolutely. Your grandmother was most passionate about the property and seeing that you inherited it."

"Now," he started once again as he dug into his briefcase, "before I leave I have another letter from your grandmother that I'm supposed to turn over to you at this particular time. Also, I need some documents signed by you in order for me to start processing the transfer of trustee to you on the trust. The ranch is required to remain in trust until you die and can be left to whomever you choose."

Eliza glanced over the documents and signed her full name, Eliza Grace Cullen.

"I think you're all set now," he said.

"I really appreciate all this. Thank you."

"It is truly my pleasure. Your grandmother was a class act. I always enjoyed working with her, and I hope you enjoy this ranch as much as she did. She treated the place with as much care and concern as if it were her child."

"I can see that. I'm looking forward to being there." Eliza watched him tuck his glasses into his shirt pocket and carefully place the documents in his briefcase.

"Please don't hesitate to call me or Chase Matthews in my office if you need anything or should you run into some type of emergency. I've included my home number on the information sheet I gave to you."

They shook hands and departed company once again. Eliza felt a deep gratitude for him and all he had done in honor of her grandmother. She knew her grandmother would have approved of how he had handled her affairs with such intentional detail and purpose.

"Yes, Grandmother," she whispered, "I behaved myself. But you, on the other hand, have a lot of explaining to do."

She headed back into the garden room and reviewed the map and directions once more. The ranch seemed to be situated at the headwaters of the Nueces River. Looking forward to the change in scenery and the discovery of a different world, her fingers peeled open the envelope Mr. Garrett had left on the table.

My Dearest Eliza,

I am so happy you have chosen to go to the hill country. I knew deep down you would be able to do it. I think you will find the natural beauty and dry air intoxicating as I have all these years. You know the Texas hill country is legendary for its scenic vistas; cool, clear streams, and mild temperatures. You will no doubt adore it.

The absolute quiet and calm have been my strength throughout my life. The way the light plays on the rocks and the incredible views is truly magnificent.

I've spent what must have been hours just sitting, looking, and listening, trying to drink it all in. I was always at my best out there, tucked in those hills surrounded by that pure, spring water. It was a complete change from my life in the city filled with social obligations and duties.

Everything in my body just slowed down when I was there. My heartbeat and my mind all seemed to take up the rhythms of the landscape. It is the perfect place to simply be still. It is another world, dear. A world I am excited to share with you. Thank you for doing this.

And don't try to get anything out of Uncle Henry. He won't relinquish anything until the perfect time.

When you arrive, you will meet Juan Carlos and his wife, Carmen— two lovely people who have lived on the ranch for a very long time. Carmen is a wonderful cook, and Juan Carlos is the foreman. You can depend on them for anything. I told them years ago you would come one day, so I know they are thrilled to finally welcome you.

Pack both warm and cool clothes, dear. I don't know what time of year you'll be going, but the weather can change so quickly.

Drive carefully and follow the directions precisely and you shall have no problem whatsoever.

Much love,
Grandmother

There were those words again—be still. Eliza scanned back up from the bottom of the letter until she found them and read them again—"the perfect place to simply be still."

As suppertime drew near and the smell of baked chicken poured from the kitchen, she folded the map, directions, and the letter, and put them in a briefcase she found in the hall closet. She planned to leave first thing Thursday morning. She still needed another day to finish up a few things, plus she wanted to check on Harold one more time before she left.

After supper she called Drew to tell him about her plans.

"I'm still not sure this is a good idea, you driving out there by your-self," he said. "Is there any way I can convince you to wait until Friday? I'll drive you out there and then turn around and come back to San Antonio."

Eliza pushed back, not ready to give up her ground. "I'm going to be just fine. Her directions really are pretty clear, and I don't think I'll have a problem."

"Well, I'm not. The whole deal has been strange from the beginning. Let me at least follow you and make sure you're safe."

"Thank you, but no. I really need to do this on my own. I'm giving both you and Ada the phone number so you can call me whenever you like. And if something weird happens, call Uncle Henry and he can get you out there. But I doubt that will be necessary."

"At least let me come see you before you go. What about tomorrow night? I've got an early dinner but could be at your house at 8:30."

"Sounds like a plan. You can help me pack the car."

"See you then. Night, Eliza."

"Good night."

Eliza ascended the stairs and strolled out onto the balcony. She looked at the platform bed her grandmother had suspended from the ceiling and thought of the countless hours she had spent there daydreaming, playing, pretending. The world had seemed so full of possibilities as a child. Her dreams had only slowly begun to erode when her grandmother died sud-denly. Now her mother was gone too.

Ever so softly, she laid down on its wooden frame, adjusting the cush-ions beneath her while the sound of the birds beginning to nest for the night drifted from the magnolia trees that surrounded the edge of the porch. She pressed her hand against her chest, feeling her heartbeat slow. *Be still,* she told herself as her eyes slowly shut.

CHAPTER THIRTEEN

DREW COULD NOT WAIT for dinner with Becky to be over. He was already feeling queasy about having to talk with her and anticipating whether or not she'd make a scene. She'd been so unpredictable lately—like a loaded gun ready to fire. And he, unfortunately, felt like the target.

Pulling up to her parents' house, he wondered if there was a way to skip dinner altogether and simply break the news to her during the ride that he was ending their relationship.

"Drew," her syrupy voice hollered at him from the balcony. "I'll be there in just a sec."

Too late, he could tell she was wound up and he'd have to endure her mindless chatter for the ride before he could even get a word in. What had he been thinking? They were so mismatched from the very beginning. He wasn't thinking. That was the problem. He had been hurt. Becky had a knack for distracting any guy, but he was no longer desperate for distraction. He was only desperate for relief from her.

Managing a smile, he opened the door and helped her into the car. Her bright-red lipstick was like a siren he wanted to shut off. As soon as he made up his mind to severe his relationship with her, everything he at one time found endearing grated like nails on a chalkboard.

Before he could ask her where she wanted to go, she said, "I've already got us reservations at the club in the grill. I thought it'd be fun to sit outside since the weather has gotten so nice. Did you hear about the new member party?"

He let her ramble, knowing his contribution to the conversation would hardly get noticed. He hadn't planned on taking her to the club. He really didn't want see a bunch of people he knew, but there was no changing her mind now. It was obvious she had planned it, dressed for it, and wanted to be in charge. He would have to wait until the drive home to call off their relationship. If he told her at the club, she'd probably cause a huge scene.

Becky's incessant chatter made the ride go faster at least. Drew helped her out of the car and noticed her red heels matched her red lipstick, which had begun to smear in the creases of her mouth. Grabbing onto his arm, she latched down with a fierce grip. Drew tried to separate himself from her, but she locked herself into the crook of his arm.

Walking inside, Drew could already make out voices coming from the grill room. He hoped no one he knew was here this early for supper. He needed to make this dinner as quick and painless as possible. Becky continued her chatter as they rounded the corner and walked into the dining area.

"Eliza?" Becky's voice practically reached the decibel of a shrill. Shocked, Drew whipped his head toward the back windows and saw Eliza searching in her purse as she was standing by a table full of her friends.

She raised her head and locked eyes with Becky and then Drew. Panic surged through his body and he froze, watching her countenance fall as Becky's voice grew louder.

"How nice to see you. We've all been praying for you. I'm so glad Drew's been able to help you in the middle of all that he's got going on. We were lucky to sneak away and grab a bite to eat tonight, just the two of us. Isn't that right, baby?"

Instinctively, he grabbed Becky's arm and removed it from his and took a step toward Eliza as if to shield her from Becky's next arrow. He saw Eliza manage a slight smile and nod her head as she hastily moved to step past them.

Her face went flush and Drew could tell she was as mortified as he was. He understood in that instant that Becky had planned this encounter to humiliate Eliza in front of him and their friends. Sick with disgust, he tried to speak, but Eliza brushed past him and the words sank in his heart.

"How could you?" He glared at Becky, his eyes wide with disbelief.

"What are you talking about?" she said, looking innocent.

"You know exactly what I'm talking about. You planned this whole thing, didn't you?"

"I have no idea what you're talking about. Now let's go sit down and eat and visit." Becky tried to hold his hand, but he jerked back from her, furious.

"No! I'm done. It's over, Becky. Your cruelty tonight was beyond distasteful. I'm leaving. Mary Grace can give you a ride home." He turned his back and stormed down the hallway, clenching his fists.

"Drew! You can't leave me here. Come back here right now. I'm talking to you," Becky demanded.

He kept walking. His stride lengthened as he got closer to the parking lot, wanting to catch up with Eliza. Frantically, he searched for her car, but he couldn't find it. He jumped into his truck and started the engine. Hopefully, she'd go straight home.

As his tires screeched on the way out of the lot, he slammed his fist against the steering wheel, cursing Becky under his breath. He knew he should have told her it was off that day when she showed up unannounced at his office. Instead, he'd let himself feel sorry for her, and now he was paying for it. Now he might have lost the only woman he had ever loved for good.

Drew swung his pickup into her driveway just as she was getting out of her car. Her face looked ashen.

"Eliza!" he shouted through his open window. "Eliza, wait!"

He jumped from his truck as she hurried to the back door and slammed it behind her. As he yanked open the screen door, he could hear her footsteps running up the stairs. Taking them two at a time, he caught up with her on the landing.

"Eliza, give me a chance to explain. It's not what you think." He bent over, out of breath.

She turned to look at him in disgust. He could tell she had been crying, but now her lips stiffened to hold them back.

"I'm so sorry," he said, reaching a hand toward her. "That should have never happened. I had no idea you were going to be there. If so I never would have showed up with Becky."

He searched her eyes for some sort of understanding, but she remained still and silent. He felt as if his heart would break. "After you left

I realized Becky had set us up. She meant to hurt you. I'm so sorry, Eliza. Please believe me."

Nothing. Eliza continued to stare at him, her body tense. She had thrown up a wall between them he wasn't sure he could climb, but he had to try.

"Against my better judgment, I took Becky out to dinner to tell her that I was ending the relationship. I needed to do it in person, but I should have just talked with her at her house. I'm an idiot. Please, can you forgive me?"

"I don't know."

He took a step closer, hoping he could reach her. "How can I make it up to you? It's over between Becky and me. Right there in the club . . . I let her have it and walked out. When I saw how she hurt you on purpose, I lost it."

"It's probably best that I'm leaving town tomorrow," Eliza said, turning her face from him. Her chin trembled.

"Why? Let me come with you."

She remained silent, not looking at him. Finally, she spoke softly and quickly. "I promised myself I wouldn't hurt you, but I forgot that you have every right to hurt me."

"That's not what I meant to do. You've got to believe me."

"I believe you, but love hurts too much, Drew. Whether you meant to or not . . . I'm not ready for that. I don't have the ability to bounce back right now. I . . . I . . ." She lifted the back of her hand up to her mouth to stifle her sobs.

Drew stood silent. He wanted to reach out and hold her and take away the pain he had caused, but she wouldn't let him.

"I can't go through life feeling this way," she said. She took a long, shuddering breath as the tears spilled down her cheeks. "I feel desperate—afraid. I've asked God to help me, like Ada told me to, but I still hear this little voice inside saying, 'You don't have what it takes,' and all I want to do is scream. What does it take?" Eliza's cry pierced his heart. "What is it? I've had nightmares and flashbacks and breakdowns and . . . and I don't want to keep living like the rejected little girl left on the swings by her daddy because he was too selfish to love me. I spent my life trying to prove I was worthy—worthy to be loved, worthy for all I've accomplished. I did a bang-up job, and I had a lot of people fooled. Truth is, I'm crumbling on the inside. The fort I built has been blown up, and what's left in the rubble is pretty frightening."

Drew wished she would look at him and see that his eyes were filled with understanding, not judgment.

"When I saw you and Becky tonight, there was that voice again telling me I didn't have what it takes, telling me I'm not worth it, telling me I'm a fake, telling me I don't even know the truth about myself. I can't live with that . . . that *thing* haunting me. I want it silenced, but I don't know how. I'm not who you think I am, Drew. I'm really not."

Drew reached to put his arms around her, and she didn't resist. He pressed his face against her hair and spoke in a hushed tone. "Yes, you are. In fact, you're more incredible than I ever thought you were. Here you are devastated, confused, upset, but you haven't given up. I know you'll find your answers. That voice is lying to you, but you need to hear the truth from your heart, not from me." He pulled her closer. "I don't want you leaving here uncertain about us because of what happened tonight. It's exactly what Becky wanted."

She stepped back from his arms and looked into his eyes. "My whole life is uncertain. You need certainty. You deserve more than I can give you right now."

Undeterred, Drew held her gaze. "I'm not afraid to love you and I'm not afraid of what you're going through. Love is worth fighting for, and I'm not giving up on us. When you go tomorrow, I want you to remember all the details of this beautiful ranch. I want to hear all about it. Don't leave anything out even down to the color of the walls in the house. I want to hear the story—her story and yours—because you get to write a new story now . . . the one your heart wants, the one it has dreamed of. When you get back, I plan to marry you, Eliza Cullen."

"Drew . . . I can't make any—"

Before she could finish, he jumped in. "Don't say anything. You don't have to have the answer. I'll be waiting for you." He turned and walked down the stairs. He could feel her eyes watching his every move, and he resisted the urge to run back and hold her. When he landed on the last step, he looked back and saw her still standing there, her head tilted gently and her hands clasped in front of her. Her lips moved as if she wanted to speak, but what more could they possibly say to one another? He gave her one last encouraging grin and walked to the door, letting himself out into the night.

Before he turned the key in his truck, he hesitated and took a deep breath. All he wanted to give her was no longer in his hands. He had handed her everything—all that was inside him and more. He turned the key and the engine began to rumble.

"Please, God," he whispered. "Please help her find her way. She needs to hear you and she needs to know you love her . . . and that I do too."

His eyes filled with tears, and the road ahead blurred as he pulled away from her house, leaving behind his heart in her hands. He cleared his throat, swiped at his eyes, and clenched his jaw, trying to subdue the welling of emotion in his heart.

"Keep her close, Lord," he said as he drove past her house and down the quiet street.

CHAPTER FOURTEEN

THE 1962 WAGONEER WAS LOADED, and Eliza finished her coffee while she waited to tell Ada good-bye. She took another look at the map and with her finger followed Highway 90 to Uvalde, then north toward Camp Wood. She noticed how sparse the countryside seemed—just little towns dotting the map here and there.

Ada walked into the house through the back door, a broad smile on her face.

"Good morning, Ada. I'm all packed up and ready to head west," she announced.

"Good mornin', baby girl. I love seein' yo' smile. Lemme pack you a lunch to take. I got some hard-boiled eggs in the icebox, so I make you a nice, egg salad sandwich real quick."

"Sounds perfect," Eliza replied, washing out her coffee cup. "I've put the phone number to the ranch on the message board by the kitchen phone. Please call for any reason.

"Also, I told Harold I'd be gone for a while visiting with some of grandmother's relatives. I asked him to call you if he needed me. He seemed to be doing all right, but he sounded lonely."

"Um hum," Ada agreed. "I reckon his house is pretty quiet these days. Nothin' can burn a man's soul like loneliness. Men just end up workin' themselves to death . . . forgettin' how to feel." She wiped her hands on the cup towel and shook her head before she added, "I guess we all go a li'l bit crazy every now an' then."

"I guess so," Eliza said. "Let's just hope I don't go crazy out in the hills by myself. I need to keep some sort of sanity if I'm ever going to make a life for myself someday."

"Now don't you go worrying 'bout the Lord's work, Liza girl. You go on an' let Him do the worryin' an' you do the livin'. He makin' a beautiful life for you just like writin' a song. You can't hear it yet 'cause He ain't done writin' the notes. But one day you'll hear it playin', one sweet note at a time. You gonna look back an' see His perfect works in your life.

"I 'member when you wuz little an' I be fryin' up some hush puppies. You couldn't wait to eat 'em, but when I take 'em out too soon, they wuz just soggy mush, so you learned to wait. An' when it came time to take 'em out, you couldn't wait to eat one right away, but you blistered yo' mouth. An' then you knew it wuz best to let 'em cool. So you waited some more an' then they be just right for eatin'.'"

Eliza laughed, remembering those days in the kitchen following Ada around like a little puppy dog. "So what you're saying is, don't rush life's hush puppies?"

At this they both nearly fell over with laughter.

"You say it, baby girl. You right though. Never rush yo' hush puppies."

Chuckling, Ada turned and handed Eliza a paper bag.

"Here's yo' lunch with a nice fresh egg salad sandwich, corn chips, an' a chocolate brownie. Now one more thing, Suga', an' no it ain't no hush puppy." Ada giggled as she turned and pulled a gallon jug from the icebox. "Here's some of my mint ice tea to keep you from gettin' thirsty."

"Perfect. I'm all set now."

"All right. You call me when you gets there, so I know you all right, you hear?"

"Absolutely." Eliza kissed Ada's cheek and hugged her good-bye.

Before she drove out, she ran next door to hug Amelia and Uncle Henry good-bye. She noticed Uncle Henry was unusually quiet, and his eyes were moist with tears.

Amelia hugged her tight. "Call and let us know when you get there, sweet girl. We love you. If you need us, we can come get you anytime."

"I will." She turned to Uncle Henry. He swallowed hard before he gave her a hug, his big arms swallowing her small frame.

"I love you, Eliza. You're such a treasure to us. Call me. I'll be waiting to hear."

"I love you too, Uncle Henry . . . very much."

They waved good-bye through a mix of tears and smiles.

With the car loaded and full of gas, she headed out toward the city limits. She drove in silence, letting Drew's words from last night linger in her thoughts and melt the sting of humiliation. She rolled down the window, and fresh air swirled through the car. She inhaled one slow breath at a time. She could see San Antonio's skyline begin to fade in the rearview mirror as she sank comfortably in the seat. The Wagoneer's engine hummed at a steady pace.

Within the next two hours Eliza was surrounded by gorgeous strands of thick oak trees as she passed the WELCOME TO UVALDE sign. She could see the hills in the distance as the landscape rolled toward her. Her heartbeat quickened. She turned up the long stretch of highway facing the beckoning hills. Her hands gripped the steering wheel, and her eyes soaked in every detail.

She filled up with gas in Camp Wood. Then she took out Ada's lunch and sat on the bench at the station, eating her sandwich. The air was filled with the smell of cedar trees and warm rocks. Stretching, she lifted her face toward the sun and spread her arms to capture every bit of fresh air she could. She could almost feel her body lengthen.

With a full tank of gas, she rolled ahead and found Dry Creek Road. Turning right she headed down the road, raising a cloud of dust. The pecan trees reached down almost as if to touch her car and guide her through their private forest. A sea of blue caught her eyes to the right and left and hemmed her in with beauty. Bluebonnets covered the sides of the road and joined with buttercups and Indian paintbrush—their colors vibrant and generous. Eliza marveled at spring's handiwork.

An old, white pickup truck passed her and raised a cloud of dust. The weathered cowboy inside waved. She reached out the window and waved back with a smile.

Then she spotted the barrel and turned left onto a bumpy road. Keeping both hands steady on the wheel, she felt anticipation building inside her and she welcomed its excitement. She crossed over one cattle guard and stayed alert for the second one. After a mile, she felt the tires roll over the metal guard as her eyes scanned the distance ahead, looking for the old gate.

Finally she saw it and held her breath as she pulled up, stopping in its shadow. She could make out the words Rancho Perdido in faded yellow paint across the warped, wooden board mounted over the entrance.

After driving through the gate, she stopped and got out of the car, stretching her back. Her eyes squinted at the reflection of the sun off the bleached road. She stood mesmerized by the enormity of the rocky hills and their majestic offering of solitude. With her eyes darting from one direction to the next, she noticed the colors and how they varied from vibrant greens to dusty creams, all set against the majestic blue sky filled with puffy-white Texas clouds. Breathing deeply, she took in the dry air and the smell of sunbaked hills.

Be still and know . . . the voice whispered in her mind.

Swallowed up by the beauty of her surroundings, it was as if God spoke directly to her heart. She felt such peace here. Even the trees and rocks seemed to stand still and listen.

"You've got a story for me, too, I can tell," Eliza said, talking to the trees.

Getting back into the Wagoneer, she drove slowly enough to drink it all in from twig to treetop and pebble to boulder. When she looked in the rearview mirror, she realized the hills now completely enclosed her. It was difficult for her to make out the direction from which she had come.

Down the road a small herd of cattle greeted her. Many were newborn calves. Their mamas rushed to push them into the surrounding brush as she passed. She noticed all the patches of springtime flowers flourishing along the sides of the hill and running up through the rocky outcroppings.

Looking to her left, she followed the flat-rock stream as it carved its way through the hillside. She slowly drove down the hill until suddenly, a limestone cliff that had been left behind by erosion peeked out at her. The stream pushed along with a stronger flow now, and the Wagoneer bounced along at its side. Staring straight ahead, she watched the house come into view.

Eliza drove carefully through the shallow water as she crossed the creek, pulled up to the main house, and shut off the engine. As she opened the car door, pure, warm air touched her face once again and the scent of fresh, clean water filled the air.

She sighed. *It is truly every bit the peaceful sanctuary Grandmother described.*

She didn't want to move from this place. All she wanted was to stay and soak in the goodness of how she felt being here. A strange sensation bubbled up inside her, and she threw back her head, laughing and crying all in the same moment. It was as if someone wanted to cleanse her from deep inside. She wiped away her tears and smiled at the hills.

Reaching for her bag, she caught the sound of a screen door shutting and footsteps on the wooden porch. She shut the door of the Wagoneer and looked up to see an older woman with brown skin and ebony hair. Her features were soft and cheerful. She waved at Eliza and called out to her.

"You must be Eliza, I hope?" she said with a thick, Spanish accent.

"Yes," Eliza quickly responded, pulling herself together. "Are you Carmen?"

"Oh, *Mija*," she exclaimed. The older woman hurried down the steps and wrapped Eliza in a welcoming embrace. Carmen pulled back and seemed to study Eliza's face. "You look like your *abuela—so bonita*. Your brown hair with sun kiss in it reminds me so much of *Senora* Dusky. I can't believe you are finally here. We are so overcome with joy. Please come inside. Juan Carlos can bring your bags in later."

Together they walked side by side up the steps and onto the porch. Eliza touched the cool walls of the house and admired the swirls of brown, cream, and blush in the stone. Each one was a perfect masterpiece.

Gazing toward the ceiling, she noticed the old cedar beams that supported stained, pine slats. The porch was wide and long enough for two sitting areas. Wood furniture with wool cushions were placed on either end, beckoning a visitor. One end had an outdoor sofa and two chairs, while the other end had two chairs with a small table between.

In the middle of the porch was a brown screen door. As Carmen opened the door, Eliza could feel her heart thumping in her throat and droplets of sweat forming on her palms.

Inside the house, Eliza's eyes followed the flat sandstone laid out on the floor below her feet. Then she lifted her eyes to see the cream-colored, stucco walls. She followed Carmen into the kitchen, trying to absorb as much of her surroundings as possible.

"Please sit, Eliza," Carmen said softly. "I've made some fresh lemonade and some *pan de polvo* if you'd like some."

"Thank you. Everything is so beautiful, just like Grandmother. It's hard to even know what to say." Her fingers reached for the dusted sugar cookies.

With a big fireplace on one side and a large worktable in the middle, the kitchen was the heart of the home, and Eliza felt her body immediately relax. The windows looked out to the side of the house where hanging baskets of red geraniums and other lush foliage spilled over their sides. She watched a hummingbird slow down long enough for a drink before it sped off toward the sky. The smell of Carmen's baking bread and the scent of spices brought her attention back to the kitchen. They both sat down in the rush-back chairs across from each other.

"Juan Carlos is out riding on the west side, checking on water for the cattle and goats. He'll be back soon and will be so happy to meet you." She patted Eliza's hand lovingly.

"How long have you lived here on the ranch, Carmen?" Eliza asked, sipping the fresh lemonade and relishing the warmth and peace that swaddled her.

"*Dejame ver* . . . a long time, Mija. I was much younger—so many years. It is hard to remember."

"So you knew my grandmother a long time?"

"*Si*, a very long time. She was a good, good woman. I miss her." She smiled softly and picked at the tiny sugar crumbs on the table.

"I do too."

"Oh, but in this house you can still feel her love and joy."

Listening to Carmen's soothing voice, Eliza focused on her dramatic gestures that brought her words to life. Soon Juan Carlos strolled through the back door. Immediately, their eyes met, and Juan Carlos tipped his hat before offering his hand to greet her.

"We are so glad to have you," he said with genuine tenderness. His eyes sparkled with moisture.

Eliza returned his smile. "Thank you. I'm excited to be here, especially getting to meet the two of you. I'm still in shock about this place. I'm having to take it all in pretty slowly."

"And you will have plenty of time," Carmen said as she rose from her chair and nodded at Juan Carlos. "We shall have supper together tonight. So for now, please show Juan Carlos where your bags are and he can help you get settled upstairs."

"All right." Eliza responded. She stood and found her way back to the front door.

After gathering her suitcase and bags from the car, Eliza followed Juan Carlos up the rock stairway of the house.

He stopped on the landing and turned to her. "Where do you prefer to sleep?" He motioned with his chin to the master suite on the right and then to the guest rooms down the hall to the left.

"I'll stay in there," she said, pointing toward the front guest room. She wasn't ready to invade her grandmother's world quite yet.

Walking into the guest room, she marveled at the expansive view overlooking the flat-stone creek and hills. It had double doors that led to a balcony with weathered chairs. Their gnarled wood framed the backs of the chairs as they sat snuggly together.

"This couldn't be more perfect," she said softly under her breath.

Juan Carlos set down her bags and smiled, backing out of the room with a bob of his head. She set her suitcase on the bed and clicked open its latch to put her things away. It was hard for her to concentrate on any one thing as she kept glancing around the room and out at the view. She hurried to finish so that she could just sit and absorb all that was around her.

After unpacking, Eliza sank down on the double bed perfectly centered on the opposite wall from the balcony. The heavy cream coverlet was soft and fresh and contrasted nicely with the dark-wood bed frame. Running her hand over the bedding, she laid back and stared at the inside of the room. A beautiful Spanish-carved dresser now held her things. An old armchair covered in a soft rose damask sat next to the window.

The lace curtains blew gently with the dry breeze, and the air coming through the open balcony door smelled fresh and pure. Eliza could hardly move. She listened as birds chattered in a nearby cedar tree. She could also hear the sounds of cooking in the kitchen below. She shut her eyes, letting her body sink into the padded mattress beneath her. Folding her hands across her stomach, she stilled her body one breath at a time.

Drew's face drifted in and out of her mind, and his last words came fresh to her heart. She grimaced, recalling her harsh words and how she had lashed out at him. She wished she had kept her mouth silent and simply told him to leave, but her emotions had decided for her, and everything she had so neatly packed away all these years scattered and lay exposed on the floor between them. She hated that it had been so easy to let it all pour out of her. Life was much neater tucked away—even though it left her empty. Now her emotions were all too raw and too close to the surface. Brushing the coverlet with her fingers, she felt regret come over her like a damp blanket.

She realized school had been just another way to avoid what she truly didn't want to face. Wearing a mask was easy. Vulnerability came with too high a price. It had been easier to hide her true self in Dallas. Alone, the pressure to perform drove her, and she accomplished what she set out to do.

Now she felt adrift and swept up in an unfolding journey seemingly written by someone other than herself. She could either choose to float or to struggle because it would be impossible to do both.

She was almost certain the advice her grandmother would give her right now would be to float. It would be easy for her grandmother to say "float" because her life was one continuous elegant stroke after another. Eliza was certain her grandmother didn't understand the kind of loss her mother had endured.

Eliza saw how the pain of abandonment had so sharply sculpted her mother's heart. It was not easy for her to love. She realized what a contrast her mother's way of life had been from her grandmother's. Grandmother seemed to stroll through life with a joy in her heart that was never compromised. She lived her life with ease and acceptance while her mother had to face a rejection that never seemed to stop talking. Eliza shuddered as she remembered how her mother, nearing death, had pleaded with her to let the walls crumble around her and learn to love.

Eliza knew how very different they were—both loving and accomplished; both strong of heart; but both at opposite ends of what life had dealt. She clenched her hands as she allowed herself to feel her own struggle, and then she opened them quickly as Ada had shown her.

I don't want to hang on to the struggle. I want the good gifts Ada said you give. I'll give up the "why" if you show me the "how."

Sitting up, she held out her hands, waiting. With her hands still cupped in front of her, she watched the sun fade behind the western hills. Rising to stand at the balcony window, she turned over her hands as if to release the invisible weights holding her back. Mesmerized, she watched the water below as it glided over the rocks. Throwing her hands over the edge, she imagined the moving water carrying away the debris of her heart.

Her eyes caught a glimpse of a red cardinal. His mate dashed eagerly in and out of a small pool nestled along the bank. Splashing water, the pair seemed oblivious to all that surrounded them. The setting sun danced on their shiny coats as they teased one another in the water. She followed them as together they flew toward a pecan tree and blended into its branches until they were no longer visible.

The rising smells of the kitchen drifted into her room, and she changed before descending the stairs for supper. Her footsteps echoed on the stone staircase as her ears followed the familiar clanging of bowls and spoons and pot lids.

The dining table was set for three with two candlesticks lit at each end of the heavy mesquite table. The reflection of the flames danced off the sheen of the polished wood.

"Ah, Eliza. Did you get settled in your room?" Carmen said from the kitchen.

"Yes, it's beautiful. I love the view." She walked toward the sound of Carmen's voice.

"I am so glad. It is good to have another heartbeat in the house." Carmen looked up and smiled at her, wiping her hands on the linen hand towel attached to her apron. "Let's get these dishes to the table so we can eat. Will you help me?"

"Of course." Eliza reached for the wooden bowl filled with rice and beef and carried it to the table. Juan Carlos came through the back door after Carmen rang the bell hanging from the back door frame and tossed his hat next to the water basin.

After they were seated at the table, Eliza adjusted her chair before taking hold of Carmen's hand as Juan Carlos led the blessing in Spanish.

"Gracias, mi Padre para la comida que teremos y por la nina, Eliza, que esta can nosotros. Amen."

Carmen passed a plate of warm tortillas to Eliza before serving the *caldo* from the clay pot next to her. Eliza eagerly sipped her soup.

"We are honored you are here, Eliza," Juan Carlos said. "I look forward to showing you the ranch. I hope you enjoy it as much as your grandmother did. I take pride in making sure that it remains as she would want it to be." He paused to slurp from his spoon.

"I love everything about it already. It would be hard to leave here. What do you think Grandmother wants me to do while I'm here? Is there a special place she wants you to take me?"

Eliza noticed Carmen and Juan Carlos exchange a quick glance before he answered. "She has thought of everything, and tomorrow you will know more. She has much planned for you, and I think a good night's sleep will serve you well. You have had to come through much to be here now, is it not true?"

"Yes, I lost my mother just over a week ago. She passed away from cancer." Eliza still struggled to make sense of the timing of the latest events. "I'm still confused as to why Grandmother waited to bring all this up now. Her timing is pretty rough, but I didn't want to miss what she wanted to tell me. I'm guessing she must have known how lost I'd feel and was hoping to comfort me."

Carmen stretched her arm across the table and wrapped her hand over Eliza's. "If there was one gift your grandmother knew how to give, it was comfort. She carried such compassion. She loved so well and so true. She was a gracious lady."

As supper wound down, the telephone rang. Startled, Eliza almost jumped from her seat as the pitch of the ring broke through the soothing calm of the night.

Carmen pushed back her chair to answer the phone as Eliza glanced repeatedly toward the hallway. Feeling guilty, she realized she had forgotten to let everyone know she had arrived safely. She wondered if Drew was calling. What could she possibly say? Her words last night had been so harsh. She wished she could erase the whole exhausting mess, but that was sadly impossible.

"Rancho Perdido . . . bueno. Un momento."

Eliza heard the receiver thump against the counter and then Carmen's footsteps.

"Eliza, it is for you."

Her legs felt heavy as she rose to take the phone call, her mind still dizzy with canned responses.

"Hello? Oh, hi, Uncle Henry. Yes, everything is wonderful." With a quick breath she continued, relieved. "Yes, I love the ranch, and Carmen and Juan Carlos are so nice. We've had a delicious meal, and I'm settled in one of the upstairs guest rooms. Will you tell Ada that I'm here and I'll call her soon? Perfect, thank you. Good night. Love you too." Hanging up the phone, she walked back to the table and gathered her dishes to help Carmen.

"Thank you for such a delicious meal. I'm so full. I know I'll sleep well tonight."

She walked into the kitchen and set her blue-painted plate and bowl next to the large sink.

"De nada, Eliza. We are so happy you are here. Please go upstairs and take a warm bath. We will clean up and lock the house."

"We live in the little house next door if you need us," Juan Carlos said. "Please know you are very safe here. We have never had a problem."

"Thank you. I'll see you in the morning then. Good night." She stifled a yawn and took her time walking back to her room.

The idea of a bath was a welcome one, and she turned on the knob to the faucet, allowing warm water to run into the tub. Her eyes were bleary from exhaustion. Relaxing, she climbed in the tub and the warm water swallowed her. She knew she needed to call Drew and at least let him know she had arrived, but she wanted to avoid any long conversations. Calling him at the office tomorrow for a quick hello was the best option. With that settled, she sunk further into the bath.

Her curiosity began to stir. With the tip of her finger, she traced the pattern on the tiles and wondered what she would uncover while here at the ranch.

How can the past be that important? What could Grandmother possibly think would have hurt Mama so deeply that she couldn't tell her and chose silence instead? What was so detrimental that it had to wait until now after Mama was gone?

Eliza's finger paused as she thought about choices she wished she could erase or choose differently.

The questions kept coming, but her mind remained unsatisfied with her suggestions. Tomorrow the doors would be unlocked and she knew better than to weary her restless heart.

CHAPTER FIFTEEN

THE SMELL OF COFFEE STIRRED ELIZA from a much-needed sleep. She threw on a pair of cropped capris with an old cotton shirt and headed straight to the kitchen where she found fresh, hot coffee and sweet rolls.

After filling her small plate, she sat down at the dining table, which was set for one. In front of her plate stood a small porcelain vase filled with several wildflowers. Pulling the coffee mug to her face, she let the steam rise over her cheeks.

A letter to the left of the yellow placemat caught her attention, and she saw her name penned in black ink across the front. Smiling, she used the back of her knife to cut an opening in the sealed envelope. She could tell that Carmen and Juan Carlos had kept this for many years, and, perhaps as instructed, left it here just as her grandmother desired. Grateful, Eliza held the letter to her chest thinking of the years of meticulous care and crafting her grandmother had worked for her to be here this very moment.

She opened the envelope and carefully unfolded the letter. Taking a sip of her coffee, she began to read:

My Dearest Eliza,

Well, I take it you have now arrived safely at the ranch. I trust Carmen and Juan Carlos have made you feel welcome and at home. I hope you are enjoying the spectacular scenery as much as I did. I used to sit on the porch for hours at a time reading, writing, and sometimes just being swaddled by the quiet.

Nothing brought me more serenity than allowing nature to speak to me. My life is in these hills. As strange as it may sound, I have shared my story more than once with every rock, shrub, and animal throughout the ranch.

Enough of my rambling, dear. I am just so thrilled thinking about you being here and wondering what you will think of it all.

Remember the other key Mr. Garrett gave to you? It goes to a closet in my bedroom. You are the only one, besides me, who will ever open it. In other words, as I desired, everything in it has been kept all this time. What's there is for your eyes and your heart only. When you open the door, you will find several thick, leather journals. I have numbered them in sequential order. Each one contains pages I filled over the years.

I ask you one favor, please read the journals in sequence. I trust you and need you to absorb the complete history as it happened. That's the only way it will make any sense to you.

In those pages you will find my life story, a very different life story from the one you have always known. It is a life that caused me to question again and again whether I was able to trust and to love and to live.

All my love to you,
Grandmother

Eliza lingered on the last sentence struck by how familiar it sounded to her own heart, her own search for answers. She set the letter aside and looked around the room, feeling a burning and a hesitation inside her all at once. She realized that once she unlocked the closet and opened the journals, she was no longer free to erase what would be imprinted in her mind whether she liked it or not. The walls wanted to go up and shield her from risk. She felt a tightening in her throat and reached to rub her neck. Fear had bound her in the past, but today she wanted no part of what it had to offer. "No longer," she decided and pushed her chair back.

She heard the creak of the back door, and she picked up her dishes to walk back into the kitchen. As soon as she turned the corner, she saw Carmen coming through the kitchen door.

"*Buenas Dias, Mija.* How was your sleep?"

"Very peaceful. Thank you for the delicious breakfast."

"My pleasure." Carmen started to clean up from the morning's baking.

"Also, thank you for the letter from my grandmother. How long have you been holding onto it?"

"Many years," she answered with a sound of reflection in her voice. "Your grandmother wanted me to give it to you when you came to the ranch for the first time. She said she wanted everything to be perfect when you came as if she was right here with you."

"And it has been," Eliza said as she stood in the brightly colored kitchen near the hanging copper pots. "Everything is incredible—the house, the river, the hills. It's easy to see her fingerprints everywhere."

"I'm glad you like it." Carmen smiled.

"Do you ever get lonely out here?"

"Oh no. We have two children we raised out here, and we always went to church in the little village not too far away. Life has been very good to us, Eliza. We are grateful." Carmen looked up to the sky and made the sign of the cross across her chest before she kissed her fingers.

"Where are your children now?"

"They are both married and live in Uvalde. Our son, Juanito, is a carpenter, and our daughter, Gloria, has three children of her own. We see them often, many times in the year."

"That's nice. I don't have any brothers or sisters. It's just me."

"I know, Mija. Your grandmother always came with many stories about you. She loved you so much, but you are our family now." Turning off the sink water, Carmen walked over to Eliza and cupped her face in her worn, brown hands. "You will fit right in, I promise. Before you know it, the house will be home to you too.

"Now I need to start my bread for the day. Would you like to help?"

"Thank you, but I'm anxious to get upstairs and see what Grandmother has waiting for me. She left pretty detailed instructions about what she wanted me to do, so I think I'll head to her room for now."

"Of course, you take all the time you need. I'll be in here or by the garden if you need me."

She smiled and turned for the stairs. Passing the phone, Eliza paused and thought about Drew.

"May I use the phone?" Eliza leaned back into the kitchen, catching Carmen's attention.

"Of course."

She dialed Drew's office number and waited for his secretary to pick up. She tapped the coiled cord in her hand.

"Drew Hillson's office."

"Hi, this is Eliza Cullen. May I speak with Drew please?"

"One moment."

The line went silent and Eliza wished he would pick up quickly. Finally, his voice broke through on the other end.

"Eliza?"

"Hey. I . . . I wanted you to know I got here and I'm fine."

"I was hoping you would call. How is it?"

Eliza was relieved to hear his voice so welcoming and easy with her. "It's really beautiful just like Grandmother described. And the ranch foreman and his wife are really sweet. It's been a good change for me."

"I'm glad to hear it. Any new information on what your grandmother wanted you to know?"

"I think I'll figure it out today. She left a closet full of journals that I can't wait to start reading."

"Sounds interesting, and I want to hear more. I've got to walk into a meeting right now, but I didn't want to miss your call. Call me again anytime. I'm glad to hear you're doing so well."

"Thanks. It's good to hear your voice. I'll be in touch. Bye."

"Bye, Liza. Take care."

Leaning against the wall, she felt a tug at her heart. Talking with Drew had been easier than she had imagined.

Relieved, she darted up the stairs and dug into her briefcase to find the key Mr. Garrett left with her. Grabbing the tag of the key, she double-checked the writing and walked into her grandmother's room.

She hesitated as she stepped through the doorway, allowing herself to take in the timelessness of her grandmother's room. A big, canopied bed covered with a soft, rose coverlet held center stage. Eliza walked over and touched the fluffed pillows trimmed with lace.

On the bedside table sat several photographs in ornate silver frames. Eliza walked over to get a better look, but the faces in them were not familiar to her. Her eyes moved past the photos to find a rock in the shape of a heart with an orange streak running through the middle. She reached out to touch it and felt its coolness as she carefully ran her fingers across the top. The white, pressed handkerchief it rested on had yellowed with the years.

Lifting her head, she moved closer to get a better look at the painting above her grandmother's bed. It was reminiscent of the scenery surrounding the ranch. She could see it was a bit faded, but its hand-carved cedar frame held it firmly in place. She stared into the colors and saw the rendition of the same hills that surrounded her now. In the distance sat the rock house tucked into the green expanse, and she saw that the rock springs carving their way through the valley looked exactly the same as those outside.

Turning toward the left wall, she walked over to her grandmother's vanity and ran her fingers along the scalloped edge. It was similar to the one at home, as that one, too, had a collection of small, colored vases sitting on a mirrored platter. Her brushes and combs were placed on the left side next to a painted Mexican dish filled with bobby pins.

Eliza soon recognized everything in her room had been preserved exactly as it always had been. The only thing missing was her grandmother—her heartbeat, her voice, her sweet fragrance of laughter and joy.

Tears sprang to her eyes as she continued to move about the room, taking her time to catch every detail. Clearing her throat, she turned back to look at the vanity and saw a dark, wooden door on the left side with a painted cross above the doorframe. She could see a separate lock from the handle and realized this was the closet her grandmother had referenced.

She slipped the key into the lock and turned it. The door opened with a creak as she stuck her head around to peer inside, her heart racing in her chest. The light from the windows in the closet brightened the dark interior, and her eyes finally adjusted to the dim light. On the top shelves sat what appeared to be her grandmother's journals. Several leather boxes with buckles rested below on the remaining shelves.

A thin layer of dust covered everything. Eliza squinted her eyes to see the back wall as she felt it with her arms outstretched. The closet was fairly good sized. Her fingers touched the notebooks and the leather boxes. In disbelief, she wondered at how long all of this must have been hidden away, tucked in time. Eliza marveled, once again, at the care and attention her grandmother took to preserve each and every object on the shelves.

By reading the numbers on the bindings, she located the first volume. Slowly, she took it off the shelf and ran her hands over the cover, leaving tracks in the thin layer of dust.

Eliza went out, shut the closet behind her, and turned the key to lock it. She heard the click and felt the bolt slip into place. Satisfied, she studied the cover of the journal in her hand and walked over to the balcony while she slipped the key into her pants pocket.

In the bright light of morning, she was able to see the worn, leather cover and the etching on the binding with the Roman numeral I in faded gold ink. The top left cover had started to peel apart, and all the corners were tattered. She gently pressed the peeling leather back into place.

Certain she had the correct journal, she decided to sit out on the covered balcony. The soft breeze relaxed her as she settled into one of the comfy chairs.

The same question remained as she opened the cover of the journal: what would have kept her grandmother bound to a silence so sacred she dared not even share it with her own daughter?

CHAPTER SIXTEEN

HOLDING HER BREATH, Eliza opened the cover and saw her grand-mother's initial entry. Slowly, she began to read the script on the pages not wanting to skip one word. Instead, she wanted to savor each letter that was so poignantly penned for this exact moment.

My Dearest Eliza,

I've spent many years of my life compiling this chronology for you. I've tried to make it as precise as memory would allow. The journals are filled with history, descriptions, emotions, and mainly people I've loved so dearly all my life.

It was my dying wish that you would one day sit with "me" here and read what I've so desperately chosen to hide most of my life and that of your mother. Time has now opened the door for you, and I welcome you with deepest gratitude.

I know it can't be easy to think of possibly rewriting your family's history, but it is truth, and I believe truth, coupled with grace, must always be heard. I don't think you will be disappoint-ed. Learn from my life, dear. Be watchful not to let time sour your heart. Let love write your story instead.

I am so pleased you are joining me.

All my love,

Grandmother

The word "sour" immediately jumped from the page and tugged at Eliza's heart. She put her hand to her chest as if to guard her own from being soiled any further. Eliza had never thought a heart could sour until now. Her grandmother had so eloquently described the turmoil she had endured for the last several months. The amount of loss and loneliness had easily left its wounds in her, but the word "sour" pierced her now and begged to be examined further. She could almost taste it as she licked her lips as if to rid her mouth of the bitterness. The walls were sour even though they seemed safe.

Intrigued by her grandmother's invitation, Eliza returned to her memoirs and found the first entry:

It was the year 1908 and I was a mature eighteen year old already battling to keep my wits about me as our small family of four suffered a devastating winter and quickly became a family of two.

The cold that year had crept in with a ferocity that none of us had ever seen before, not even the elders of our town. The frigid winds seemed to take their time leaving, slapping us in the face as we braved the chill. In the dusty, frozen cemetery on the edge of our small Texas town of Eagle Pass, my father and I buried my mother and my younger sister. It had felt as if each tear was frozen to my cheeks, and I remembered Father pulling his cowboy hat down upon his head, trying to cover his ears from the biting cold.

It was such a dark time filled with an abominable silence that I wanted to crush it between my fingers.

Losing my mother left me in the precarious position of running the affairs of our home, caring for Father, and polishing my skills in female maturation. Not easy tasks to master while battling my grief. My resources for perseverance were limited, and I relied on the memories of the way in which my mother had lived to help me get through.

Because Father was gone so much due to his cattle brokering business, my mother and sister and I were often left together for weeks on end. On a typical day our home by the river would be filled with friends and acquaintances. An elaborate buffet of foods and delicacies was presented every Sunday for many people. We held church picnics and baptisms in our backyard as the preacher used the river to immerse new believers, and we hosted many a celebration to welcome those young and old in their newly-found faith.

Mother moved about the house with an ease and gentleness that mesmerized me as a young girl. I so wanted to mimic her every move and become the dignified beauty she was. Her gorgeous red hair was flawlessly poised atop her head with soft tendrils outlining her tender features.

We had a delightful, two-story home with a farm close to town. Father provided well, and we had field workers and maids who helped Mother with the daily chores. Sister and I spent much of our time schooling at the Catholic girls' school in town. We went in our carriage pulled by our beloved horse, Pet.

When Sister fell ill, Mother worked tirelessly caring for her. She was adamant that she tend to her and left the rest of the housework to our help, Eva and Marianna, as well as me. Elizabeth was only twelve and much younger than I and seemingly more feeble. Father was in Mexico and not due back for two more weeks.

As the days passed and Sister grew worse, I began to hear Mother's chest rattle as she too struggled to take a deep breath. It was only a matter of days after that when Mother's face paled and she ran a fever. She refused to rest, though, for fear my sister, Elizabeth, would slip away. I remember her arguing with Doc Richards day after day.

"You won't be no good if ya don't slow down, Mrs. Lane. You are plumb worn out, an' I can see a wanin' in your eyes. That fever gonna set in 'fore you know it, and I can't do nothin' after that."

"I'll be fine, Doc. You tend to Elizabeth and let me be. I just need a quick rest and I'll bounce back," Mother said as she coughed.

"I hope you're right 'cuz I can't convince you otherwise."

Sadly, she didn't listen and she sank into such a state that her fever never subsided. Her obstinacy was, no doubt, her downfall.

Father arrived home when he got word at the border and continued to do all he could to save them. Unfortunately, his efforts were futile at that point. Mother's fever took her in the night a week before Elizabeth passed.

I felt so incredibly guilty as I sat with Father the night of Elizabeth's funeral. I felt I had let him down. Tears of desperation and anger poured from my eyes and seemed not to stop for weeks. I couldn't speak for several days, and my eyes burned from endless crying. Our once-happy haven of life and love was swept away into an abyss of silence and grief.

I couldn't understand how God could take my mother and sister. Where was He? Why couldn't I have taken ill instead and been saved from the utter misery of this consuming grief? Many nights I slept, clutching our family's Bible, praying God would answer my cries. I buried my head in the quilts so no one would hear me sob, especially Father. He sat solemn night after night, day after day, trying to stay strong, immersing himself in business.

When the sun rose I would run to Eva's house next-door, shadowing her throughout the day, hoping to find purpose, hoping to hear an echo of hope. I couldn't find comfort no matter what I occupied myself with and no matter with whom I spoke. I remained restless and angry.

As soon as the winter winds quieted and the days held tinges of warmth, I went to the river and fed off the memories of sweet, full times of laughter and promises of life. My fingers dug into the earth, and I pulled on the small shoots of winter grass as Mother's favorite Scriptures ran through my head. I strained to hear her pronounce the words. I strained to linger in the memories of the past when death was far off and we knew nothing of it, nor prepared for it.

I remember questioning the Lord day after day. "If love never fails, why do I remain hopeless and lost?" It was safe to say I felt betrayed by love, and anger seemed the better friend at the time. A silent, dignified anger overtook me that I only spoke of in the wide open where I knew God could hear me. I challenged Him to prove me wrong. I wasn't going to work on my faith any longer. It was His turn. We lived a righteous life that spilled over with generosity to others and were dedicated to prayer and obedience. He failed me, or at least that is what my young heart determined to believe.

I wanted out of the house and begged Father to take me the next time he went away on business to Mexico. Springtime was coming, and I felt caged and hopeless. At that moment I hated Eagle Pass, the small border town where we lived. I detested the silence in my heart. Nothing seemed right in the world without Mother and Elizabeth.

I gave Father an ultimatum to either take me with him, or I was going to set out on my own in search of the hope that would shatter the bars I felt closing in around me. He was overwhelmed, and I was utterly undone. I am sure he couldn't fathom toting his daughter with him, but I couldn't fathom staying at home. The last several months were cruel.

I did not consider myself capable of withstanding the abuse of loss any longer. My heart cried out for fresh faces and a new landscape far away from the gray shadows of our house.

This wasn't an easy decision for Father to make. The cattle business between Mexico and Texas could be very dangerous at times. Father's prominent ranching contacts in Texas employed him to go into interior Mexico and buy cattle throughout the year.

It was a time-consuming and tricky business. When Father would receive a buy order, he headed to Mexico—usually into Coahuila where he had good contacts. After several weeks, perhaps even a month of sorting and buying cattle, he would then arrange for the cattle to be shipped to the border by railway.

Father always carried much cash with him, and this made him a prime target for banditos and robbers in Mexico. It wasn't unusual for a train to be jumped in the night and the people on board held at gunpoint. Therefore, Father was insistent on riding the train with the cattle he was bringing back. He knew many people depended on him to deliver what they had bought and he delivered—even at the risk of losing his own life. Father understood that he could be murdered at any time on the train, but he was determined to conduct business and that is why many in Mexico and Texas considered him to be the best cattle broker. He was sought after constantly, even by folks as far away as Oklahoma.

It was understandable why he did not want me to go with him. He paced the floor night after night as I pleaded with his heart to let me go with him, knowing I could never penetrate his logic.

"Dusky," he said, "I am always in danger whenever I go into Mexico or am returning. Agents on the border know I carry a lot of money with me not only to buy the cattle but to pay them off when I come back through. All it takes is one of the policia *on the border to tip off a bandito about when and where I am coming through and then they will jump me. It happens more than you know. That's why I depend on good contacts in Mexico to help me get there and back in one piece, but it can all turn on a dime." He slapped his hand down on the table as his piercing Germanic eyes stared me down.*

I never flinched, but sat erect in the chair ready for another standoff until he yielded to my request.

"I know you're sad and angry, but my job is to provide and protect you, not lead you into the hands of danger. The school up the road run by the nuns has agreed to let you board there and be an assistant teacher.

"Going with me makes absolutely no sense," he continued, his voice rising in volume. "I cannot even imagine what your mother would think. You are a young lady, Dusky. It is my job to see you rise up and embrace your station in life. I know nothing of training you to be cultured and poised, but the nuns do and they have raised many fine young ladies in their institution. I am grateful they will have you."

"No!" I was furious but tried not to show the level of my anger.

Calming myself, I spoke carefully. "Father, please, I will keep to myself and do what you say. I beg you to let me go. My soul will crumble if I stay here with the nuns. There is no future left for me here. Can you not see that?

"I must leave. I will wither if I stay. You are right that I am no longer a child. Then I should be allowed to have a say in my future. I'll leave Eagle Pass. I would like to accompany you, but if that is not acceptable then I ask you to make arrangements for me to go to San Antonio and stay with Aunt Maggie."

Finally, he relented and agreed that come the end of April he would head south to Mexico and take me with him. I was elated at the prospect of leaving this town and being free from the darkness I felt growing inside of me.

Spring passed quickly due to the promise of freedom in April. I made preparations with the servants to look after the house and pack my trunks. I took special care in packing Mother's belongings and Elizabeth's personal items, preserving them for my return.

A few new dresses arrived on the train, and their soft pastels lulled me from the dreary tones of winter's sting. The freshness of the crisp fabric and the impeccable embroidery were a welcome and cherished sight. Oh, how I missed Mother and Elizabeth.

"These dresses would look so handsome on her," I thought as I held

one against my body in front of the mirror. I could almost imagine Elizabeth tugging gently at my pleats to let me try one on, her timid giggle getting the best of me.

Mother had planned to take me that spring to San Antonio to stay with Aunt Maggie and enjoy the Battle of Flowers parade and other celebrations. I had waited years to be of age and to stay in San Antonio with Mother and Aunt Maggie, taking part in the weeklong celebration.

The rich history of the Alamo had always intrigued me. Mother often told stories of the Alamo and its brave men, recalling the few last letters penned by William Barrett Travis to his fellow Texans, pleading for aid on behalf of him and his men. His famous words "Victory or death" still scourged the hearts of Texans across the state.

I wondered if the sour wounds of the Texas revolution still festered in the hearts of many in Mexico. Perhaps that is what made Father's business so treacherous and profitable. The unpredictability of dealing with a culture still smoldering from a humiliating loss made my father a rare gem in the cattle business. His savvy ways earned him quite a reputation. He was held in high esteem on both sides of the border.

I was intrigued to know more about the man I called "Father" as he was all that I had left.

Father finally received his buy orders as April drew near. He discussed his plans with me. I sat attentively at our dining table so grateful he had conceded and said yes to my going with him.

"Dusky, sit down here and let's talk awhile about goin' to Mexico." I sat quietly and listened to him speak, his deep drawl rolling out each word. "See here, I've got two different buy orders for Mexico crossbred cattle with plenty of age. What that means is; I have to make two trips back to back to get these fulfilled."

He continued without falter. "Now I've taken the liberty to contact my good friend Señor Eduardo Roberto Peña de la Cruz and let him know I am comin' to buy cattle from him and that I'm bringing you. He is one of the wealthiest men in all of Mexico and a longtime friend and business contact. I buy many of my cattle from him and from the villages that surround his ranch in the mountains.

"I received word back that he and his wife, Penelope, are delighted to have us, especially you. Now when I return with the first shipment of cattle, you will stay with the de la Cruz family at their headquarters near Muzquiz, Coahuila. I will come back again, fill my order, and return to the United States for the second fulfillment. Then you will return on a different train with an escort from the de la Cruz compound. It is just too dangerous for you to come back with me."

"Oh, thank you, Father!" I exclaimed and hugged his neck.

I felt weightless for the first time in months. I knew Father was nervous about me going, and I worked hard at proving myself a worthy traveling companion. I also worked hard shutting out the pain of loss and the nagging questions about God. All I could think about was freedom—freedom for my heart.

We left within a week, and I never looked back. Our house was like a cemetery, and the journey ahead was life. I felt light and curious once again. I didn't know much about Father's world, but the thought of learning about his life in the cattle business brought a feeling of expectation and a much-welcomed purpose.

Father conducted most of his business at the Eagle Hotel where cattle were bought and sold over a drink. I was quickly fascinated with studying the men's faces and expressions.

We sat for what seemed like hours, meeting different men and listening to different deals. Father was well-liked. I could easily tell by the way others approached him, their postures almost submissive as they advanced to shake his hand.

I was allowed into a world mostly hidden from women. I began to understand the sacrifices he was making to allow me to accompany him. I stayed in the shadows as Father filled out the necessary paperwork and permit applications, his weathered hands meticulously marking the papers.

"It's more than ya realize, Dusky. Not only do I need to know how to play the game, but win it as well. Gettin' these cattle across the border requires difficult cooperation on both sides. That's why I carry so much money. I'll be shufflin' it through hands on either side to ensure the cattle get through undeterred. If I don't get 'em back here healthy, then they're *just about useless," he said, never looking up from the task spread out before him at the table.*

I studied his face as he offered more.

"Even when I arrive with the cattle at the Mexican border, it isn't a guarantee they will be allowed to cross. A new dance starts then as my permits can easily become invalid if I don't have any money to offer the officials to keep my cattle moving. It takes one crooked eye to cause me to stagnate and stale my herd. We call it modido. *It's how men like me pay off the government inspectors to keep our cattle moving on through without difficulties or fake penalties.*

"You'd be surprised at what comes up if you don't know what you are doin'. Those officials can smell it too. I've seen them pick off those rookie brokers like locusts in a cornfield. I've seen them forced to leave their cattle at the border pens to rot."

"How do you know you will be able to get the cattle through?"

"That's just it. You don't unless you've been in the business a long time and have connections on both sides of the border. Even when I get a nod to unload the cattle at the border, I've still got to get them through quarantine for our Texas officials to inspect and draw up paperwork. And most likely it will depend on an inspector's mood that day. Sometimes an order can be bottlenecked indefinitely."

"But couldn't that ruin your business?" I was aghast at what a ruthless process it seemed to be.

"Ruin you, go broke, lose your temper, and get put in jail. I've seen just about everything. That's why having friends on both sides of the border is crucial to foreseeing a successful transfer."

"Mr. Lane," a young man announced as he approached our table with his hat in his hand and his khaki pants covered in mud and dirt.

"Johnston, sit down if you will."

"Thank you, sir. Don't mind if I do. Ma'am." He nodded in my direction, and I met his gaze from the corner of my eye.

"Sir," Johnston said, "I need your help. I've got 'bout 350 head of cattle I'm tryin' to get through up to the panhandle for a new client near Amarillo, but they won't let me pass. I've exhausted every option I can

think of. It's gonna be the end of me. You know as well as I do, if they don't get sick and die, then they'll probably get stolen. I'll never get my buy order filled and delivered." His eyes were almost wild with fear as he pleaded his case.

"Go ask for Antonio Herrera and tell him I sent you," Father said. "Hand him your paperwork and he'll sign off on it as long as you take care of him. If you can't get past him, then I'm afraid there's not much I can do."

"I 'preciate it, sir. I'll go see 'bout speakin' to him right now. I can't afford another night here."

He stood up quickly, almost knocking his chair over in hopes to right his circumstances. I could see a spark return to his eyes as he hastily made his way through the other patrons, leaving through the double doors off to the side.

"That's a fine example of what I've been talking about. If it was summer, it would be even worse. It isn't unusual to see men with buckets in the summertime, dosing their overheated cattle with river water and hoping they'll last until the paperwork gets processed. A high death toll presents a pretty rotten stench plus more labor and time to drag off the dead carcasses. The only time I let my guard down is when I have safely delivered all the cattle to my clients. Precision, patience, and connections—that's what it is all about. And if you don't have those you won't make it."

"Well, what about him? Is he going to make it?" I asked leaning forward into Father's shadow.

"He'll do all right. Antonio will take care of him this time, and hopefully, he'll get some bigger clients that can help pay the way. None of it is a guarantee. Any one of these men can turn on you in a snap." He paused to pull out his stopwatch from his pocket. "Our train is leaving shortly. We need to meet the porter on the platform, and I need to stop by the border offices before we get on."

Father put me on the train while he finished wrapping up business at the border office. I began to get settled in our quarters anxious to feel the tug of the train underneath me. I smoothed my skirt over my petticoats and sat back into the cushions, my eyes catching the last swirl of passengers *waving tickets and hoisting their luggage into the train. The frantic sounds of the last-minute rush filled our quarters.*

Father made it just as the last call was being announced. Standing, he secured our bags and checked the tickets.

The train lurched and started toward the open stretch of countryside I could feel my heart humming with the changing landscape. Never having left Eagle Pass until this moment, I cherished every mile we drew further away from my hometown. It seemed as if my every limb grew longer.

As night fell and we finished dinner in the dining car, I could hardly think of sleeping. Every mile we covered took me further away from the grief and ugly memories of cold death. My focus had now become to learn to live again.

Eliza paused at the last four words her grandmother had penned. "Learning to live again" struck a chord in her own heart. Looking out at the hills, she understood that her pain was no longer unique. Loss had swept through her grandmother's heart too.

Eliza pulled her arms close. She could relate to that feeling of restlessness her grandmother had so eloquently described. She could feel it beating now in her own chest—the pull to walk out and away from what had once been the sweet sound of familiarity and leap headfirst into the risk of the unknown.

Eliza's thoughts were interrupted by the sound of Carmen ringing the bell. She picked up the journal and stepped inside to look at the clock. It was high noon. She put her grandmother's journal back in the closet and closed the door carefully. Reluctantly, she left the room and meandered down the stairs, her head full of the story she had read.

But risk doesn't always mean freedom.

CHAPTER SEVENTEEN

WHEN ELIZA'S EYES OPENED, she yawned and stretched, feeling refreshed and grateful for the luxury of an afternoon nap. She couldn't remember the last time she felt relaxed enough to drift off to sleep completely unaware of her surroundings. The hammock off the front porch had been an enticing reprieve in the stillness of the day. She could no longer hear Carmen in the main house, and she saw Juan Carlos' pickup parked down the hill.

Swinging her legs over the hammock's netting, she steadied herself and walked into the house. She noticed a note from Carmen on the table.

"Eliza, we are home for siesta. I'll be back at 4:30 to start dinner. Enjoy some dessert."

She bit into one of the lemon squares and put down the note as the fine sugar stuck to her skin. Licking her fingers, she climbed the stairs to go back to her grandmother's room. Picking up in the journal, she opened it where she left off. Sitting on her grandmother's bed, she plucked a fallen crumb off the page, found her place, and began to read again.

After two days on the train, we arrived in Muzquiz. The town was abuzz with activity and life. We unloaded our belongings and called a porter to help us. As I descended the steps, I took a deep breath and realized it smelled nothing like home. A rush of gratitude engulfed me.

Leaving our bags with an attendant, we walked across the road to the main inn—Hotel Colonial. The grand, stone columns in the front framed the worn entrance. Father approached the main desk to see if Augustino, one of the ranch hands from Rancho de La Cruz, had left his name. With the unreliability of the trains in Mexico, he wasn't sure if Augustino would be there.

"Si, Señor." The clerk nodded in the direction of a group of men talking by the small bar to the left.

"*Gracias,*" *Father replied as he tipped his hat and walked over to them. Sticking out his hand to a man with a black mustache, they shook hands. The man patted Father on the back. I stood near the entrance and Father led him over.*

"*My daughter.*" *Father extended his arm in my direction as Augustino's eyes lit up.*

"Con mucho gusto, Senorita." *Augustino bent over at the waist as he lifted his hat from his head. "Please follow me."*

Delighted, I smiled.

He led us to a beautiful, brown- and cream-colored carriage stationed in front under a clump of towering trees. I climbed in and peered out the glass as he and Father gathered our bags from across the road. Several men on horseback joined our convoy as we headed out of town.

Muzquiz was a beautiful, busy city. Exotic-looking men and women in colorful garments sold vegetables, dried beef, and crafts. I took in every flavor, smell, and sight. Life here was so very different—so fresh . . . or so it seemed that day.

"*Señor Lane, your ride here was safe?*" *Augustino asked Father as they sat opposite me.*

"*Couldn't have gone smoother. How is the ranch?*"

"*We could use more rain, but it is good. The family is good and our cattle are well taken care of, you will soon see.*"

"*I don't doubt that.*" *Father chuckled as we rode toward the mountains. My eyes were wide as I saw their majestic shapes rising in the distance. The smell of junipers and firs filled the interior of the carriage. The desperation of the past year began to dissipate and roll off my shoulders as I let hope chip away at the walls of grief.*

"*We should be there before sunset.*" *Augustino leaned in as he watched my eyes fixate on the passing expanse. "And you won't be disappointed. I promise."*

Timidly, I responded, "I can't imagine that I will. My heart is already healing." I could feel Father studying me as I kept my head turned toward the glass.

The sun began to wane, and in the distance I could see what appeared to be a large fortress with massive walls and trees all around. Much larger than I ever dreamed, it was an oasis in the arid hills. Its enormous size demanded attention as it sat steadfastly in its place, taking command of its surroundings.

"This is the Hacienda de La Cruz, Dusky. This is where we will be staying with Hacendado Eduardo and his family."

Speechless, it was obvious that even among the tall mountains, the hacienda dominated the landscape. I began to make out various roof sizes and what seemed like a tower. Huge, arched gates were positioned at various spots along the walls. On the left side was a river of crystal blue water, flowing unobstructed among the cream-colored rocks. The vegetation was lush along the river bottom, and it spread out to the edges of the hacienda with thick, green grasses and flowers.

"How did they build this?" I asked not really expecting a response.

"With sun-dried bricks made of mud. We call it adobe," Augustino offered. "You can tell by the different colors from the dirt like brown and cream. Over there are the main gates with the de la Cruz name carved in stone above it. We call the main doors portones. See how they are made with dark, heavy wood and lots of bolts and locks to hold them together? On a beautiful day like today, we keep them open for people to pass through. You can even fit two carriages at the same time."

The horses tugged and lurched as we passed through the gates at the sudden movements of the grounds alive with people, horses, cattle, and carts. It was as if we had entered another town. An entire village existed behind the walls—completely self-sustaining.

Augustino pulled down the quarter-glass panel so he could whistle to the footman. The sounds of people talking, bargaining, arguing all at one time filled the space around us along with dust from horses trotting by and women strolling together with huge baskets tucked under their arms.

Father had told me grand stories of the haciendas he visited and their elite hacendados—hacienda owners—but I didn't have the depth to imagine someplace as extraordinary as this. He described Mexico's social life as a dynasty. Marriages were arranged, much like those of European royalty, to ensure mergers of great wealth and land.

The peasants, or peones *as they were called, were often indebted to the hacendados and had to work for life on the estates. The wealthy were extravagantly wealthy, and the poor stayed poor and dependent upon their superiors.*

Many families, like the de la Cruz, were direct descendants of the Spaniards. Their ancestors received large land grants from Spain's monarchy and came to Mexico to increase their already deep pockets.

After the French were expelled in 1867, Señor Eduardo's family, along with many others, confiscated land that belonged to French sympathizers. This act alone propelled the de la Cruz family to be one of the largest hacendados in Northern Mexico. Most landowners had at least a couple of hundred thousand acres. The de la Cruz family, Father told me, owned close to a million.

"Over here is the workers' quarters," Augustino said, rolling on with his narrative describing and pointing out all the details. "This is the place of everyday life, if you will. See how everything sort of spills out of the windows and onto the porch—the laundry, dogs, children, chairs."

He stopped to give a whistle and a wave. The small children caught a glimpse of our arrival and ran alongside, waving and cheering.

"Over on the opposite side is the commissary where people barter, buy, or swap goods. It is always the busiest place in our village. And to the back right are the stables and the large barn. As you can see, the corrals and pens are filled with horses, cattle, and goats."

"And in the middle right here?" I asked, pointing to the one building settled in the midst of all the chaos.

"Ah, yes, that is our chapel and bell tower. We have it perfectly placed at the end of our zocolo *or square as you may call it. It is used daily for prayers by everyone. And now, we are making our way to the main hacienda."*

With gorgeous vines covering its walls and dripping in yellow flowers, the main home was a cathedral of color. Flowers were set in large terracotta pots scattered along the top of the walls, and huge trees guarded the perimeter. Their large, heavy branches hung low over the walls and brought shade to the dry, dusty road outside the hacienda. The lushness of the main grounds contrasted sharply with its arid surroundings.

"Senorita Dusky, bienviendos to Hacienda de la Cruz," Augustino said as he turned and smiled at me. The carriage came to a stop at the entrance, and we were greeted by a flurry of servants. "Come let us show you the jewel of the mountains."

The door opened, and I could feel my heart beating in my throat as I stepped down onto the ground. I felt overwhelmed and shy all of a sudden. I took Father's arm, and we walked into the large colonnade that led us straight to the doors. Huge columns of carved wood lined the walkway, along with heavy, hollowed-out rock planters filled with enormous agave plants. Bougainvillea dangled overhead, running all the way to the doors and down the walls. The pink blossoms littered our path like colored confetti.

Two well-dressed men in white linen shirts greeted us at the doorway, while a parade of household help fell in behind us carrying our luggage. We were escorted through lush courtyards smothered in red geraniums, vibrant yellows of the esperanza plant, cacti with blossoms all nestled under the canopies of glorious oak trees. The lawn was carpeted in deep, green grass, surrounded by vegetation of every color and size.

Gardeners, housekeepers, cooks, handmaids, and butlers scurried through the courtyard, carrying out their duties in obedient silence. Eye contact was minimal except when they stopped to acknowledge our presence on the accidental chance our paths crossed. It felt strange to be treated so royally.

"Senorita, you will stay in this room, and Señor, you will be in the room next-door. Please let us know what else you need. It was a pleasure to meet you." Augustino turned to me, bending his head.

"Thank you, Señor Augustino . . . my pleasure as well." I stepped into my quarters and began to put away my belongings.

Eliza closed her eyes and soaked in her grandmother's words—the vivid descriptions and emotions. Her body relaxed into the cool bed cover, and she glanced toward the photos on the bedside table. In the back corner sat a portrait of a young lady. Eliza drew closer and examined the eyes of the girl as they seemed to examine Eliza's. The familiar softness spoke to her. She opened the frame to read the back of the photo. It read: Dusky Victoria 1908. It was taken a year before the journey to Mexico.

The long shadows cast by the sun fell upon the bed, and Eliza wondered what time it was. As she turned toward the window, she could see the sun hanging low in the hills. Undoubtedly, Carmen would be downstairs.

Setting the journal aside, Eliza walked down to the kitchen and peeked around the corner. Carmen was busy preparing a tray. She caught Eliza's eye and smiled.

"I thought you'd like to continue your work upstairs, so I made a tray for you."

"Thank you, that's really thoughtful," Eliza said, wondering if she should mention the journals. "Carmen," she began hesitantly, "how did you and Juan Carlos come to work here?"

"Well," she responded, wiping her hands on a red dish towel tucked in her apron, "Juan Carlos came from Mexico with his parents when he was very, very young." She stopped to clear her throat and wiped down the butcher block in the middle of the room.

"They had work here," she continued, "and Juan Carlos stayed all the years because he loves the ranch and loved your grandmother so much too." Carmen brought her hands toward her face and then stopped to cup them on top of her chest. Smiling, she paused and offered no more.

Eliza decided not to press further and picked up her tray of food. Before walking out, she turned toward Carmen. "Thanks again for taking such good care of us . . . me and my grandmother. It's comforting to know how much you all care and how long you have been here."

"You're welcome. It is our pleasure, truly."

When Eliza left the kitchen, she got the feeling Carmen knew more about her grandmother's past than she cared to share at the moment. Strangely, she felt reassured by Carmen's restraint.

CHAPTER EIGHTEEN

WITH THE TRAY IN HER LAP and the journal in front of her on the small table, Eliza continued poring over the handwritten pages.

My clothes were filthy, and I welcomed the chance to splash cool water on my face. Dust from the ride had literally covered every inch of my bare skin.

"Buenos tardes," a small voice said from the back of the room. "My name is Maria. I will be your chambermaid while you are with us."

"Gracias. I'm Dusky. Thank you for your help."

Maria moved swiftly to hang all my garments in the wardrobe. I pulled out one of my finer dresses since supper was always an event, especially tonight. We would not be the only guests. High-ranking government officials from the President's cabinet would be joining the de la Cruz family this evening.

"This is lavender oil for you," Maria said as she placed a small bottle in the palm of my hand. "I learned how to make it from my grandmother. She was French, and many years ago the French had much influence here in Mexico and brought many gifts. My grandmother taught me how to grow and tend the herbs. Allow me."

She dabbed a few drops on my wrist and the sweet, mild scent filled the room. I rubbed my wrists on my neck and inhaled.

"Thank you, it smells so fresh."

"Let's get you into your dress now." Maria moved to unbutton the back bodice of the limp garment draped on the bed, and I walked over to the basin to fix my hair.

A knock came at my door shortly after. Father stood waiting outside with Juan, one of the servants, who came to escort us to the family's private dining courtyard.

"*You look lovely,*" *Father said as he offered his arm.*

"*Thank you, and you look very handsome,*" *I replied as I reached up to slip my arm through his.*

We walked through several porticos, porches, and gates. We made our way through what seemed like a maze of plants, vines, and flowers that covered every inch of the hacienda property.

We passed the main fountain crafted from carefully chiseled cantera stone. Tiers and tiers of carved layers trickled water from one level to the next and landed in a splash in the ornate basin. The birds dashed in and out and fluffed their feathers with the cool water.

Finally, we arrived at the courtyard lit with luminescent candles, music, and the warmth of people. Immediately, a tall, handsome gentleman came over and embraced Father.

"Ricardo, mi amigo," *he said, smiling brilliantly and hugging Father. Father greeted him warmly as well with a tight squeeze.*

"*Eduardo, please let me introduce you to my daughter Dusky.*" *Father turned to me.* "*Dusky, Señor Eduardo de la Cruz, the master of this castle.*" *Father finished with a grand sweep of his arm and Señor Eduardo approved with a laugh and a pat to his back.*

"Señor de la Cruz, con mucho gusto," *I responded with a slight bow.*

He took my face in his hands and smiled. "*You, my dear, are a beautiful addition to us. Your father did not warn me he was bringing such a gorgeous woman to my home. He knew what chaos would erupt between my three sons. I will delight in the competition that ensues over such a beautiful lady's attention as yours.*" *He winked at Father.*

I ducked my head and felt my face flush crimson with embarrassment.

"*Come, Eduardo,*" *I heard a melodic voice say.* "*You must not scare this perfect angel just yet. She's bound to flee before I even get the chance to welcome her and enjoy getting to know her.*

"*Dusky,*" *she said as I lifted my eyes to meet hers. She took my hands.* "*I'm Penelope. Welcome to our home, my dear. We are honored to have you with us this summer.*"

"*Thank you, Señora de la Cruz. I am so grateful to be here with you as well.*"

She held my hands firmly and looked into my eyes, "I am Penelope to you, dear. You are family to us." Her gentle touch was reminiscent of my mother's.

"Thank you," I whispered, looking into her sweet, blue eyes. She was absolutely regal with her petite frame, fragile features, and fair skin. Her golden-brown hair was pulled up into a bun with flowers woven between each wisp. She smelled fresh, like a bouquet of roses. Her skin was radiant . . . not a blemish upon her face.

We walked arm and arm toward the table, and Penelope casually began to chat with me.

"So, Dusky, tonight we have government officials from President Dîaz's cabinet dining with us, and the conversation will no doubt become very intense before the night is over." She leaned close to me.

Her persona was warm and attractive. She moved with ease through the gathering of people, taking the time to introduce me to everyone.

I listened closely as she told me about Mexico's current political state.

"It is no secret we are one of the most influential families of Northern Mexico. Many hacendados of the North do not want any government interference of their operations. However, we are on friendly terms with Porifirio Dîaz, and he continually sends his men up here to keep his relations with us in good standing. I think he hopes we will one day influence our good friend of Chihuahua, Hacendado Luis Terrazas, to consider Dîaz a friend rather than foe.

"Even since the colonization of New Spain, hacendados have resented forces of centralized government. We have no need to depend on outside sources for labor or materials. Our vaquero *work forces and their families are dependent upon us and fiercely loyal as well."*

She continued on in quiet confidence without losing her tranquil smile.

"For years Dîaz has been looking to strengthen his alliances in Northern Mexico, but he is growing old and so are his supporters. Talk of a new government, a smaller government, is in the air. I am sure tonight Mexico's future will be on the table.

"I do hope you are not bored with the details, but our very livelihood hangs in the air as we continue to press for our independent needs." She

winked as she smoothed the front of her long, red skirt. Her gold bangles fell down her arm like synchronized chimes.

The hacienda system was very intricate and massive and more similar to the European feudal systems of the past than I ever realized. As the bell rang, everyone made their way to their places marked by cards at the table. To my left sat Señor Peña and to my right sat Penelope's second oldest son, Gustavo. He was a strapping seventeen year old with a startling flash in his eyes and the physique to match.

In looks, Gustavo took after his father with his dark-brown hair and intense, brown eyes. His strong muscular build was the perfect complement to his strong ideas.

Across the table and down toward Penelope sat Gustavo's youngest brother, Miguel, who seemed much quieter and more observant. At twelve, he had not earned the privilege to comment on a man's world. Because his juvenile frame had not matured, it was hard to tell whom he would resemble. He had Señor Eduardo's caramel coloring but Penelope's slight features.

As he tapped his glass, Señor Eduardo commanded the attention of the group. "I would like to welcome our guests Señor Ricardo and his daughter, Dusky."

I blushed as the attention of the table turned to me. I caught the eyes of Roberto, the eldest of the three boys. Seated across from me, he was clearly the leader his father was and every bit the diplomat like his mother. His face held a strong resemblance to hers. He had her gorgeous blue eyes and perfectly balanced features along with her sun-streaked brown hair. He was the most handsome man I had ever laid eyes on in my life.

We smiled cordially at one another before Señor Eduardo continued with a blessing.

Servants fluttered about the table as the meal was lavishly presented in several courses, all served on colorful porcelain platters or bowls. I tasted foods mixed with chiles, tomatoes, chocolate, corn, beans, cinnamon, almonds, and citrus—every course exotic and foreign to my South Texas taste buds.

"I hope you are enjoying yourself," Gustavo said without completely turning his head toward me. "We enjoy the presentation more than the consumption if you haven't realized that yet."

I smiled as I reached up to cover my mouth with my napkin.

"Don't feel as if you have to eat all that is placed in front of you. We take pride in spoiling our guests with extravagance."

"I see that," I said. "You certainly do a beautiful job. I feel quite spoiled already."

"Good, then our hospitality is doing its job." He slurped his soup and lent an ear to the conversation developing on my left.

"Why would we want to confuse our workers with various forms of authority?" Roberto said. "Right now, they work, earn money, and live safely within these walls. Bigger government only adds more confusion and less productivity for not only the country's people, but for the country's treasury as well."

The entire table suddenly fell quiet. The passion in his voice rose. I watched as his hands elaborated along with the words coming from his lips. For the first time in my life, I was completely mesmerized by the presence of another.

It was obvious Roberto had been groomed well for his role as the next hacendado. At twenty-one, his mind seemed at ease sorting through the minutia of business and politics. Daring to ask the questions others shied away from, his inquiries provoked thought and agreeable silence. I watched and listened carefully like a perched songbird, poised and alert as he negotiated the turbulent topic of simmering political leadership.

"Yes, Roberto," Señor Peña chimed in, "but you've forgotten, my friend, that we want to work with you side by side, providing for all."

"You fail to realize, Señor Peña, we are self-sufficient. We take care of our people socially and economically. We don't need to work with you, but we choose to tolerate a president and his politics to present a unified Mexico. However, you must never forget we are the backbone of this country. Without the haciendas, Mexico will never stand. It will crumble into corruption and extreme poverty for all of its people.

"Northern Mexico alone contains over one million head of cattle. If you do your math, that puts the value close to twelve-million pesos. Not to mention the various other holdings many of the northern hacendados have in mining, lumber, and banking.

"We believe in a unified Mexico, but we know true authority lies in the hands of the great haciendas."

Roberto stopped and sipped his wine calmly while waiting for a response. Our eyes met through the candlelight, and my body tensed at his stare. Breathless, I shifted my gaze to my plate. I was unfamiliar with the swirl of curiosity and confusion building inside me. I tried to muster a tidbit of intelligence or enlightenment to add to the dinner conversation, but nothing that came to my thoughts sounded fitting.

General Hernandez spoke to Señor de la Cruz from the other end of the table. "Eduardo," he said, chuckling, "you have trained your boys well in your ways. Dîaz and his supporters are aware you contribute to the greatness of our country. We want your ways to continue. There is no doubt about that. With Dîaz getting older, turnovers can become dangerous. We all know that fact, so we must stick together and keep Mexico moving into the twentieth century as a powerful and rich country."

Roberto's father looked pensive. The guests respectfully waited for his response. Through the flickering candlelight, I could see the look of concentration on his face. He brought his elbows to the table and folded his hands. His voice was deep and slow.

"Gentleman, we recognize that under Dîaz' presidency, trade with foreigners has expanded immensely. We have had peace in our rural lands, and a good foundation for a modern economy has been built. But he must not forget how our country rose to its current state." Eduardo's finger began to shake as he pointed it toward the faces of the Dîaz men. "We, the hacendados, have shed our blood and our own children's blood to achieve financial success for this country!

"The cattle industry alone has brought recognizable status with the United States and earned Mexico a prominent place in trade. A greedy government will only ruin our chances of growth. We are the ones who keep Mexico alive. Dîaz is merely a spokesman—a puppet, for that matter—for this country. Vain attempts to control our liberties will bring riotous behavior and strain the very threads of our entire existence. All will suffer alike."

Everyone at the table was silent after Eduardo's reproach.

I saw Miguel shift in his seat and look up at me with a smirk on his face while pretending to twirl his hair in his fingers. I covered my mouth as I smiled at his gesture to make me laugh by mocking the intensity of the conversation.

Penelope reached over to press his arm while she listened to her husband. Miguel was sweet and not yet fueled by the fire of politics like his brothers. His peculiar sense of humor was refreshing. I could tell he and I would be quick friends.

Eduardo continued unaware of Miguel's antics at the opposite end of the table. "I support Dîaz and will continue to encourage support from other northern haciendas. You have my word. In turn you and Dîaz must assure us all that your party will recognize our independent spirit and will uphold the freedoms of each hacendado.

"Now," he said as he abruptly pushed back his chair, "I would like to offer you gentleman cigars on the back terrace."

With his authoritative invitation, the heaviness around the table lightened, and I felt myself begin to breathe normally again. Señor Eduardo put his hand on Father's shoulder and smiled.

"It is never boring here is it, my friend? You alone are the perfect example of our success."

I watched Father as he smiled and nodded. Pushing back my chair, I heard an inviting voice over my shoulder.

"Allow me." I looked up to see Roberto standing behind me and offering to pull out my chair.

"Thank you," I said gently, meeting his blue eyes. I took his arm, and we strolled back through the main patio.

"You are a patient woman to put up with the unruly passions of men and politics," he said, smiling down at me.

"I find it more interesting than you might realize. I appreciate your family's passion to protect what you all have worked so hard to create. Your parents seem like wonderful people."

"Well, we always value the honest opinion of a beautiful young lady such as yourself," he replied.

I nodded and felt a flutter rise in my stomach. I looked toward the ground and fiddled with the pleats of my skirt. His charm and genuine words were refreshing to my soul and yet terrifying.

Oblivious to my bumbling, he continued without falter. "I would be honored to show you some of the property. Perhaps you would care to join me within the next day or two on horseback? We could tour the river bottom. I'll have the cooks prepare a lunch."

"That sounds delightful. I would like that very much."

"Very well, I'll have arrangements made with the stables."

We stopped outside my door, and I couldn't help but notice the way his eyes dazzled in the soft flicker of the lantern.

"I trust you will sleep well tonight, Senorita. I look forward to our ride. And, I promise not to talk politics."

We both smiled and said our cordial good nights.

Once inside my room, I collapsed on the bed and placed my hand on my chest. The unmistakable beating of my smitten heart was obvious. Taking a deep breath, I stared at the ceiling, wistfully delighting in the memories of Roberto's dashing good looks and warm personality. I had to convince myself he wasn't a dream. I was really here in Mexico, and my heart was beating with joy, not grief.

On Monday morning I was up and dressed when Maria arrived with my breakfast tray. She set it down on the table under the window and laid out the napkin and silverware. Then she refilled the vase with fresh-cut geraniums from the flower garden and arranged them quietly.

My stomach was a bit jittery with nerves. I was hesitant to eat, but the warm, thin, corn tortillas and fresh butter were too tempting to pass up. Slowly, I sipped my hot tea and looked out my window into the guest quarters' courtyard.

Already several workers in white pants and shirts were out watering and weeding the various floral beds, one of them fussing with the flowering vines that wove their way up the roof.

I saw Father pass by the window and heard his knock on the door.

"Good morning. Roberto tells me he is planning on taking you horseback riding with him and several attendants today. Is that right?" he asked.

"Yes, he asked the other night if he could show me the river. Would that be permissible?"

"As long as you are chaperoned. You are in good, safe hands with these folks, and I trust them implicitly. I will be going horseback in a couple of days. However, my trip won't be one of leisure but of work. Right now I am going to discuss with Augustino our options of round-up stock available.

"Since the property is so vast, it will be a time-consuming process to gather the livestock. We'll be taking a team on horseback as well as a cooking staff, so I suspect there will be several long nights spent out in the open. The cattle are scattered throughout the ranch, and with my order so large, it'll take a good amount of time to fulfill. From what I hear of late, the predators—men and animal alike—have been pretty fierce, so we will go with no less than thirty to forty men. I'll see you this evening and let you know what day we plan to head out."

He kissed the top of my head and walked toward the house.

Shortly after he left, a soft knock came to the door and a young male attendant escorted me to the stables. We walked in silence through the courtyards and out the front colonnade as my high-shank leather boots clicked against the stones.

Going through the gate, we stepped into the bustle of men, women, and children moving throughout the grounds attending to the needs of their daily lives with a casual calm before the heat of the day rose and all would retreat for a customary siesta.

We turned to the left and walked toward the enormous barn and its corrals. Chickens scurried under my feet, pecking furiously at the ground while goats devoured their hay in the back pens. The pungent smell of manure, hay, and feed moved with the breeze. I adjusted my hat and put on my leather gloves as we approached the shade of its covering.

Finally, we arrived at the back end of the barn and I could make out Roberto's strong silhouette against the sunlight. With his hand atop the saddle, he talked casually and jokingly with the stable boys. Hearing our approach he turned and smiled welcomingly. I felt my cheeks warm and hurried to distract myself by fidgeting with my glove before looking up at him.

"*Good morning, Dusky. Have you had breakfast this morning?*"

"*Yes, thank you. Good morning. What a lovely day for a ride.*"

"*Indeed it is. We are finishing saddling up, and we will be on our way shortly.*" He turned to the stable boy and pointed to the girth on the other horse. The boy checked the strap and slid the bit into the horse's mouth. As Roberto draped the reins over the horse's neck, he beckoned me to his side.

"*Allow me,*" he said as he offered his hand. The stable boy brought a step stool, and I climbed onto the smooth, leather saddle with my legs in sidesaddle position. I took the reins and waited for Roberto to mount his horse. Once seated, he walked his horse over to mine. A small entourage fell in behind us as we began our procession to the back gates.

"*This is so lovely,*" I said, smiling at him. "*I'm enjoying myself already. Thank you for taking the time to show me your gorgeous countryside.*"

"*It is my pleasure. This land is who I am and I love nothing more than to share it with others. My family has been here a long time, and I look forward to continuing the legacy that has been bestowed upon me.*" He continued without hesitation, his chest proud as he sat upright. "*My father's family has been here from the start of Mexico's colonization. His family led the way for many others to come and prosper in New Spain. I, too, plan to continue his traditions with my brothers as we usher in this new century. Mexico is ripe with opportunity.*

"*Tell me about your city in Texas. I have not traveled to the United States, but plan to make a trip across the border soon. We have property in Texas as well. In fact, much of our wealth is in banks up there.*" He turned to me and waited for my response, his eyes flickering under the brim of his hat.

"*Well, it certainly isn't as pretty or as peaceful as this, I can assure you. It's truly just a busy, border town that thrives on the cattle trade and its mercantile business. The name, Eagle Pass, comes from the flight of the Mexican eagles along the river. It's really dusty and dry most of the time . . .*" My voice trailed off, and I looked down at my horse's mane, hoping Roberto didn't notice the tears welling up in my eyes.

"*It must have some redeeming feature,*" he remarked.

I hesitated to answer, feeling the lump in my throat, but I pushed through until I heard the words form with the movement of my lips. "*It is *good for business, of course. Father has done quite well for himself . . . It just doesn't feel like home anymore with my mother and sister gone now. I guess my fondness for it is buried with them as well. . . . It's been a long winter." I focused on the cracked leather of the reins between my fingers.*

Lightening the conversation, I smiled. "Nothing compares to the beauty of your home and land here though. I always loved it when Father returned from his trips. He was full of rich stories of the grand castles of Mexico and the incredible beauty surrounding them. I'd sit for hours completely mesmerized by his descriptions.

"Mother, my sister, and I lived so quietly in comparison. We spent many nights by the piano and afternoons by the river. My sister and I loved to play duets and entertain our mother. We lived so peacefully and contentedly on the edge of town in a beautiful, two-story home filled mainly with Mother's family heirlooms. Her father was a doctor in Maximilian's army, so that is how she ended up in Texas.

"She and father met in San Antonio, and he began to seek his fortune in the cattle business. They settled in Eagle Pass because of its prime location between San Antonio and Mexico, especially with the new railroad established. Father was gone most of the time due to his business travels, so Mother truly raised Elizabeth and me by herself."

Looking up toward the sky I smiled, remembering with fondness the richness of my childhood. Roberto's attention was focused so intently on my words and mannerisms, it was almost uncomfortable. Never had I been in the presence of male company alone without supervision, and his sincere interest in my every word made thinking difficult.

"So you play the piano?" Roberto asked casually.

"Yes," I said, nodding. "I do. It's very relaxing for me. I love the way music and melodies fill up a room with the stroke of one key."

"Then you must play for us. Nothing adds beauty like music. I will insist." Roberto chuckled.

He pointed toward the cluster of trees hugging the riverside. "There is a little spot tucked right over there, where the river slows over the rocks and waterfalls hide small caves. My brothers and I played for hours down here in the summers as young boys. We splashed and bathed in the crystal-clear water. It was easy to hide behind the small waterfalls and scare each other. It holds many fond memories.

"My mother still believes these waters have special meaning. She finds rocks in the shape of hearts every time she comes. She tells us they represent the miracles of God in our lives. She has collected them and placed them in the gardens throughout the hacienda. Whenever one of us gets sick, she has this water brought up to the hacienda and has Padre Antonio anoint us and pray for healing."

He grinned and relaxed in his saddle as our horses walked under the shade where the smell of oaks and firs was thick in the air.

"So," he continued, "you are welcome to search for and keep any heart rocks you may find."

Taking a deep breath, he said, "I don't know what it is, but anytime I come here and drink in this pure air everything seems at peace within me."

He turned back and began to give his staff orders to dismount and prepare lunch. Immediately, one of the cowboys came to my side with his hand extended and placed a stool on the ground. I slid off my horse and thanked him for his help.

As I pulled off my gloves, I strolled toward the river and stood waiting for Roberto under the shade of a large oak tree. The thick, dark branches hung low with the weight of age. I reached up and touched the leaves with my fingers as I heard Roberto's footsteps behind me and turned upon his approach.

"Shall we wait for lunch down by the bank? I can show you the waterfalls."

"Absolutely," I answered eagerly.

I was curious to touch this gorgeous blue water I heard moving over the rocks. We walked a short way and stood at the edge of a small bank. It was a grassy spot where the ground gently melted into the water and rocks. It was just as Roberto described. Several small waterfalls spilled into the river and created puddles between the stones before it flowed into a grand, clear pool. I sat on the edge astonished by its clarity and sharpness. Every shape beneath the water's surface was clearly defined. Fish darted in and out of rocks at the flicker of a changing shadow. I stretched my hand out to feel the water, as I was almost certain it was an illusion.

Roberto sprang forward and landed on a rock halfway submerged *in the water. He quickly made his way to the next one and beckoned me with his hand to follow. Giggling, I extended my arms and started cautiously over the stones.*

Roberto waited and took my hand as I came closer. Soon we reached the waterfall with a small entrance tucked behind its ribbons of water. We ducked through the water and landed in an alcove unscathed, but damp.

I started laughing, feeling the moisture on my hair and face. It must have been contagious, and Roberto, too, began to laugh. We both wiped the water from our faces and dried our hands on our damp clothing.

It was a small space, enough for the two of us to stand or sit shoulder to shoulder. Roberto turned toward the rock wall and pointed above him.

"Here are some paintings that are from ancient dwellers that must have been here before. It is hard to tell what they are trying to say, but you can definitely make out animals, perhaps bear or deer and warriors hunting. Who can say?"

I followed his finger with my eyes as he traced each depiction. It was hard to make out the story, especially with the muted colors of rust, mustard, black, and brown. The years had eroded the crisp lines and blurred many of the figures. My gaze was transfixed on the wall and ceiling around us.

"I have never seen anything like this before. It's absolutely fascinating," I said in a whisper.

"My brother and I pretended to be warriors of this tribe, holding secret meetings in this cave, planning our next ambush. We would spend hours getting lost in the details of our game until we would hear Franco, one of Father's foremen at the time, yelling for us. Father was rather strict and had fairly high expectations for us even as children. When we did not show up for duties, he sent Franco to find us and bring us to him. We were skillful in knowing how to fluster Father and evade our duties, but now I understand and appreciate the importance of his discipline. At the time all we could think about was sneaking off.

"I believe it is time to eat. I know a small feast has been prepared for us on the bank. Shall we?" He dashed through the water one last time and step for step I followed him.

We carefully made our way back over the rocks and followed the path. Looking toward the bank, the cooks had set up a table and chairs in the shade.

"Welcome to lunch," Roberto announced.

"How perfect," I said, my face full of amazement as I was seated across from Roberto at a quaint table. My fingers unfolded the white linen napkin, and I pulled myself toward the table. "This is quite an affair, thank you."

Roberto smiled and we fell into a comfortable conversation over lunch.

"So you decided to come to Mexico because . . .?" his voice trailed off, coaxing me to pick up where he'd ended.

"Because I knew I couldn't stay in Eagle Pass. I needed to leave. I begged Father to take me or send me to San Antonio. Either way I was afraid of what would happen to me if I stayed."

"What do you mean?"

"Grief, sadness . . . they both seemed to follow me around like a shadow. I needed to know that there was a world bigger and different than the only one I had known. I didn't want what they had to offer—a life of isolation and fear. I wanted to test my heart. I needed to know I could live again despite all that had been lost."

"Then I would say you have succeeded. Wouldn't you say so?"

"I've succeeded in knowing my heart still beats and that is victory for now."

"I would agree." Roberto smiled and let his eyes linger on me. I could feel his curiosity as I continued with my meal.

His voice broke the silence. "If it would please you, we will take our siesta here by the river. The staff has set up cots for us under the shade."

"I'd like that very much."

After we finished our meal, I welcomed the quiet of the afternoon and easily drifted into a light rest, listening to the rush of the waterfalls. Upon awakening, I noticed everyone was still napping. Quietly, I rose from the cot and tiptoed toward the river with my hat in hand. Fixing my hair, I stopped as the sun's rays warmed my face. I closed my eyes and listened to the steady flow of the water.

I was stirred back into the moment by the warmth of a hand on my shoulder.

"Were you able to get some rest?" Roberto asked as he studied his surroundings.

"I did, thank you. I am truly refreshed. Who wouldn't be? This place is so special."

"So glad to hear that you were able to rest. The servants are packing up, and it is time to ride back. Believe it or not, dinnertime will come quickly. So, we must say our good-byes here, but I promise to bring you back soon. The horses are ready. Shall we?"

"Roberto," I ventured timidly, "if it is hurried when we return, I just want to properly thank you for such a delightful day. I know you are busy and for you to share your time is quite generous of you. It has been truly lovely."

"I, too, enjoyed myself. I don't get down here as much as I would like anymore. I take my job as eldest seriously. It is my duty to see to it that our guests are well entertained, is it not?" He grinned.

With that we turned and walked toward the horses. Roberto excused himself and moved ahead to instruct the workers and oversee their duties. Looking back, I felt a tinge of regret as the formalities seemed to return between us.

Touching the back of my horse, I walked to its side and stepped onto the stool awaiting me. I mounted properly and listened for the others. Roberto brought his horse around the large oak and gave a signal for our small tribe to commence the trek back to the homestead. Without a single twitch from me, my horse fell into a rhythm and found its place with the rest of the group. While Roberto worked accounting for his men and their wares, I rode silently, making notes about the day. I didn't want to forget a single moment.

We seemed to arrive back at the hacienda so quickly, and before I knew it I was walking back to my quarters with the same gentleman who delivered me to the stables hours ago. As I suspected it was busy when the ride ended. Roberto and I had exchanged quick but warm thank yous before we parted.

"How was your day, senorita?" Maria asked as I entered my room and found her turning back the covers for the evening. She approached and handed me a sweet-smelling sachet of rosemary. "This is for remembrance."

"It smells heavenly," I replied, studying her smile and trying to conceal the unspoken thoughts of my heart.

"Enjoy. May I pour a bath for you?"

"Yes, thank you."

After my bath I dabbed on the lavender oil and chose the soft, cream dress with delicate lace along the bodice for supper. My hair was a touch unruly from the day, but I managed to sweep it up gracefully, and I placed Mother's pearl comb amidst the wavy locks.

Father knocked on the door, and we walked slowly through the courtyard to dinner.

"I trust you had a good day with Roberto?"

"It was . . . very lovely. The river is so beautiful. I'm so grateful you allowed me to come with you."

Father smiled and patted my hand tucked against his arm.

"I'm glad you convinced me. It's good to see you smile again."

"It's what they would have wanted . . . for us to be together and going on with life in the best way we know how." I stopped to look up at him before I continued. "We're allowed to love again, we're allowed to enjoy our lives and let our hearts beat again. As cruel as it may seem at times, it truly is the best gift we can give them."

Father's eyes filled with tears. He wiped his handkerchief under his nose and swiftly looked away. "You're right. It's just hard. All my life I lived to care for the three of you, and somehow I feel like I failed because they died. I still can't get past the anger I feel toward myself. I let your mother down. I left her alone to face an enemy bigger than her."

"Please, Father, no. Look at me. We never wanted for anything because you made everything possible for us. Mama knew how much you loved her. None of us saw what was coming. It blew in one night and never left. All that could have been done was done, I can assure you of that."

"I hear that, but it is my senseless nagging of duty that haunts me

still today. All I know to do is to keep doing what I've always done and hope that one day the plague in my soul subsides."

"Father, love is a choice and you must choose it. God didn't tell us to choose fear and regret and sadness. He said to choose love and He will make all things new."

"That He did. I'm trying, sweetheart. I promise, I'm trying."

I continued without compromising the moment or giving in to his weakness. "Even though I grieve, I will choose to love. Even though I mourn, I will choose His joy. I can't do it alone. I see it all clearly now. Surely we will live with great love or surely we will wither and die and neither of us is ready for that."

He rubbed his hand over his mouth and worked to loosen the clenching in his jaw. I stared intently into his eyes, begging for his agreement, but he averted his glance.

"Come, I'm sure they are waiting on us now."

Quietly, I took his arm, determined on the inside to break through his encrusted exterior before summer's end and our return home.

When we arrived at the family dining room, the table was set for seven: Father, myself, and the de La Cruz family. Intricate wooden candelabras dominated the tabletop, one posted close to each end. White linens with embroidered napkins featured the family seal. Each goblet was filled with red wine that reflected the candlelight like tiny burgundy mirrors. Everyone convened simultaneously, and we each sat at our assigned places. Penelope was at my end of the table with Miguel and me on either side of her. Father was to my right next to Señor Eduardo's left. Directly across from him sat Roberto and then Gustavo between his brothers.

Soon we were served and flanked by servants on either side of the table. I heard Penelope in discussion with Miguel about some apparent antics that had happened in the cooking quarters earlier.

"And none of the help would go back in. They refused to work, thinking someone had put a curse on them when they found the live frogs in one of the clay cooking pots. You wouldn't happen to know who would do such a thing would you, Miguel?" Penelope raised her left eyebrow as she glared at her son.

Miguel sat frozen in his chair.

Penelope continued, obviously not amused by his silence. "Finally, I got the priest to come and he blessed the room with holy water."

Miguel could no longer contain his mischief and broke out into a loud laugh. Reaching over to pinch his ear, Penelope admonished him. "That is foolish and irresponsible. Next time I will tell your father and you will have to take his lashes. Really, Miguel, you are almost thirteen—practically a man. In a few months you will sit by your father. He has no tolerance for child's play. Be warned!"

He flashed me a quick smile and bit his lip. I turned the other way not wanting to fall prey to his merriment.

The night ended uneventfully, and the men retired for cigars and more talk of business while Penelope and I said our customary good nights.

In bed later that night, I held the sachet of remembrance as each part of the day replayed in my head. Happiness was taking root in my heart once again. I prayed it would last.

Eliza could feel a smile break out over her own face. The warmth in her heart was growing. The testimony of her grandmother's fervent fight to love stewed in her mind, building a cord of strength Eliza had lacked before.

Night had begun to overtake the sky and the hills grew dark. Gathering her things, she walked inside and down the stairs.

"Hi, Carmen. I'm so sorry. I've been so caught up in Grandmother's story that I haven't given much attention to anything else. I've forgotten my manners."

"Goodness no, Mija, you are fulfilling your Grandmother's dream. That is what she wanted more than anything. We are only here to help. You take time for yourself and her. Please, don't think about it for one more minute."

"You are so kind," Eliza replied as she placed the empty tray near the sink and made a cup of hot tea. Carmen laid out some sweets on the table, and Eliza put a few on a small tray and walked to the living area. She sat near the fireplace, opened the journal, and continued to read by the slow crackling from the fireplace.

CHAPTER NINETEEN

DREW SLUNG HIS BRIEFCASE across the seat and started the engine of his truck. He planned to meet Mitch after work for a plate of barbeque by San Pedro springs. His tires hummed over the asphalt road as he made his way through downtown. He thought of Eliza and their brief conversation earlier.

He was grateful she called to let him know she had made it and was fine, but he wasn't willing to let their relationship revert to shallow talk. He could feel the fight for her rise up inside of him. He had let her go one too many times, but no longer.

He passed by the church and stopped in the parking lot, rolling down his windows. He needed a moment to clear his head. He let the breeze drift over his face as he leaned his head against the frame and closed his eyes. With so much talking all at once, it was hard to make sense of truth.

He could feel the tension between letting her figure out her heart and wanting to pull her in and rescue her from the pain of struggling with it all. He knew how to fix things. He was always good at sorting out problems, developing strategies, and executing a formula that would bring results, but suffering was new territory for him. It wasn't something he could lift off of her no matter how much he wanted to.

He stared at the front of the church and its closed doors. The low sun dulled the stained glass windows, and the grounds were strangely silent. He didn't like how closed off he felt and how the church seemed to mirror his current state.

"If I rescue her, I'll cripple her," he said aloud. He studied the locked doors of the church. "The same way I would damage those doors if I pried them open without the key. But what's the key for Eliza?"

His mind swirled back through their conversations before he caught sight of the time on his watch.

He put the truck in reverse and pulled out of the parking lot. The silent, closed church was poised in his rearview mirror unstirred by his unexpected visit.

The parking lot at the restaurant was already filling up, but Drew managed to find a spot close to the entrance. He saw Mitch standing off to the edge of the porch and extended a wave. Drew pulled off his tie and shut the door of the truck.

They sat outside among the other patrons who crowded the picnic tables scattered under a grove of oak trees.

"Good to see you," Mitch offered as Drew took the seat opposite him.

"You too. How was the job interview?" Drew asked before ordering ice tea and the brisket plate.

"It went well. They pretty much offered me the job, but I just need to let Mr. Parker at the bank know I'm going to be leaving."

"That's great news, Mitch. The investment world will never be the same with you trading stocks. I hope you take care of me once I pile up enough savings to dabble in the stock market."

"You know I will. Hey, heard you had kind of a rough week in the ladies' department."

"News travels fast, huh?" Drew peered over his glass.

"Apparently so . . ."

"Yep, it's been a heck of a week. Things with Becky ended in a blowup I didn't anticipate, but I'm guessing time will smooth that out. She just took our relationship a lot more seriously than I realized. I was hoping to let things die down easily, but it didn't pan out that way."

"Sounds like you didn't have a choice." Mitch said.

"Basically not. I hope we didn't make too much of a scene."

"I think it will all be old hat after a few weeks. You know how girls can be. They've got to talk about it with everyone before they let it go."

"For Becky that is definitely true, but with Eliza not so much." Drew wiped his hands on the paper napkin and took a swig of tea.

"How is Eliza by the way?" Mitch asked.

"I don't really know. I think she's doing the best she can. It's hard to tell. She's gone to the hill country for a few days . . ." Drew's voice trailed off as he tried to think of a more substantial answer, but he couldn't draw on any more than what he truly knew, which wasn't much.

"Are you concerned?" Mitch prodded. Drew could tell Mitch was able to read between the lines.

"Yeah, I guess I am. It's just been such a struggle for her . . . and for us for that matter. I'm not willing to let her fade away again, but I don't know what to do. I'm not even sure if she trusts me after that whole ordeal at the club the other night with Becky. It pretty much blew a hole in all we had reestablished."

"She knows you better than that."

"I thought so, but she was pretty shaken, and rightly so. How else could I expect her to react? It looked pretty bad."

"And knowing you, you're still trying to figure out how to fix it."

Drew smiled at Mitch as he leaned back, allowing the waitress to remove his plate and set down a serving of peach cobbler in front of him.

"Exactly." Drew picked up his fork and broke through the sugary crust of the cobbler.

"How do you plan on doing that? Not sure nuts and bolts can put back together a shattered heart."

"I have no idea. Any suggestions?"

"You're asking me? I haven't managed to even date a girl for longer than three months much less mend broken hearts. I'm lost when it comes to relationship rescues."

Drew chuckled and tapped his fingers on the table.

"True, you've got some miles to run before you get the joy of mending matters of the heart. The good news is that by then I'll have a wealth of information for you. I'll have probably tried every possible scenario and can give you some solid how-to advice."

"I'm counting on that," Mitch mumbled through his mouthful of dessert.

"That's what I'm here for."

"What are you doing tomorrow? Spring turkeys are gobbling so I thought I might run down south to do a little hunting at my uncle's place on the Medina. Welcome to come along if you'd like."

"I sure might. I'm wrestling with the thought of driving to the hill country to check on Eliza. I just don't want to sit back and let things play out. I did that before, and I'm definitely not doing it this time."

"Then I think you ought to go," Mitch said. "As long as I've known you, you've been one of the most trustworthy, honorable guys I know, and my guess is Eliza knows that too. I don't think her struggle is with you; I think it's with herself. She's worth fighting for. As much as you've tried to date other girls, it seems like ya'll just keep coming back around to each other. There's a reason for that. I'd pay attention."

"I've had the same thoughts. I just don't want to push her too much." Drew looked past Mitch, his eyes glazed over as he searched to answer his dilemma.

"No matter what it looks like right now, she needs you, man. Go see her. We can hunt another time."

Drew nodded his head in agreement and stood to leave after paying his check and parting with Mitch.

He knew his mind wouldn't rest if he didn't pursue the path his heart had already taken. Slowly, he backed his truck up and drove toward his home, the dark of the night folding over him except for the glare of his headlights. With the windows down, he could hear the steady rumble of the deep engine.

Surely, love is on my side and won't fail me now, he thought to himself.

CHAPTER TWENTY

BEFORE RETURNING TO HER READING, Eliza heard a lonely howl of what she thought might be a coyote in the distance. She waited for his companions to reply, but his cry went unanswered. Getting up, she walked to the door and opened it. Staring into the darkness, she strained her eyes, looking for any sign of movement.

She sympathized with the coyote. Crying out into the darkness, waiting for an answer, but hearing nothing back. He mimicked all she had felt these past few months . . . a lone voice. Again, he let out a howl to signal his brethren and finally she heard a faint response from the other direction. Relieved his attempts were successful, she closed the door and settled back into the chair.

She thought of Drew and how he had always seemed to be the tender voice answering her back . . . encouraging her, honoring her.

He judged so little and gave so much . . . always, and in ways she had not been able to recognize until now. He was the hero that stood in the shadows and reached out to pluck her from peril and then receded again until he was needed once more. *Who else does that?*

Her grandmother's words had already opened her up to trusting the tenderness inside that she had ignored before. The way her grandmother had allowed herself to be so vulnerable and pour out her heart like an offering and solely for Eliza . . . solely for the purpose of inviting Eliza to lean on the courage mounting inside her own heart.

Looking around the room as the flickering light from the fireplace danced on the walls, she turned her attention once again to the stories woven in front of her.

With Father gone to gather cattle, I had easily slipped into a comfortable daily routine at the hacienda. It was hard to imagine three weeks had already passed since we first arrived.

The sun had ushered in another glorious Sunday, and I was walking with the family to the chapel for a private family mass. We entered the quaint church quietly and sat down with hands folded. I sat next to Penelope and waited for Padre Antonio to begin. It was a long service that unfortunately tended to send my thoughts elsewhere. Roberto and I had not had the opportunity to visit as we had weeks ago on horseback. Work had kept him by his Father's side, and I dared not make any suggestion of another encounter.

I began to reason with myself and bring some logic into my youthful emotions. I knew Roberto's family more than likely had arranged a marriage for him, which therefore made any type of relationship between us impossible and out of the question. However, I couldn't stop my heart from dreaming.

Church finally ended, and we walked somberly to the door. Outside Penelope announced an outdoor picnic for lunch since the day was so perfect.

"I couldn't possibly have kept us indoors on such a glorious day so the cooks are assembling an outdoor feast under the oaks next to the springs. We will eat and take our siesta down by the cool of the river," Penelope proudly told us all.

My heart leapt. After changing into riding clothes, we met at the stables and rode out to the springs. Miguel and I found each other riding side by side. We chatted continuously on the trail as he recounted his latest tales of mischief.

"Do you ever give the help a break?" I chuckled.

"Now that wouldn't be much fun, would it?" Miguel said, grinning. "I've only got a couple of months to enjoy being a boy before I'm turned over to Father. He won't have any of that."

"You can count on that," a deep familiar voice piped in from behind us. "So I see you two have had no trouble getting into the adventurous spirit today. What are you all giggling about, if I might ask?"

Miguel and I exchanged playful glances and I answered. "Miguel always has a good joke or two to share, don't you my friend?"

"No doubt about that," Roberto responded. "Miguel, ride up by Father please. He wants to fish with you today and asked for your assistance." Roberto flashed a quick smile toward me.

Miguel rolled his eyes and kicked his horse forward.

"You have had no trouble fitting in with our family." Roberto looked toward me with a light grin on his face. "I wasn't sure what to expect when Mother announced you would be spending the summer with us, but you seem like you've been with us from the start."

"That's very kind of you to say. It truly has been wonderful for me. I didn't know I could ever feel so relaxed . . . and at peace."

We smiled at one another, and Roberto held my gaze. I felt my cheeks flush and looked down at the horse's mane. I ran my fingers through the coarse, cinnamon-colored hair.

"I do hope you'll forgive me if I have seemed preoccupied," he said. "This is a busy time in our family's business, and Father needs me with him. Each quarter our conciliatory from Texas visits to discuss our holdings and their financial state. Plus with a large cattle sale coming up, we are busy reviewing the books. Don't mean to bore you with this, but it would be my pleasure in the near future to accompany you on another ride and show you more of the ranch. I enjoyed being your guide for the day. Would you care to join me again soon?"

"Of course," I said without hesitation. My heart beat in my chest ready to take flight.

"Very good, I'll see to arranging it as soon as my schedule lightens."

Our arrival at the springs was an event. We were greeted by more than ample staff as we dismounted. All of us, dressed in our Sunday best, looked like white butterflies scattered along the riverbank. I made my way, unintentionally, to the same spot I had last stood with Roberto.

Miguel scurried past with a fishing pole and a wide grin. I decided to scamper behind him so as not to miss any of the action. Gustavo joined us as well at the riverbank, and they each began taunting one another about who would catch the first fish. I was caught between cheering for them both.

"Okay, out of the way little brothers. The one who taught you will once again demonstrate his masterful fishing techniques." Roberto's tall figure stood proudly next to Miguel's boyish frame.

"No way, Roberto," Miguel said. "You lost your touch years ago. We all know I am the true fisherman now. Even Father said so."

"Guilty as charged." I heard Señor Eduardo's gruff voice as he approached me.

"I told Miguel how great he was, but it has been too long since all four de la Cruz men fished side by side. How can anyone not take notice of the greatness of this event?" he asked, looking toward me with his arms outstretched.

"I have the best-looking boys in all of Northern Mexico. You each hold greatness in you." Señor Eduardo's proud words landed on each of his sons' shoulders, and they all turned to pay their respects to him in agreement.

"This is a good day for you, Señor. I am honored to share it with you," I added warmly.

"I am too." He patted my arm and signaled the servants to bring chairs for us.

"I am glad lunch is not provided by the boys . . . we wouldn't eat until twilight I'm afraid," he said, chuckling.

We both laughed and caught view of the smirk Roberto threw toward the sky. Penelope had been correct; it was a glorious day.

"It seems like yesterday I stood shoulder to shoulder with my own father and listened to him pass the time with stories and directions for the future. And now here I am again with three strong sons to share in the blessings others bestowed upon us. What does the future bring? That we know not, but we know who we are and that will determine our course." Señor Eduardo raised his cup in a toast. "To the future of our dynasty. A good name makes a man, but a beautiful wife completes him. To my darling and her sons, may we remain mindful of all that we've been given and be faithful through whatever may lie ahead."

"Bravo, Eduardo," Penelope cheered from her seat as she leaned over the table to touch her cup to all of ours. Sitting back down, she blew him a kiss and dabbed her cheeks.

Roberto and I caught each other's attention, and he held his gaze momentarily with a calm assurance over his face. Hardly knowing what to make of it, I ducked my head and refolded my napkin.

"I have another surprise," Penelope announced as I watched her face

filled with warmth and beauty and her white-linen collar ruffling in the slight breeze. Around her neck hung the pendant she wore always. The sun highlighted the detail of the heavy gold medallion with a cross set in the center surrounded by rubies and diamonds laid flat in the gold filigree outline. Atop the cross was a crest or perhaps a crown. It was a good size piece of gold—much larger than a traditional ladies' cameo and more similar in size to a large Spanish doubloon. She appeared to wear this piece always. No matter what other jewelry she put on, her pendant was centered on her neckline. The sunlight set off a sparkle of the tiny encrusted jewels, and in the brilliance, they danced like flashes of stars.

"Now," Penelope ventured boastfully, "a treat arrived yesterday by caravan . . . chocolate truffles from France." She lifted the cotton napkin from the cream-colored, porcelain platter and revealed the deep, dark chocolate mounds each powdered differently—some with tiny, hand-colored crystals of lavender or pink and others rolled in a fine powder of chocolate or white sugar. They were a sight like no other I had seen. Even the butterflies passing through seemed to take delight in them as well. One daringly landed on the centerpiece with the iced-pink frills.

The help passed the platter to each one of us, and we all made our choices carefully and with much commentary.

"I still do not understand the desires of a hacendado's wife," Eduardo began in good fun. "Here we have everything in this new and plentiful country, and yet, we are still importing goods from Europe and China."

He shook his head and bit into his truffle. The soft chocolate disappeared between his lips. "It is a woman's madness no doubt, but it certainly has its benefits." He nodded and gestured to the servant with the platter. He plucked two more off the plate and popped them into his mouth.

Penelope smiled at Eduardo's words.

"Ah, Eduardo, mi amor, it is the small pleasures that define the luxuries in life, and we shall not deprive ourselves of such soulful treasures. Let's not forget, dear Eduardo, we are European first and therefore it is our duty to bring culture to this land. Our sons must be kept abreast of worldly sophistication. Certainly you expect them to marry within our class and keep educating their territories and families."

"I am more concerned with their knowledge of business than china patterns, dearest. Nevertheless a woman's world shall always remain a complete mystery to me." With a gentle smile toward his wife, Eduardo concluded the conversation. "I thank you, dear Penelope, for a wonderful lunch. I shall excuse myself to the tent by the river to recline for a bit."

With that, Eduardo put his napkin on the table and pushed back his chair. All three boys followed suit. Penelope instructed the help on cleaning up and walked to the river with her parasol.

I, as well, retired to the small tent set up for me where I laid down upon the cot. I thought back to Eduardo and Penelope's conversation. Even the remote seclusion of the massive hacienda could not deter the influence of worldly wealth.

My mind then drifted to Father and his affairs. By now he was traveling back to Texas, hopefully pleased with his cattle purchases. Sleep gradually took over like a sweet song, and I gave in to its rhythms.

The ride back was filled with conversation among the men with regard to an upcoming ranch rodeo that was to be hosted by the de la Cruz family at the hacienda in the next few weeks. The two eldest boys would compete as well as several of their top hands. The hacienda would be full of neighboring families, some wealthy, some laborers, but people of all classes competed in this yearly event.

Turning to look back, I bid good-bye to the riverbank and its sweet song of friendship.

Eliza's eyes grew heavy, and she closed the journal before heading up the stairs to bed. Her head was swimming with the imagined scene of her grandmother and Roberto on the riverbank. It seemed a little like the rocky creek that ran through this ranch.

By the time her head hit the pillow, her eyes had already closed and the tender sounds of her grandmother's life, lived before her, lulled her to sleep.

CHAPTER TWENTY-ONE

DREW WOKE UP THE NEXT MORNING determined to drive to the hill country and see how Eliza was doing. He packed an overnight bag before calling Henry and asking if he could come by and visit. Without specific directions to the ranch he would be lost, but he knew Henry would have the details he needed.

Picking up the phone he dialed Henry's number and made arrangements to meet him in an hour. Drew knew he was taking a risk with Eliza. She might be offended at his driving out there to check on her, but he believed her heart would hear his and override any disapproval.

Pulling up to Henry's house he noticed the lights on in Eliza's kitchen next door and guessed Ada was probably there checking on the house. He decided to knock on the back door and say hello. He rapped on the screen door and heard Ada's footsteps approaching.

"Well, how you, Mr. Drew? Come in here an' let me get you some coffee."

"Good morning, Ada. I just came by to say hello. I'm actually on my way to talk to Henry next door."

"Well, you got some time for some coffee. I'll heat you up a biscuit too. Come on an' sit down."

Drew watched as she pulled out the chair from the kitchen table and motioned for him to sit while she moved toward the counter.

"All right, sounds good. How are things here at the big, white house?"

"All is quiet an' good. Not much goin' on here with Miss Liza girl gone, but 'nough to keep me busy. How 'bout you?"

"I'm all right." Drew took a sip of his coffee before continuing. "I'm driving up to see Eliza today so I came to visit with Henry and get directions. She doesn't know I'm coming, but I believe I need to get out there." Drew watched Ada for her approval or disapproval, but she kept her back to him in silence as she plated a buttered biscuit with ham. "I'm not willing to let her slip away this time."

"I think you's makin' the right choice," Ada finally said. "You know that girl as best as anyone. She needs to know she can love again an' not feel guilty 'bout goin' on with her life."

Drew took a bite of the warm biscuit Ada placed in front of him.

"When Liza was little, she'd get mad at Miss Hope or Miss Dusky and stomp outta this house, makin' a big noise with them little feet. I'd hear the back screen door slam. I used to tell her the Lord got ya' now. You can't outrun Him. Where you goin', He goin'. She would turn an' look at me with that pouty mouth. Good thing He had mercy 'cause there's a time or two I coulda used a wooden spoon on that behind of hers."

Drew laughed as Ada's chuckle spilled out into the kitchen.

"Ya' can't outrun Him, no sir. He always got His arms open an' is ready to catch us. I think Eliza is already figurin' that out."

"Have you talked to her at all while she's been away?" Drew asked.

"Naw, Mr. Henry just told me she's there an' doin' all right. I expect she's workin' through what Miss Dusky left for her to figure out. That gonna take Eliza some time. She don't like to feel the sad days."

"What do you mean the sad days?" Drew wanted to understand.

"The days that ya' sad or upset or cryin'—the days that don't make no sense. It's days like that when you rest in the Lord an' He will see to ya'. He gotta way of takin' the sad days an' makin' somethin' new—somethin' pretty. But you gotta let Him have 'em 'fore He can take 'em."

Drew nodded as he followed her words, taking in her wisdom.

"It's time she turn an' see you, Mr. Drew. You is faithful and kind."

"I appreciate you saying that. It's been difficult to know what to do, but last night I made up my mind I wasn't going to let her shut me out again because of grief. She needs me and I love her and I plan on marrying her if she'll say yes."

"Oh Lord have mercy!" Ada cupped her hands to her mouth. "Sweet, sweet Lord. I knew you wuz the one for her. I just knew it in my heart." She reached over the table and put her hand on Drew's arm. "You a fine man, Mr. Drew, and she know that too. I know she love you."

"Thank you."

"You go get that girl. The Lord gonna lay out your steps for you." Ada smiled and rested against her chair.

"I'm hoping you're right. Thank you for the coffee and breakfast."

"Anytime. I'll be waitin' to hear and I'll be prayin' too."

Drew stood and hugged Ada before he turned to leave. Her lighthearted approach to life was a relief to him. He followed the footpath around to Henry and Amelia's house and knocked on the door.

"Drew, come in," Henry offered as he held open the door.

"How are you today?"

"Doing fine and yourself?" Henry answered.

"Well, thanks. I appreciate you visiting with me this morning. Like I said over the phone, I need to go check on Eliza for my peace of mind." Drew sat in the small leather chair in Henry's study.

"I'm glad you're going and listening to your gut. I think it will be good for Eliza."

"So you don't think she will be upset with me?"

"No, I think she is going to want you there. My hope is that all Dusky is sharing with her now will release her to live without guilt or regrets."

Puzzled, Drew asked, "What is she sharing with her?"

"Everything that she wasn't able to share until now."

"What does that mean?" Drew pressed as he watched Henry stare toward the window.

"Dusky held much back that she endured before Eliza was ever born. It was a difficult and gut-wrenching journey that she chose to conceal from her own daughter, but she wasn't willing for it to die completely. She left a series of journals for Eliza to read. Dusky wanted to seed into Eliza's life in a way that she couldn't until Hope had passed."

"Why? What could be so terrible that Eliza's mother couldn't even know?"

"I think perhaps heartbreaking would be a better way to put it. I don't think Dusky wanted to burden Hope's life with heartbreak, and I'm not sure if Dusky could handle carrying Hope through the pain of it all. As dear and strong as Dusky was, she suffered greatly. She needed to raise Hope on a platform for the future, not the suffering of the past. She was protecting herself and her daughter."

Drew tightened the muscles in his jaws. "Are you able to tell me what happened?"

"I am able, but I think it's best to allow Eliza to share it all with you."

Disappointed, Drew rested against the back of his chair. "I guess I'll have to wait then. Thank you for giving me what information you felt you could."

"It's for the best until you hear more from her. In the meantime, let's get you out there to see her." Picking up his reading glasses, Henry reached for a piece of paper from his side table. "I've written down the instructions here. Glance at it and let me know if you can read everything I've written. If you leave soon, I'd guess you'll make it right after lunchtime."

Drew took the paper from Henry's hand and read over the directions. "I think you've pretty well spelled it out. I should make it just fine. Where do you suggest getting gas? Uvalde?"

"Probably so, or even Camp Wood would have a station that's probably open on a Saturday afternoon."

"Perfect, it will give me a chance to see what kind of gas mileage my new truck gets." He smiled and looked up at Henry. "I've got one more question I'd like to ask you."

"Of course, please." Henry pulled his glasses down on his nose and looked over at Drew.

"I'd like to ask Eliza to marry me and I'd like your blessing."

Drew saw tears spring to Henry's eyes as he stood and held out his hand toward Drew. Drew reached to shake his hand, and Henry put his other hand over his.

"Not only am I honored to give you my blessing, but you have honored me by asking for it. It is my distinct privilege to say yes and bless you."

"Thank you."

"Do you have a ring?"

"Not yet, but I was planning on calling Edward, my friend from high school who runs the jewelry shop downtown with his father."

Henry put up his hand and Drew paused. "May I offer something?

Something that has been in Eliza's family but she knows nothing about, at least not yet?"

Henry walked to a small cabinet in his study and pushed on two books. Drew watched as the books slid into the wall and a panel popped open beneath. Henry bent down and reached inside, pulling out a small, black box.

He handed it to Drew. Carefully, Drew opened it and gazed upon the emerald-cut diamond mounted in platinum with several smaller diamonds accenting each side.

"Are you sure?" Drew looked up at Henry, stunned by his offer.

"Yes, this ring belonged to Dusky. She asked me to save it and give it to Eliza at this very time when Eliza had read her story. I can think of no better timing than this."

"Thank you, sir. I'm honored you would offer this."

"It will bless so many in ways you will soon understand. I've watched you and Eliza over these past years and she will be fortunate to have you for a husband. You live out the definition of honoring and loving no matter what the cost."

"I appreciate your confidence in me, sir."

"Go and love her and bring her home with her heart full."

"That's exactly what I intend to do."

Drew thanked Henry again as he tucked the ring in his pocket and folded the directions. Walking to the front door, he felt a tingle in his stomach as his dream to marry Eliza was now becoming a long-desired reality. His only hurdle was getting her to say yes.

CHAPTER TWENTY-TWO

ELIZA WASTED NO TIME waking and getting ready for the day. She was eager to pick up where she had left off the night before. She hurried down the stairs and grabbed a cup of coffee before getting started. Passing by the phone she paused and stared at the receiver resting snugly in its cradle. She had begun to so desperately miss Drew, it was becoming ridiculous. Perhaps a quick phone call and the sound of his voice would put her heart at ease.

She set her coffee on the side table and dialed his number, hoping it wasn't too early for a Saturday morning. As his phone rang on the other end her heartbeat accelerated with each passing second, but after the fifth ring she realized he most likely was not going to answer. Disappointed, she placed the phone back in the receiver and picked up her coffee. He was probably playing an early round of golf or maybe had gone to see his parents out toward New Braunfels. She regretted she hadn't called him last night, but waved it off and walked upstairs. She would try again after lunch.

Sitting on the balcony she perched herself amidst the trees and the singing birds and allowed her fingers to flip to the marked place in the journal.

Her grandmother's entries continued chronologically scattered with detail. On June 28 she noted that Grandmother finally received word that her father had made it back to Texas and completed his delivery.

Señor Eduardo summoned me one morning to his study. I was curious as I made my way across the gardens to the main house. His study overlooked a private garden and was filled with gorgeous books, each one with an elaborate binding of encrusted worn leather. The smell of cigars and saddle oil hung in the air, announcing the threshold into a man's world. The office rarely held the presence of a woman unless she was requested due to business matters. This space was solely occupied by the male gender. I perceived his summons must be about Father.

I stood in front of his desk, admiring the inkwells and various writing accouterments, as he finished his conversation with Gustavo and one of his top hands. When he turned his attention toward me, he gestured for me to have a seat.

"Dusky," he began as I sank into one of the barrel-back leather chairs across from him, "A telegram has arrived from Texas in regard to your Father. He completed his delivery on June 20 and will wait for his next buy order, which he predicts will arrive in a couple of weeks. I'm sorry for the tardiness in getting his word to you, but as you are aware we oftentimes receive information on somewhat of a delay.

"He did make note that temperatures are exceedingly hotter than normal and perhaps may slow his return to Mexico. You, of course, are to continue to stay comfortable with us however long it is necessary. You are like family to us, and I know Penelope has enjoyed having a female counterpart. Your presence has been a welcome addition for all of us." His eyes smiled at me over his spectacles, imparting a fatherly warmth that settled around me.

"Thank you, Señor. I, too, have so enjoyed myself more than I thought possible. Your hospitality has been most gracious. Thank you for sharing the news in regards to Father. I am glad to know all is well with him."

"Yes, I also," he added while shuffling papers among the maps on his desk. "Well, by now you have seen all the preparations underway for the rodeo. I think you will find the festivities, as well as the people, charming and most entertaining."

"I am looking forward to it."

"Good. The de la Cruz team has never let me down yet, and I believe us to be stronger than ever this year. We are leading the charge on taking back the win from the Castaneda family. You must realize my comrades and I are extremely competitive. We may boast of strong ties and kinship, but all we care about now is winning and bragging rights for the next year. Roberto is our captain. With his skills and clear thinking we will be victors again," he said, chuckling and grinning with amusement.

Eduardo's eyes told his secrets too well. If he was pleased or dismayed, one would only have to read his eyes to know his thoughts. His passion for family and life was so fierce it sometimes overwhelmed me. Yet I was easily swept up in his reverie today.

The next several days were filled with talk of arriving guests and planning. Slowly, throughout the next week, the hacienda became more crowded and guests buzzed with excitement. By mid-July all had arrived for the annual gathering of fellowship and talent.

On the evening before the commencement of the larger events, there was an elaborate garden party. Friends, families, dignitaries, and the like were reunited and gathered to catch up on the latest news.

Maria graciously educated me on the guest list and the customary exchanges. "Senorita, you will stand in the receiving line next to Penelope because you are considered a family guest. She will shake hands, hug, greet, and pass the guest on to you. You will introduce yourself followed with the title of 'family guest.' The Senora always likes order at these events, so these are her requests on how it is to be done."

Maria then reached and opened the large brown box she had brought with her.

"She ordered a dress for you and wants you to wear it tonight. So let us get you ready."

The dress was absolutely stunning. Made in a shade of creamy yellow, it had a light cotton inset with strips of lace and sewn pearls along the shoulders. Its fit was flawless. The curves of the dress flattered my silhouette, and there was also a beautiful, woven shawl in matching lace. I was speechless. It was utterly gorgeous and regal in every way.

"Maria . . . this is so exquisite. I'm almost afraid to wear it for fear of ruining it," I said in a whisper as I studied myself in the mirror and ran my hand along the delicate fabric.

"Yes, it is truly beautiful," she said as she peeked over my shoulder. "But so are you, Senorita, so let's finish. I don't want the Senora to wonder where you are."

Maria's hands worked to quickly button up the back of the dress, and then she helped me with my hair. She wove fresh gardenias onto two combs and pressed them carefully into the sweeps on the sides. In the back my hair fell in cascades past my shoulders.

"I can't help but feel like a princess," I told her and smiled.

A knock came at the door, and Maria opened it to find Roberto's butler. I bade Maria good night and thanked her profusely. As I walked through the door, Roberto stepped onto the porch.

"Mother asked me to escort you to the party. I hope that is all right with you?" he asked with tenderness in his eyes.

I stepped forward and pulled the shawl over my shoulders before taking his arm.

"You are radiant, Dusky! Absolutely beautiful! We will be fighting off every eligible man here tonight, won't we Juan?" He turned and included his butler.

"You look very handsome yourself," I said. "Thank you for escorting me to the party."

I was so full of excitement, nerves, and anticipation I could hardly beckon my legs to work. I took a deep breath and tried to let Roberto's ease and gentle manner calm me, but it was a touch hopeless. My stomach would hear nothing of it, and I held fast to his arm to steady my steps.

He, on the other hand, talked casually of the party as we strolled through the patios, but I didn't hear a word. If my feet ever touched the ground, I failed to remember. I was enraptured in the moment walking next to him. Even though being with Roberto was an impossible situation, my heart disagreed and that night I gave in to what I knew I had felt all along.

As the eldest son he was destined to marry for more wealth, more land, and more alliances . . . of which I had none. Nevertheless, my heart didn't understand all those conditions, and logic played no role in its longings.

When we arrived at the reception, I took my place alongside Penelope. Roberto squeezed my hand as he left to stand with his Father across from us.

"That dress is utterly divine on you, Dusky, as I thought it would be." Penelope smiled and brushed my cheek with her hand. "I love the flowers Maria put in your hair . . . you smell heavenly."

"Thank you. I am so honored to be here. What an enchanting night."

She giggled. "We'll see, my dear." She winked and cued the musicians to start in the far corner.

Leaning toward me she whispered, "Now I do have someone in particular I want you to meet. He is not only gorgeous, but intelligent. His father is a longtime rival, but a friend as well. Even though we have had tense moments with his family, we all remain strong allies. It is really the stubborn competition that breeds in men. Half the time there is absolutely no need to be so coarse about things. However, I cannot change that.

"He is the second eldest in his family even though he is Roberto's age. His family has ties in Texas, and I think you might be a delightful match. I hope you don't mind, but I took the liberty in letting his father know you are here, so I know he will be looking for you. His name is Fernando. His older brother Gabriel is quite the entertainer and is engaged to a wonderful girl by the name of Susannah."

Even though my head was spinning with Penelope's announcement of matchmaking, I worked hard at remaining calm. I ran my hand across the front of the dress to smooth its soft curves and then took a deep breath. As I fixed my shawl, I looked across the patio and could feel Roberto's eyes on me. I softened and smiled at him even though I felt as if I had somehow betrayed him. He cleared his throat, adjusted his collar, and smiled back.

As the guests began to flow into the grand gardens, Penelope whispered the name of the first guest, and soon Roberto and I were separated in a sea of people. The crowd was thick with colorful gowns, jewels, flowers, and laughter.

"This next family has a daughter we would like to see Roberto marry. As a matter of fact, Eduardo intends to speak with her father this week while they are here," she quickly whispered.

Reality crashed into my heart. I steadied myself with thoughts of duty and obligation, whispering encouragement to myself under my breath.

Penelope was simply playing the part she was raised to play. Seeing her boys marry into arranged marriages was part of her maternal duties. The fact that she would inquire of me to another family was flattery *in itself, and I quickly reminded myself of what high regard she must hold for me, otherwise, my future would be of no interest to her.*

Had this been the plan all along? I began to examine Father's part in all of this. A widower who was gone most of the time left with a daughter of marriageable age, what else was he to do? I didn't blame him or her, not for one moment. They both were taking care of me the very best way they knew how. Part of me was completely grateful, so why wasn't I ecstatic at the thought of meeting a potential suitor with regal credentials?

Pulled from my thoughts by a flurry of kisses and hugs, Penelope and I were both engulfed by bustles and silk. Her distant cousin, Alicia, and her three daughters smothered us in giggles and small talk. I beat back my emotions with the constant reminder that duty and obligation came first to all here tonight. It was power that held these families together. Their destinies were interlaced like a web precariously stretched across one another.

The stream of people seemed endless. Their colorful clothes and entourages quickly filled the grand patio. The night became alive with movement, chatter, and sheer excitement; it was undeniably electric.

As I mingled with the guests, I watched curiously as Roberto glided across the patio with his dance partner, the beautiful and petite Isabella. Her jet-black hair and porcelain skin were the true mark of Spanish aristocracy. Her fragile, delicate hands rested lightly on top of Roberto's. There was no doubt they seemed perfectly suited for each other. Her delicate stature melted perfectly into Roberto's gorgeous physique. His masculine presence filled the space around him. I noticed he was guarded, yet attentive, in his actions.

"Dusky." I was startled from my thoughts at the sound of Penelope's voice. "Here you are, dear. I want you to come meet Fernando and his father, Señor Alejandro. They are most interested in meeting you."

"Of course." I adjusted my shawl and skirt and followed her through the guests.

"Señor Alejandro and Fernando I would like to present to you our dearest friend, Dusky Victoria."

"With pleasure, Senorita." Señor Alejandro took my hand. "My son,

Fernando, has been most anxious to meet you after we received Penelope's letter. You are as beautiful as she described."

I smiled and turned to Fernando who gently took my hand. Our eyes met and I shied. His face was just as handsome as Penelope described with olive skin and blue eyes. His light-brown hair was combed neatly to the side.

"May I have this dance?" he inquired with a confident tone.

"Of course."

"So, how do you like Mexico and life on the hacienda?" He led me onto the dance floor.

"I like it very much, thank you. The de la Cruz family has been most gracious and loving. It will be hard to return to Texas."

"Perhaps arrangements can be made for you to stay longer?"

I admired his tenacity and candidness. As handsome as he was, he had the confidence to match. To my surprise, I was rather enjoying myself.

"Are you planning on attending the rodeo tomorrow?" he asked as he whirled me across the patio.

"Yes, I am looking forward to it."

"Well, it will be a shame the hosting family will lose, but so it shall go." He grinned sheepishly.

"Yes, I hear you all have quite the rivalry going."

"That we do, but the last several years we have managed to come out ahead, so at some point they will get tired of losing, don't you think?"

"If they did it wouldn't be as fun for you, now would it?" I enjoyed the banter that had developed between us.

"Quite true and a good observation. Are you always so observant, Dusky? It is so refreshing coming from a woman."

"I just take great interest in what is going on around me. I've always been that way."

"I do hope, then, that you will take a great interest in me."

We both smiled, and I giggled. I had never met someone as precocious as him.

"May I?" I heard a deep voice break through our laughter.

"Ah, Roberto, dear friend, how are you?" Fernando replied with a hug. "I see you've spotted me dancing with this gorgeous lady. How like you to recognize beauty when you see it. If I must relinquish this one time, I shall. Dusky, promise me another dance later tonight?" He gave a slight bow.

"I look forward to it, Fernando, thank you."

Roberto stepped forward and took my hand while placing the other on my back.

"I see you have met Fernando," he said as he guided me away.

"Yes, your mother introduced us."

"She did?" He looked perplexed for a moment. "Well, I am glad you are making friends. We have had you all to ourselves. We have been rather stingy, have we not?"

"I would hardly call it that. These have been the most wonderful weeks in my life. I selfishly don't want them to end. How has your night been?"

"The usual polite gestures, dances, and all the while finding myself uncharacteristically preoccupied."

"I'm sorry. Business must be quite heavy, or is it tomorrow's rodeo?"

"No, none of that. I just can't take my mind off one particular person, and I am having the hardest time figuring out why."

Roberto kept smiling and dancing with such lightness and freedom. I just let myself enjoy him even though I knew it wasn't meant to last.

"I see your new suitor coming this way. I shall be the gentleman and acquiesce. Don't leave before I get another dance. She is all yours, my friend."

Fernando picked up where he left off, and Roberto walked to the edge of the dance floor. I saw him look back before he turned to greet an approaching guest.

The dancing seemed endless, and my feet and head began to get weary.

"Fernando, I thank you for a wonderful evening. I must get some sleep before tomorrow. I look forward to seeing you then."

"May I walk you back to your quarters?"

"Thank you, but please, stay and enjoy yourself. One of the butlers will walk me back."

"If you insist. Until tomorrow . . ." He kissed my hand and disappeared.

I said my good nights to the family and made my way to the edge of the party. Juan met me and we began to walk through the colonnade.

"Dusky," I heard Roberto call out from behind me. "Allow me to walk with you," he said as he caught up to me.

"I would like that." I smiled at him, my heart speeding up.

When we walked around the corner out of sight of the party, Roberto stopped.

"Dusky, I must apologize. I had no idea what my mother was up to with Fernando and his family. I realize our ways are not your ways, and she did not mean to insult you. She lives in tradition, and I am concerned her customs may have hurt you."

"Not at all. I understand and appreciate her concern for me. I am flattered she would go to such lengths just for me. It is a compliment, truly."

"You are not upset then?"

"You and your family have been so dear, how could I be?"

"Are you pleased with Fernando then? Is this arrangement something you want? Because it can become quite serious from this moment forward. All Señor Alejandro has to do is agree to an engagement. With your Father's consent, this may happen faster than you realize."

"Well, I . . . I don't know what to say. No, I mean, I am grateful but I don't know Fernando. He seems like a gentleman, but I am not ready for that. I fear I may insult your mother but . . ."

I couldn't come up with the right words. They seemed stuck in my throat. I fought back tears and wanted to run. Instead, I turned my head toward the fountain behind us to calm myself.

"Dusky, are you all right? I feared this put too much pressure on you. My mother is out of line. I must tell her to stop."

"No, Roberto, please. She only has my best interest at heart, and I fully respect her for that. I cannot turn down what fate has brought to my door. Nothing has to be decided tonight, and I know my Father well enough to know he wouldn't agree to anything without asking me first, of that I am sure."

"Very well. I just wanted you to know I could put a stop to this."

"Yes, perhaps you could, but then what, Roberto? I go back to Texas and wait for fate to come again? It is different for a woman, Roberto. We don't marry for power, but for preservation. And sometimes the one chance comes along when you marry the one you gave your heart to, but that is rare, because men seek advancement and hardly ever allow their hearts to dictate their future. It takes bravery to lift the veil of tradition and risk to love." I felt strength pour through me as I stood before him.

I turned abruptly and left without looking back before he could respond. I knew I had insulted him beyond the normal boundaries of a woman, but I had spoken the truth, and it had freed us both whether he realized it or not.

CHAPTER TWENTY-THREE

ELIZA KNEW THAT FEELING of regret all too well. It had been brewing in her chest since the last night she saw Drew when she had used such heated words. Now miles apart, she hadn't been able to reach him, partly because she had been afraid until today. Her words felt so final. She wished she could take them back and start over, but it was impossible. As levelheaded as Drew was, she realized she had pushed him to the limits of compassion and reason.

Hoping to find an answer or some solace she continued to read.

I hardly slept that night, tormented by my harsh words and wishing it had gone so differently. How I wished Roberto had said he didn't agree with tradition and would vow to marry for love and not for duty, but those wistful thoughts soon fled and I was left with the reality of what poured out of my mouth and my heart.

I knew I must get dressed and meet Penelope for the women's brunch she was hosting. Maria had already laid out another dress Penelope had purchased for me in a lovely shade of turquoise with white lace piping. It set off the few auburn highlights in my hair, and I pinched my cheeks with a bit of rouge.

Staring into the mirror, I decided in my heart to give Fernando a chance and to quit toying with an infatuation that wasn't meant to be. Grabbing my parasol, I walked out the door and met the sun with a hopeful heart—a heart that gets to choose, I reminded myself encouragingly.

Juan led me to the gardens, and I secretly hoped he had not overheard the tiff Roberto and I had the night before. Approaching the covered trellis, I heard the continual chatter of women already lounging on the patio.

As I stepped under the flowering canopy, I saw an enormous display of various foods. Succulent fruits dripping with nectar and exotic berries were placed throughout the table. Even fresh pineapple, an indescribable luxury, was displayed. Fresh roasted meats and homemade breads filled the other end of the table. The ladies casually pecked their way through the buffet.

Parasols touched one another, trim to lace, and swirled around the perimeter. This was their life, another typical day amidst immeasurable luxury. A noble woman was designed for lavish relaxation and adornment—to be revered by their men and worshipped by their heirs. It was difficult to imagine myself fitting into their lifestyle.

I made my way to a group of young ladies whom I had met the previous evening. My favorite among them was Susannah, a very distant cousin of the de la Cruz family. She was positively spunky and energetic in every sense of the word—much different from most of the other female guests I'd met.

"Buenas dîas, *Dusky*. You look lovely as usual this morning," she said as we embraced cheek to cheek. Susannah's rich-red hair set her apart from her peers instantly. She wore an ice-blue linen dress, which set off her clear, blue eyes. Her skin was delicate and fair and perfectly flawless.

"And you as well. What a breath of sunlight you've been to me."

"Tell me," she whispered as we strolled arm in arm through the grounds. "You danced quite often with Fernando as well as with Roberto last night, two of the most gorgeous men this side of the border I might add. Which one did you give your heart away to or is it yet to be decided?"

Caught off guard by her brazen question, I stumbled to conceal my true feelings. "I have . . . I have not the slightest idea. Where my heart lands remains to be seen. I'm sure Roberto simply took pity on me and there is nothing more to make of that."

"I wouldn't be so sure of that, dear friend. He seemed rather enchanted by you. I don't think I was the only one who noticed either."

"You must not say such things," I insisted. "Everyone knows his parents desire him to marry Isabella, and I certainly don't want to create a scandal over a dance. We must be respectful. I do not want to insult the de la Cruz family. They've been nothing but dear to me. It would be dishonorable of us to speak of such things."

Susannah stopped and faced me. "I'm sorry if I've upset you. It was only an observation. Besides, I think Roberto would have to put up a fight at this point. I hear Fernando has found you to be quite a lady. His mother has been chatting about it all morning, waiting to meet you."

I smiled, feeling a faintness wash over my face.

"What is it, Dusky? Doesn't that please you? We would actually be sisters! With my marriage to his brother Gabriel less than a month away, we could end up being sisters before the year's end. Isn't that a marvelous thought?"

"Yes, it's just . . ." My voice trailed off and again the words failed to follow through.

"What? Are you nervous? There's no need to be nervous. You're perfectly divine looking and smart. I think they've all fallen in love with you. You fit in just wonderfully."

"Maybe so . . . I . . . I just wasn't expecting all this."

"Maybe not, but look what's at your door. This is a chance of a lifetime. Unless of course, you have someone at home you're in love with. Do you? Oh dear, I could see how that could be a problem."

"No, it's not that. Not that at all."

"Then what?"

"How did you do it, Susannah? How did you tell your heart this was it and to be pleased and grateful and exuberant?"

"I expected I would do nothing less, and, of course, I prayed God would bring a good match for me and that my parents would see it too." I stared into her eyes with a flat expression. Oblivious, she continued. "Yes, this has happened quickly, but where I come from you are quite fortunate. Many girls are betrothed to older widowers or given to a convent. What Penelope did for you is a gift. In fact, there are several mothers still trying to figure out how you snuck in and stole him."

"I do see that, Susannah. I'm not ungrateful in the least bit. I think it would all make sense if I could speak with my father. If this is his wish for me, then yes, I shall make it mine too."

"My best advice is to enjoy the moment—two marvelous men vying for your attention . . . one forbidden to love you, the other destined to win you. What could be more romantic than that? Come, let's join the others before they think we are conspiring against them."

"Of course." If this was a game, I certainly wasn't going to be any good at it. The queasiness in my stomach was already a foreboding sign.

"Senora Castaneda," Susannah called out, "let me bring Dusky to you."

At that moment it seemed as if everyone's eyes fell on me. Penelope met us as we walked over to Senora Castaneda's seat.

"Hello, Senora," I managed.

Her touch was so sweet and generous. Surprisingly, I instantly liked her. I was taken aback by my reaction. I couldn't help but want to sit next to her.

"Dearest girl, you are as pretty as my husband said you are, and as gentle in spirit as a dove. Please, tell me about yourself." She was the opposite of her gruff husband and Fernando's bold ways. Her words were heavy with sincerity and warmth.

As I began to talk, the others who had once surrounded us milled with the crowd and we sat alone in privacy.

"My, you have had a journey, haven't you?" She squeezed my hand. "It is hard to know where one's heart is after loss such as that. I remember when I was a bit younger than you and my parents were killed in a house fire on our ranch. Fortunately, my eldest brother survived, as did his wife. I fell into her care, and her compassion gave me back my heart. It is hard for men to know how to speak into that tender part of a woman. It takes another woman's gentle ways to speak into us what we can't remember of ourselves."

She brushed my hair off my face. "I see your heart, Dusky, and it is good. You don't want to let others down or disappoint. But my dear, one day you will have to choose, and the disappointment for the others will pass. Regret, however, can last a lifetime."

Curious as to what she saw in me, I stared into her eyes wondering.

"Now, dear one, don't be hasty. I realize men want answers, but I want truth not only for you, but also for my Fernando. He may be a man, but he is still my son and as bound by tradition as we all seem to be. Love still finds a way."

"*Thank you, Senora.*"

"*You're welcome. Now, if you'll excuse me, I must get my rest before the afternoon presents itself. She turned and summoned her help as she rose slowly to her feet. Her heavyset frame wobbled before she gained the balance to begin walking.*

Susannah walked over. "Isn't she lovely?"

"*One of the loveliest women I have ever met and so wise. You will be so fortunate to have her for a mother-in-law, Susannah. I cannot think of a more gracious woman. She loves her family with such honesty. I admire that.*"

"*She is rare and sometimes the talk of disgruntlement comes around as she doesn't always keep to traditional ways. That tends to infuriate those who stick to tradition as you can imagine.*"

"*I can imagine. She is refreshing.*"

As siesta approached, we all retired to our rooms, and I was ever so thankful. I lay on the cool cotton coverlet and closed my eyes.

Maria's soft footsteps woke me from my sleep.

"*Buenas tardes, Maria.*"

"*Buenas tardes, Senorita. Did you have a good sleep?*"

"*Yes, thank you.*"

"*You were tired. There will be much excitement this afternoon at the rodeo. The men are busy with the horses. It is a big honor to win. You will not be disappointed. All year the* charros *and the hacendados have been preparing, as well as all the ladies.*

"*The winning team not only wins prestige for the ranch, but also for their ladies, as they honor them publicly with the presentation of roses. So we must make you pretty in case you attract the attention of a certain señor.*"

I got up and secretly hoped I didn't attract any more attention. I had had enough sorting the affairs of the heart in the last twenty-four hours. It would be best to remain anonymous tonight.

Maria's hands worked quickly to tuck my hair up and pull loose a few wavy strands near my ears. She powdered my face and added color to my cheeks and lips.

"*Your natural beauty is most attractive, Dusky. Let's put a small bundle of orange blossoms right here for an accent.*"

"Your touch works miracles, Maria."

Maria left as I finished dressing and fastened a turquoise necklace around my neck.

Juan's knock at the door was my cue to leave for the rodeo.

Arriving at the outdoor arena, I was seated near Susannah and her friends in the shade. The older, married women sat behind us. They were flanked by servants standing alert.

Excitement and frenzy flashed through the air. To my right I spotted Señor de la Cruz and his comrades. Even though they no longer actively participated in the rodeo, they dressed in fashionable charro attire with silver-buttoned pant seams and elaborate stitching. A round of cheers and bets were placed as each team was introduced.

All eyes were on the riders entering the arena on their groomed mounts. My eyes involuntarily searched for Roberto as the de la Cruz troupe circled the arena. He and his brother, Gustavo, were the captains who led the eight-man team. Ropes swirled as the men practiced with their lassos and exercised their horses.

I spotted Roberto on the far side of the arena with Gabriel, his match in talent and in looks. I watched their mannerisms filled with bravado and grit. Fernando rode up on Roberto's left and began to make what appeared to be small talk. Roberto stiffened in the saddle at his approach, but did not retreat. He nodded curtly to Fernando and paid no attention to his remarks.

As I watched the two men, I couldn't help feeling sorry for Fernando. Roberto paid him no more attention than he would a small child. It was seemingly uncharacteristic of him. He extended his grace so generously to others.

Smiles flashing and with expanded chests, the participants rode around the arena amidst the flurry of swirls and dust.

"How do you like it so far?" Susannah asked from beneath her parasol.

"I'm not sure. Tell me more about what goes on."

"Well, only the top ranch hands and hacendados' sons can ride in this charreada. *It truly is a game of skill and privilege. Whoever takes the title earns the prestige and respect of his comrades."*

She clapped furiously as Gabriel rode up and stopped in front of her. Susannah beamed and blew him a kiss. With a simple gesture of his hat and a flash of his charming smile, he gave his chestnut mare a swift kick and took off for the gate. Fernando was quickly on his heels but took a moment to throw a grin my way. That brought giggles from the girls around me and from me too.

"You are unabashedly beaming, Susannah," one of the other girls remarked.

With a twirl of her parasol, she gushed, "Truly, he is utterly delectable."

We all bubbled with laughter at her racy comment.

Our attention quickly turned as a flag was raised and the musicians began to play, signaling the commencement of the competition. The teams retreated to their places near the sides of the pens to wait their turn in various events after the musical introduction.

Suddenly, the arena was filled with steers kicking dust and ropes flying through the air caught between the thumping of horses' hooves and whistles of the cowboys. We watched as each team worked with precision and timing. Playing off one another's shadow and energy, they gauged their accuracy. Ropes became like graceful ballerinas, twirling through the air. Yet once entangled with their target, the loop was pulled tight by thrashing horses. The breath of man and beast permeated the air. The steers strained as their eyes bulged from the pressure of taut ropes. Their legs whipped frantically against the dirt.

The charro jumped from his horse and raced to the restrained steer. His hands worked furiously as he tied the steer and threw his arms in the air with a grand gesture at the completion of his sweaty task. The time it took for him to tie the steer was recorded, and the next team soon got their opportunity to overthrow the fastest opponent's score.

When the Castanedas entered the arena, loud calls and whistles erupted. The young ladies squealed. When Susanna turned to me, her eyes flashed with excitement and pride. Her eyes darted to Gabriel, and she began to fan herself feverishly as she squeezed my elbow.

"The moment of truth, Dusky. I can hardly stand the anxiety. My stomach is twisted in a ferocious knot. I feel as if I cannot breathe. Surely I

am going to faint before it is all done." She tugged at her dress and moved to the edge of her seat.

I smiled and searched out Fernando on his mount. His confidence soared as he leaned into his saddle and made a loop in the air with his lasso. I was impressed with his demeanor.

Gabriel rode past our seats. He was the solo competitor in the Cala de Caballo. His goal was to gallop his horse the length of the arena and then with fierce precision come to a dead stop in a designated area. We watched in anticipation as he pulled off each move without hesitation and spun his horse in a gallant display of horsemanship. Everyone was breathless and on the edge of their seats. As he finished, he gracefully nodded and backed his horse out of the ring. Susannah erupted into glorious applause, rising to her feet.

"Bravo, mi amor! Bravo," she yelled. "Isn't he just the most splendid gentleman this side of the Atlantic?"

All her girlfriends nodded in agreement and added their approval with the perfection of a choreographed chorus. Their voices rose in unison, mimicking one another. I marveled at the spectacle witnessed by the guests and the dashing charros.

A fleeting shadow on my right caught my attention. The de la Cruz team was making its way from the backside of the arena. This event was called the Pielas en el Lienzo where a young mare comes galloping down the long corral and the mounted contestants wait to rope the mare's hind legs and bring it to a complete stop. Each charro secured his rope on the large horn of his saddle.

I could hear Roberto calling to his men in a deep, loud voice, and each one responding from their positions in the main ring. Without a moment's notice, a black mare came rumbling toward them from the long sleeve and burst into the ring.

Yells, whistles, ropes, and dust erupted. The mare was pulled to a stop after Carlito's horse stumbled and fell into Gustavo's mount. Roberto leaped off his horse and pulled Gustavo from beneath the downed mare. Gustavo lay motionless as Roberto frantically called to the other cowboys for water.

Behind me I heard Penelope let out a whimper. I searched for Señor Eduardo. Silence and stillness impregnated the air. No one moved. I watched Roberto. His face was fixated on Gustavo. He splashed water onto his brother. Soon, Gustavo revived and regained color. Roberto spoke to him before he helped him to stand and walk away. Gustavo stumbled through the dust and waved with his right arm while Roberto held him on the left.

I could hear Penelope mumbling prayers and fanning herself. Her friends joined in her prayers and tried to give comfort. I sat motionless in awe of Roberto and his integrity and pure motives. He gave up any desire he had with regard to winning the competition in order to honor and protect the one he loved—his brother. He knew that losing focus of the outcome could cost them the title, but I could tell his heart overrode his ego. It didn't take anyone long to figure out he was a man, not only of his word, but of his heart as well.

"Are you all right?" Susannah inquired of me.

"Yes, just a touch stunned, I guess."

Señor Eduardo made his way to the edge of the arena and met both his sons. I watched as he patted Gustavo's shoulder and talked with Roberto.

"It seems every year someone comes close to tragedy. In fact, two years ago one of the junior charros was thrown into the wall during the leap of death. He suffered a concussion and had to be carried out. None of us thought he would live. It was Roberto, in fact, who rode up and told us the charro was breathing, but not awake. My mother called for the priest and we all began reciting prayers.

"The riders were determined to finish the rodeo, but it was painful to watch for fear another cowboy might be hurt. Finally, we all began to come around and cheer the teams through to the end, but it certainly put quite a damper on the day."

"I can only imagine," I replied as I adjusted my dress.

"Yes, well, because it was my brother's team, my family felt responsible. Father became very strict after that about who he allowed to compete. The boy was only fourteen. Although he recovered, he never regained good balance or eyesight for that matter. Now Father has age limits and certain restrictions for anyone who wants to ride on the team."

"Susannah, Susannah," her younger sister interrupted in a high-pitch voice, "Su amor *on the paint!'*

"*Must you make such a spectacle, Francesca,*" Susannah replied. "*I do not wish to be a complete fool surrounded by giggling girls every time I am in his presence.*"

Francesca giggled with her young friends. She was Susannah's younger sister and seemed to take great enjoyment in embarrassing her elder sibling. She, like Susannah, was feisty in spirit and enjoyed keeping the conversation exciting.

"*Keep your voice down, Francesca,*" Susannah snapped. "*You have no idea how silly you sound!*"

"*Definitely not as silly as you talking about your precious Gabriel,*" Francesca mimicked as she made a smooching sound with her lips and burst into laughter.

"*I shall pretend she does not exist at this moment.*" Susannah settled into her chair and turned away in disgust. "*She absolutely enjoys making me furious, and I simply cannot stand it!*"

Susannah took a deep breath and turned her attention back to the arena and the late afternoon's final event. Just as she had described to me earlier, the paseo de la muerte—the leap of death, was complicated and extremely dangerous.

"*Only the most skilled and bravest of the charros compete as they must ride bareback full speed alongside an unbroken mare. The teammates assist in positioning the animal all the while remaining at full gallop. At any given moment the charro leaps from his horse onto the wild mare's back and can only grab the mane for support. He must stay mounted until the horse comes to a stop.*" Susannah sat back in her chair as if exhausted by simply describing the whole event.

"*What happens if he misses?*" I asked.

"*I don't even want to imagine it. Thankfully, I've never seen a miss happen. Look.*" She quickly pointed. "*Fernando is competing for his team. That is quite the honor.*" Susannah nudged me and grinned. Fernando raced alongside the wild mare while his team whipped and yelped on their horses beside him. As he came up beside the mare, he gave his horse one final kick before he leaped onto her back. The wild horse's eyes gave way to surprise and fear as Fernando landed on her back. He grabbed her mane as he swung his right leg over her side and steadied himself. With a huge grin, he brought her to a halt and let out a loud cheer.

"Tremendous! Bravo!" Shouts erupted all around me, and we all instantly rose to our feet for a standing ovation and much jubilation. As his mount became agitated, he leapt off and threw his hat in the air. On bent knee he caught his hat and took a bow. He covered his heart with his hat and nodded in my direction. I couldn't help but smile. He was daringly flirtatious. He continued to look my way as he rose to his feet. Even the other competing charros gave their approval and congratulatory gestures.

"That was tremendous, Dusky," Susannah said. "How absolutely dashing he is! He is not afraid to lay claim to his skills or his seeming affections either."

I shook my head and laughed. "How utterly complicated this has all become."

"I don't think so for him. He seems quite determined to win your affections, my friend. Trust me, the Castaneda men are relentless when it comes to something or someone they are passionate about. Look, we must watch now. It's Roberto's turn. If anyone can show up Fernando it will be Roberto. He is a master at this event."

Susannah tucked her skirt beneath her legs and seated herself once again. Her voice trailed off as I watched Roberto ride his prancing, gray-dappled stallion with the proud neck and high tail. It was the same horse he had ridden to the river. Horse and man came flashing out of the chute toward the ring in pursuit of the wild mare.

Roberto balanced on his powerful mount as they came up on their target. With a swift shift of his body and legs, the stallion knew at once to lean in toward the mare to help Roberto land in the correct spot. Roberto grabbed the mare's mane and within seconds had brought her to a complete standstill.

Cheers and applause rang out from the gallery as we all gave him a hero's tribute. He was modest in his acceptance of such grand attention and gave the crowd a bow and a wave of his hat. I looked over at Isabella to see her beaming at her friends crowded around her.

Roberto whistled, and his stallion took his place next to him. Roberto mounted and rode toward the stands.

I held my breath as I waited for him to acknowledge Isabella with a special gesture. She, too, stood attentively on her feet while her friends hovered around her almost holding her up. However, he strode up to the center of the ladies' box and gave his mother a nod.

"Well done, my son! Excellent job. Bravo," Penelope encouraged from the back of the box. As he turned back toward the gate, he glanced toward Susannah and me. I smiled with admiration. He quickly returned the gesture and rode back toward his team.

Susannah squeezed my hand without saying a word or turning my way. Neither of us wanted to give away anything that might potentially harm Isabella, or Penelope for that matter. I couldn't even look at her for fear of spilling my heart, so I just gave her hand a squeeze back and stood motionless.

All the riders made a grand parade through the arena before lining up and announcing the winners. The men sat proudly in their saddles, and the hacendados joined their teams. With trumpet fanfare, the victors were revealed. The de la Cruz team had recaptured the winning title from years past even with the close call of Gustavo's fall. Shouts and cheers filled the air. Roberto and Gustavo embraced, and Señor de la Cruz beamed with great pride. The Castanedas rode over and congratulated them.

I stood in the ladies' box and cheered along with Susannah.

"This is good," she shouted over the applause. "It keeps the spirit of competition alive whether Gabriel realizes it or not."

"Yes . . . I believe you're correct."

Penelope was exuberant and continued to applaud her husband and boys. The team rode over and presented Penelope with the winning roses. She was showered with affection and the blanket of red flowers.

When the trumpeters blew their horns, all the riders made their way to the gates to exit the arena. We began to gather our things and make our way to the celebratory dinner and dance. The women were uncharacteristically muted, but I overheard some say they felt Isabella had been shunned or perhaps forgotten due to the jubilation.

"Dusky, promise we'll sit together at dinner tonight?" Susannah asked eagerly as we walked together.

"Of course. Unless Penelope seats me elsewhere, I would love to sit with you."

"I'm still reeling over the fact that Roberto didn't acknowledge Isabella. Her mother must be fuming. No telling what story Penelope will have to create to cover that up. Roberto certainly has a mind of his own, wouldn't you say?"

"Yes, I believe he does," I responded.

"It would certainly be quite the talk if Roberto does not agree to the arrangement. He is the eldest and will clearly make decisions not only for himself, but also for his family. I am just quite curious what statement he is making by his actions today."

"I don't think I understood all of this to be such an ordeal."

"Oh yes. It is customary and apropos to publicly confirm a marriage arrangement, especially when we see one another so infrequently. This is how our families survive. Roberto is on the threshold of his destiny and must choose. He will make the right decision, and neither one of his parents will fault him for that. He has never been one to give in to folly. He was born a leader. Even Penelope will agree to that. She may not like his independence, but she respects it."

"To what do you attribute his sudden change of heart?"

"Do you really have to ask me that?" She laughed. "You, of course. It is quite obvious."

"Oh! You are quite wrong, Susannah. Roberto has never made any suggestions or confessions to me. We are merely good friends."

"You really believe that? Is that what you have been telling yourself? Dusky, time brought change and it brought you. Roberto will always do what is honorable. However, his affections for you are not hard to see. He treats you with considerable care unlike he gives to anyone else. Perhaps it is difficult for you to notice because you didn't grow up within this protocol, but I see it."

Had my heart known all along and I had simply dismissed it?

"I think you complement one another quite well," Susannah continued oblivious to my introspection. "Poor Fernando. He'll really have his work cut out for him now."

We both giggled, but I was not convinced of all that Susannah had to say. I was not about to let trivial observations direct my heart. I knew better than that.

We approached dinner and I excused myself to go find Penelope and be of any assistance.

CHAPTER TWENTY-FOUR

THE SOUND OF GRAVEL CRUNCHING beneath his tires made Drew slow down even more as he pulled into the gas station Henry had described. It was on the edge of Uvalde and surrounded by towering pecan trees. He waved at the attendant as he pulled close to the pump. Rolling his window down, he could smell freshness from the sycamores and pecan trees lining the streets.

"How you doin' today, sir?" the attendant asked as he approached the driver's side of Drew's truck.

"Doing fine . . . and you?"

"'Bout as good as it gets with this mighty fine spring weather . . . and that is pretty darn good."

"Yes, sir, I believe it is," Drew added, noticing the gap between the older man's teeth when he grinned.

"You need a top off or are ya fillin' her up?"

"Looks like I'll need to fill up the tank. I've still got a ways to go."

"Where ya headed?" the old man inquired.

"Up 55 toward Barksdale." Drew could see the man squint his eyes as he pulled the gas cap off.

"Yep, you'll need a fill up all right."

Drew nodded and stepped out of the truck to stretch his legs. He pulled the folded paper from his pocket and reviewed the directions Henry had written down. As he slid them back into his pants, his fingers brushed the velvet box. He tightened his hand around it and pulled it out of his pocket.

The sun caught the luster of the center diamond as he carefully peeled back the hinged lid. It was even more brilliant in the light of day than he remembered in the soft lighting of Henry's study.

"Surely the blessings of others will make a way now," he said under his breath. He looked up at the rich, blue sky. "I'm counting on you. I'm trusting you to ready her heart for me."

Drew then closed the box as if to seal his and placed it back in his pocket. He heard the clink of the gas pump and turned back toward his truck.

"Think I've got ya' all set," the attendant announced while placing the gas pump handle back into its cradle. "Good lookin' truck ya' got here."

"Appreciate it and thank you. Been saving up a long time for this one." Drew smiled and handed him eight dollars. "Keep the change," he said as he shook the old man's hand.

"Appreciate ya'. Have a good one."

Drew climbed into the truck and grabbed the door. "You too," he added before shutting it.

He looked at his watch and figured he had about two hours left before he arrived. The tires gripped the asphalt as he turned the wheel to head down the last part of Main Street before joining Highway 55.

After rolling down the windows to enjoy the crisp breeze flowing into the truck, he tuned in a radio station. As he drove out toward the edge of town, he glanced over at the Nueces riverbank that lined the left side of the highway. Chalk-colored cliffs stood on the far side. He thumbed along with the beat of the radio until he heard a thump from the right front tire. Immediately, he slowed his speed and pulled off onto a dirt road.

Drew shifted the truck into park and turned off the engine. He felt certain it was a flat. As he rounded the hood of his truck, his suspicions were confirmed. Rolling up his sleeves, he loosened the spare and dug for the crossbar.

He began to work to prop up the front tire when he heard a car pulling in next to his. Sliding out from the undercarriage, Drew stood to see who it was.

"Looks like you need some help," the Hispanic man offered as Drew slapped the dirt from his backside.

"That would be most appreciated, sir." Drew extended his hand to shake.

"Juan Carlos," the man said, accepting Drew's hand.

"Drew Hillson."

"Looks like we are headed in the same direction, yes?" Juan Carlos offered him a jack.

"Maybe so. I'm heading up to close to Barksdale." Drew said as he took the jack from Juan Carlos' hand and bent down to place it under the frame of his truck.

"I believe we are. I live over there. I'm just heading back now from the market." He squatted next to Drew and handed him the tools.

Drew unfastened the lug nuts, and pulled off the flat tire. Juan Carlos helped him slide on the spare.

Tightening the lug nuts, Drew wiped the sweat from his forehead onto his shirtsleeve, "I sure appreciate your help."

"No problem. I travel this road many times, and I have had a flat as well. It's always nice to have an extra hand. Do you come through here often?"

"No sir, this is actually my first time. I'm going to visit someone staying at a ranch near Barksdale." Drew rolled the tools back into the faded cloth and handed them to Juan Carlos. Together they picked up the flat tire and slung it into the bed of the pickup.

"Do you need any help finding the place? I have lived up here all my life. I pretty much know everybody."

"I think the directions are fairly clear but . . ." Drew's voice trailed off as he reached into his pocket and pulled out the folded paper. Opening it, he handed the paper to Juan Carlos and noticed the man's eyes widen as he rubbed his hand over his mouth.

"Yes, I know the place."

Drew waited for Juan Carlos to continue, but he stared at the paper a bit longer before handing it back to him.

Confused by his sudden coolness, Drew probed further. "Do you think these directions will get me there?"

"Yes. Maybe. Probably so." Drew watched as Juan Carlos turned to pack the tools back into the steel toolbox locked to the bed of his pickup truck. Drew followed him and pushed a little more.

"You seem a little unsure. Is there something else I need to know?" Drew was hoping Juan Carlos would offer a bit more certainty.

Drew remained still as Juan Carlos turned and faced him, peering at Drew from under his tattered cowboy hat. Drew felt the steeliness from his stare as he waited for Juan Carlos to speak.

"May I be bold and ask a question?" Juan Carlos adjusted the brim of his hat.

"Please." Drew was quick to respond, trying to figure out the sudden tenseness that had developed between them.

Slow to answer, Juan Carlos finally spoke. "Who are you going to visit?"

"Well . . ." Drew paused, wondering what the man would do with the information once he shared it. "I . . . I'm going to ask someone to marry me." Relieved he had actually said it out loud, he noticed Juan Carlos raise his eyebrows. Unsure if he should continue, Drew waited.

"I see. I like your answer, but what of hers?"

Drew felt like Juan Carlos was baiting him. "I'm hoping it will be a yes but she's been through a lot lately and it seems like grief and strife have tried to drive a wedge between us."

"But you feel she is worth fighting for?" Drew could tell Juan Carlos wasn't letting up at this point.

"Yes, sir. She is worth everything to me, and I'm not willing to lose her again." Drew was rattled by his own emotions, which were beginning to stir inside of him now.

"Lose her again?" Juan Carlos pushed.

"Yes, we've been separated by distance at one time, and recently she coped with caring for her mother who died of cancer and pretty much shut herself away from the world. Now she's dealing with a situation that her deceased grandmother wanted her to know about and, truthfully, I won't let anything else come between us."

Drew waited for a reaction from Juan Carlos, but the man remained stoic as he leaned back against the truck.

"And you feel she loves you too?"

Exasperated, Drew answered, hoping to satisfy the man's curiosity so he could get back on the road. "I believe she does. In fact, I know she does, but . . ." Cautiously, he let the words spill from his heart. "I'm just not sure if she knows how to trust that love."

"Ah, I see." Juan Carlos looked at Drew, and Drew leaned in ready for the answer he felt Juan Carlos was about to share. "Then you go. You go and let love have its way. Love will win. You must trust in it. She will feel your confidence, and it will allow her to follow you. Your call, your duty as a man, is to love her well no matter what. The more you love well, the less fear is allowed to speak. I think you are making the right choice. It is clear you love her and have given this a great deal of thought. You can follow me. I'll get you to the ranch."

Even though he was reassured by Juan Carlos' encouragement, he was baffled at his invitation. "Thank you, but I'd hate to interrupt your day."

"Oh, you are not an interruption at all."

"Well, getting me there isn't going to mess up your plans?"

"Not at all. I'll be right on time."

Completely confused, Drew watched Juan Carlos walk around to the driver's door of his pickup. "How is that possible?"

"I live there. I'm the foreman of the ranch," Juan Carlos quickly replied before shutting the door. Leaning across the seat, the man looked out the window at him standing there in shock. "Let's get moving. My wife, Carmen, won't be happy if I don't get these supplies to her, and you and Eliza will need some quiet time before supper." Juan Carlos winked at Drew and turned the ignition.

Taken aback, Drew let out a laugh and almost fell backward. *Of course, the one man who stops to help me is the foreman from Eliza's grandmother's ranch. God, you've got quite a sense of humor.* He shook his head.

CHAPTER TWENTY-FIVE

ELIZA KNEW IT WAS LUNCHTIME, but she couldn't pull herself away from her reading. She walked inside to look at the clock, which only confirmed her thoughts. She wanted one more hour, and then she would try to call Drew again. She picked up the journal and searched for her spot.

As I came around the corner, I heard Penelope's voice.

"What shall I tell Isabella's mother?"

I stopped and remained out of sight.

"Well . . ." Señor de la Cruz began, "you tell her nothing."

"Nothing? Nothing! Eduardo, we have been planning this for years. We all gathered this weekend in anticipation of a formal proposal from Roberto to Isabella, and we've seen nothing of the sort. I cannot tell her nothing."

"My dear, you women flitter and worry about the littlest details. It will all work itself out. Let us not forget, Roberto is a grown man. We must consult with him before we speak for him. He will one day be the voice of this family, and we must honor him, not manipulate him."

"I am not manipulating him, but I am demanding he answer to his intentions from here forward with Isabella. Everything has been perfectly arranged. It was distasteful what he did."

"Oh Penelope, you are getting worked up. I beg you to calm down and regain your composure at once. This is nothing to be overly concerned about. I will talk with Roberto tonight and inquire over this matter, but you must promise to stay silent until he and I have had a chance to talk."

"Very well. I will try to avoid Senora Nunez as best I can."

I quickly retreated to the party and mingled with the other guests. Fernando caught my eye and approached me.

"Did you enjoy yourself today?"

"*Immensely, I had no idea how entertaining a rodeo could be.*"

"*Well, unfortunately for us we let the title slip away this year, but we shall prevail next year and regain our crown!*" *Fernando jovially replied.*

"*I'm glad to see your loss didn't dampen your spirits.*"

"*Quite the contrary. I rather enjoyed seeing us lose.*" *Just as we both laughed, Gabriel and Susannah joined the conversation.*

"*Having a good laugh over our loss, brother?*" *Gabriel said.* "*Hard to imagine, but I didn't find it as humorous as you did.*"

"*Come now, Gabriel, if we can't laugh at ourselves then who can we laugh at?*" *Fernando grinned.*

It was fun to watch the interaction between them. It reminded me of Roberto and his brothers.

"*Dusky!*" *Miguel's voice cried out.* "*Dusky, I've been looking for you. Mother asked me to escort you to your seat. Excuse us, please.*"

We all broke into smiles, and I proudly took Miguel's arm.

"*Save me a dance, Dusky!*" *Fernando called out as we made our way to our seats. I turned toward him with a grin as Miguel led me to the table.*

"*As today's victors, we will sit together at the head table on the upper patio,*" *Miguel informed me.*

When we arrived at our places, I could hear Eduardo and Roberto's voices coming from inside the house.

"*You must inform me of your decision, my son. Your mother is distraught over this. If you have changed your mind, then please be honorable at this very moment. I cannot go out there and continue to pretend. Masquerading is a lie.*"

"*Father, I cannot commit.*"

"*You cannot commit. I see. Does that mean right now or ever? Because I might possibly be breaking an alliance with Hacendado Nunez tonight if I must inform him that my son finds his daughter distasteful and us liars!*"

Roberto's voice rose louder. "*Father, I never said she was distasteful.*"

"*You didn't have to say it. From what your mother told me your actions spoke for you! Roberto, I am not commanding you to marry*"

Isabella. I would never condemn any child of mine to a perceived life of misery, but I am commanding you to be forthright with your intentions because arrangements must be made with all concerned parties. You are not the only son I have, and I cannot subject this family to a scandal.

"Our fortune is not at stake here. We are blessed in that regard, but our reputation is at stake! Over a year ago this was your seeming desire, and preparations were put in place specifically for this weekend for an engagement announcement. So you can understand how shocked your mother and I are that quite the opposite has taken place!"

"Father, I realize my actions have created confusion, but I cannot go through with this. It would not bring honor to Isabella or myself."

"I want honesty, Roberto. Have you been involved with another woman?"

"No, absolutely not . . . I . . ."

Eduardo cut him off. "It is finished then. I will see to it that this arrangement is dissolved. I am inclined to offer her Gustavo's hand instead for the sake of unity. Would that offend you?"

"I believe that to be the best, Father."

"Find me Gustavo and your mother at once. This matter must be settled before the night is over."

"Yes, Father."

Roberto burst through the patio doors and out into the party. Miguel waited by the table, making small talk with the other charros and their wives. No one else seemed to have heard their discussion other than myself.

Waiters passed cool limonada *and white wine. I took a glass and stared toward the party guests as Miguel continued in lively conversation. Out of the corner of my eye, I caught Penelope and the boys entering the house through the side patio doors. I moved closer to hear the conversation. I couldn't help myself.*

"Penelope, Gustavo," Eduardo began, "Roberto and I have had a frank conversation over his presumed engagement. I assured Roberto, as eldest in this house, his desires are our desires. Even though as parents we may have aspirations for each of our children, none of us are bound by them. Therefore, I have given Roberto our blessings, Penelope, to

relinquish his obligations to Isabella and pass them to Gustavo . . . should Gustavo accept."

Penelope let out a small gasp and cleared her throat before she spoke. "I am . . . of course, I am in agreement with your father's decision, Roberto. Your happiness is our deepest concern, and yours too, Gustavo."

"Gustavo," Eduardo interrupted, "before you consider this arrangement, you must realize the implications it carries. Isabella is Señor Nunez's eldest daughter. They have no sons. Your marriage to Isabella will then require you to leave the Hacienda de la Cruz and become hacendado of the Nunez family. It was different for Roberto as he would have run both, but perhaps this is a better opportunity for you, my son."

"Father, I see this as a great honor and an opportunity to keep alliances strong. Isabella is a respectable, beautiful woman. I accept."

"Very well. It is settled. I will speak with Señor Nunez before supper begins. Penelope, make sure supper is prepared, and we will begin after the boys and I speak with Señor Nunez. Roberto, bring him to my study."

As the sound of feet scattered, I moved quickly to the table. Roberto had relinquished a legacy tonight, and all for what? Only he knew.

"Hello, all," Penelope said to the gathered crowd. "Dinner will be served shortly. Sorry for the delay. We've had a few matters that needed to be settled. Dusky, will you come with me and help me organize for a moment?"

"Yes, I'd be delighted to."

"Thank you, my dear. Miguel, keep entertaining the others. It will only be a moment." She patted his arm and moved passed him.

Seemingly breathless, she turned toward the steps and I followed. With her back to me, she said, "I need a few moments, Dusky, to catch my breath. Go make sure the staff knows we will eat in twenty minutes so they can seat the guests. Thank you." Then she hurried toward her private quarters.

I found the head staff and relayed Penelope's orders. I was a touch bewildered by it all. What was Roberto thinking?

Finally, dinner was served and we ate with casual chatter, recounting the day's victory. Penelope was a touch quiet, but seemed to perk up toward the end of the meal. The guests began to stir and make their way to the dance floor or gather in groups to continue their conversations. Over my shoulder, Fernando popped up behind me.

"May I steal this beautiful lady from your table?"

"Fernando, dear," Penelope said, extending her hand to him, "you are most gentlemanly. Please enjoy yourselves."

She nodded in my direction. Fernando took my hand and led me to the dance floor. Gustavo followed our cue and excused himself from the table.

"Another gorgeous night," Fernando said, twirling me around. "I am hoping you will come for Susannah and Gabriel's wedding next month?"

"I would love to, but it all depends on Father's return and what his plans are."

"I see. Perhaps I will come back and visit you then?"

"Yes, that would be nice."

We wove through the brilliant colors of potted flowers and ladies' gowns, the aroma of perfume and sweat heavy in the air. Faces blurred as other dancers whirled past us. I looked toward the hills as twilight gave way to darkness and stars began to pop out on their blanket of black.

"Thoughts?" Fernando whispered.

"Umm . . . thoughts. More like choices. Like stars scattered in the night sky, each possibility leads to even more possibilities. A gift or a curse; sometimes it's hard to decide."

"Well . . . what if you allow someone to decide for you?"

As dear as Fernando was, I knew he wasn't the one. But one must always give fate an opportunity on the slight chance that the door is unlocked.

"I think it's best to decide for myself. Will you excuse me?"

"Are you all right?"

"Yes, I just need a moment."

"Here, let me come with you."

"No, please. Thank you . . . enjoy yourself. I'll only be a moment."

"If you insist."

"Yes, please." I left the dance floor and walked to the backside of the veranda, out of sight of the party. I ascended the side steps to a balcony.

The air was clear and crisp. I shut my eyes and pulled my shawl over my shoulders. While my head still hummed with the melodies of the night, I was transported back to the river . . . the sweetness and the freedom. The ease of that day.

"May I join you?"

Startled, I turned to see Roberto standing behind me.

"Please. I was just enjoying the simple sounds of the night from here."

He leaned on the railing beside me. "I can see that. Today has been a busy day."

"Most certainly. You must be exhausted yourself."

"Surprisingly, no. How about you?"

"A touch, yes."

"Do you like it here, Dusky? Our home? Mexico?"

"Why, of course. It is so lovely. You all are blessed with such beauty and family. It has been so special to be with you all this summer. I shall never forget your generosity."

"It pleases me to hear that. I hoped you would approve. This is all I have known—our ways, our customs, our land. I am glad we have not overwhelmed you."

"No, being here has restored my hope in life and in living. I don't have words to thank you all enough. It will be quite hard to say good-bye."

"Who says you have to leave? What of the friends you have made here? Fernando?"

I couldn't help but giggle.

"What?" Roberto began to chuckle himself.

"It's not you I'm laughing at Roberto, it's Fernando. Not him, but the whole introduction. I . . . I'm sorry what I said the other night. It was out of line to be so harsh with you. You only meant well, and I didn't understand.

"As dear as Fernando is, Roberto, I don't believe that he and I are meant to be. I'm afraid we will just end up confusing one another. We are both so vastly different in personality. Am I making any sense?"

"Yes. I, too, believe you to be opposites in character, but that belief wasn't for me to make public."

"Your mother meant well, and I certainly don't want to disappoint her."

"You must not concern yourself with her whims. It is you who must live with the choice—not her. She simply cannot let some matters unfold for themselves. I, for one, this very night have made a commitment to myself to pursue liberty and freedom in all circumstances, including the concerns of my heart.

"I have always been driven by duty and direction to assume my position. But lately, and so unexpectedly, I have found myself questioning my heart's desires.

"What I'd like to say, Dusky, is . . . ever since you arrived your beauty has touched me—changed me to the point that I walked away from my engagement to Isabella tonight."

He gently took my hands, and I felt his outpouring of sweet passion sweep over me. I steadied myself with his touch as my chest rose with nervous excitement.

"Your words flatter me, Roberto. I am at loss at what to say," I managed breathlessly.

"Then say you won't leave, and say that today and the rest of the days you will be my wife and raise our children and love me until our breath has ceased." He cupped my face in his hand.

I swallowed as tears filled my eyes. "Yes, I'd like to say that," I whispered as he brought his lips to mine and tenderly kissed me. He took me in his arms and we embraced, and all that we had held back came gushing forward in that moment. Words could not suffice. His strength and tenderness spoke for each of us. I felt his breath upon my neck and his cheek warm against mine.

He broke the silence with his whispers. "I promise to fill your days with beauty and love just as you have mine." He kissed my forehead and pulled me to his chest. In that moment, the stars held their brilliance in the night sky for us. Their shimmering shadows laid witness to our hearts' promise.

"What of your parents, Roberto. Have they given us their blessing?"

"I had no intention of mentioning my affections for you until I was certain you felt the same. I needed to know that you had not fallen for Fernando."

"He had quite the opposite effect on me, really. I soon realized how much I deeply love you. No matter what the outcome, I'd rather leave Mexico than live here without you."

"My dear, your words thrill me. Let me handle Fernando. He understands the game of love better than most. I so deeply desire to have your father's blessing, and I would like your permission to ask him. With his return still uncertain, I believe it would be best to send him a telegram. May I have your consent?"

"Of course. Father will be pleased, I think."

"Tomorrow after our guests leave, I will speak with my parents and ask for their blessing. Perhaps then we can arrange for a telegram to be sent to your father. I want to celebrate with you. Let us go dance. The others will just have to wonder what mischief we've been up to."

Roberto offered his arm, and bent down to kiss my cheek once more. Flushed, I took his arm and laid my head against his shoulder. The door to my future had been unlocked, and I was walking through.

Eliza carefully placed the leather journal in her lap and closed the cover. She let her fingers linger and began to laugh in disbelief.

Grandmother about to marry this prince of Mexico from a time long forgotten. And, she called my mother spirited.

What a story she kept this hidden all this time! Why? I still haven't figured that part out. And who was Roberto? He certainly wasn't the grandfather I remembered.

Eliza stared curiously at the grouchy mockingbird fussing at Chula the cat on the rock patio below as she sunbathed carelessly in the agitated bird's territory. This duet went on for a few more minutes before Chula sauntered off to a more secluded spot.

Carmen knocked and opened the door.

"I brought you a small tray. Lunchtime is almost here, and I thought I would bring this up before you stopped to go downstairs. Here you go, Mija."

She set the tray on a small side table.

"It looks delicious, thank you."

"Are you doing all right?"

"Yes. Just losing track of time. I apologize."

"No apology necessary. That is what you are here to do. Sit and eat and stay with your work, please."

"Will you sit with me a moment?"

"Of course, dear. I love this spot. It was your grandmother's favorite place to read and write."

"What do you remember most about my grandmother?"

"Well, there are so many things, but one thing stands out the most for me. She was gracious, but gracious in a way that is hard to put into words." Carmen turned to stare at the hills. "She never seemed restless but very peaceful about her life.

"When she came here, I watched as she spent most of her days down by the springs that run in front of the house. She had a very special spot with an old bench and rocks she collected from the property."

"Is it still here?"

"Yes, we have moved nothing—just kept it clean all these years. I don't remember a day when I didn't see her down there." Carmen's voice drifted as she turned toward the river.

"Just behind the big oak," she said, pointing, "is her garden of rocks. She wrote on each one. Some are faded now, but you should go down there when you need a break.

"She was always very grateful even without telling you. Maybe it was a look in her eyes or her considerate ways, but I never felt uneasy around her."

"Yes, I understand what you mean," Eliza responded thoughtfully. "Even my littlest concerns were important to her. She never rushed or hurried when it came to matters of the heart. I cherished that about her. I miss her compassion."

"She took it all to heart. You are right, Eliza. So to me being gracious means living in love even when the world doesn't understand loving in that way. Now I must leave you. Juan Carlos should be back from town soon, and I want to put the supplies away before resting. Also, you've got more reading to do I see."

"That I do," Eliza added.

As Carmen shut the door to the bedroom, Eliza leaned over the balcony to peek at her grandmother's retreat by the springs. She remembered how much her grandmother loved the outdoors—always gardening and gathering in the backyard.

And what she had, I have too. I can draw from her courage. Eliza decided to call Drew.

After several rings, there was still no answer. Eliza sadly figured he was out to lunch. Not hearing his voice as she had anticipated made her realize how much she missed him. She couldn't imagine what he must be thinking at this point. He said he would wait for her, but she wished Drew was here with her now.

Her grandmother's legacy of courage had begun to erode the walls hidden inside her. It was unlike any gift she had ever received or even knew how to give.

"I'm listening, Grandmother. My heart is listening. My heart, too, still beats."

CHAPTER TWENTY-SIX

ELIZA WALKED BACK UPSTAIRS to the balcony and looked toward the road. She didn't see Juan Carlos' truck returning, but she had been fairly preoccupied. Perhaps she just hadn't heard him drive in.

The day is turning out to be as gorgeous as it promised this morning. Everything seems to be more vibrant and alive than it has the last several days . . . or maybe it's just me. Maybe I'm more alive, and the life I feel inside is changing my view of the world.

"If that is the case, then whatever you are doing inside of me, I want more," Eliza said as the breeze gently brushed her cheeks. "Change my heart to see the way you see, God."

She sat down and laid her hands in her lap, closing her eyes to allow the stillness to have its way. With slow breaths, she inhaled and gave herself permission to relax.

All in His time, she heard her own voice reassure her.

She reached to pick up the journal.

The guests had finally left after a long day of farewells and good-byes. Susannah and I bid one another sweet good-byes and promised to correspond frequently. With her wedding coming up, I wanted to be there for her.

Roberto had sent me a message earlier to meet him on the side patio in the private quarters at dusk. I imagined he had broken the news to his parents and this would hopefully be an informal celebration.

Penelope and Eduardo were seated next to one another. They smiled as I approached.

"Dearest girl," Señor de la Cruz held out his arms to embrace me and then kissed my cheeks. "You have made our son most happy. We are delighted for you both."

Penelope rose and took me in her arms. "I completely mismatched everyone this past weekend, and I am truly sorry. What turmoil I have caused so unknowingly. We are thrilled, dear. And I mean that with all my heart."

"I have so much to be grateful for. Thank you both," I responded, grateful for their love and acceptance.

Señor Eduardo took charge and announced a toast. "It is with unexpected pleasure, Dusky, I welcome you to our family. Nothing is dearer to my heart than my loved ones, and their happiness is my utmost concern. I see how you make our son jubilant, and we give you both our blessing."

He raised his cup and we all followed suit. Roberto stood with his arm around my waist. The moment was perfect.

"May God bless you both with all that He has blessed upon Penelope and me. May each day of your lives be filled with more and more of His goodness."

Roberto bent down to kiss me, and my eager heart met his. I chose love. My heart was full, and more importantly, my heart was at home.

That evening Señor Eduardo sent a telegram to Father asking on behalf of his son for my hand in marriage. The words he wrote were this:

Ricardo, I hope this telegram finds you well. All is good here. It is with great honor that I come to you on behalf of my eldest son, Roberto. He wishes to ask for your daughter's hand in marriage. Your blessing would be an honor to us all.

We waited for his reply, and after many days, Señor Eduardo announced the receipt of his telegram. I knew Father would be pleased, but still my stomach was in tangles. Señor Eduardo gathered Roberto, myself, and Penelope in his study. I sat across from him with the great mahogany desk sprawled out between us. I was poised on the edge of my chair with Roberto standing next to me, his hand upon my shoulder.

"We have received word from your father, Dusky. His telegram reads:

Hacendado Eduardo: I am honored by your request. I send my blessings to them both. I will return by the end of the month to give my daughter away. Give Dusky a hug and kiss from me and tell her I am most pleased.

"So . . . I believe we have a wedding to plan," Señor Eduardo said as he set the paper down and removed his glasses. His eyes met mine, and we both beamed. Roberto bent down and swept me up in his arms.

"We will have the wedding six weeks from now," Roberto announced. "Plenty of time for your father to arrive and for us to make plans."

"Hardly time," Penelope chimed in. Dusky felt lightheaded. "Gloria and I will work furiously to pull this together. Dusky, we cannot waste a single moment."

Señor Eduardo stepped out from behind his desk and walked over to us. "It is our privilege to host this grand occasion, and more importantly, to give you both the gift of a home." He turned to Roberto. "I want you to work with Carlos and pick out a place to put your homestead. Whatever you desire shall be done. Now, we must let the lady of the house begin preparations for she has quite a celebration to host."

Penelope rose and hugged each of us. "Darlings, what a wonderful time to be young and in love."

The whirlwind that ensued over the next several weeks left me breathless at times. Penelope insisted on having her gorgeous wedding gown fitted just for me. Tiny pearls were sewn all over the collar and the bodice. In between each pearl was a crystal that glimmered every time I moved. The gown flowed gloriously to the floor and spilled out the back into a small train. The lace veil was outlined in the same pearls and crystals along the scalloped, delicate edges. The gown was regal in every sense of the word.

After the final fitting, I stood in front of the full-length mirror in my future mother-in-law's quarters. "Penelope, this is divine. I feel like a princess in this."

"You are. You're Roberto's princess." She smiled as tears spilled from the corners of her eyes. "This was crafted in Old Spain. The crystals came from Sweden, and the pearls from the Far East. My family was quite proud, I dare say, and spared no expense. It brings me unspeakable joy to see you in it now, Dusky."

I felt tears sting my eyes as I realized my life was moving forward, farther away from Mother and Sister. And on the other side their great loss had led me to love—glorious, beautiful love. Such a sacrifice. And yet God had brought about great good from such tragedy.

"Are you all right, dear?" Penelope inquired.

"Yes, I'm just thinking of my mother and my sister, that is all. Because of their deaths, I've been given a chance at a new life. It's quite humbling."

"The gift of resurrection, an enormous gift at a lofty price . . . more often than not at the expense of the death of a loved one. You will honor them with your smile, your spirit, your joy, and your love. Don't waste their gift, my dear. You've risen from the ashes, and it is time to take flight. Cherish the freedom and inspiration this brings."

With those words she left the room silently, and I stood looking at myself in the mirror. Her words encircled me and swathed me.

Yes, it was time. Time to walk ahead and no longer dwell on the past. I knew neither Mother nor Sister would want me to carry the burden of sorrow for them. Bowing my head in silent prayer, I reflected with an expectant heart.

Nights and days melted into one as the entire hacienda was set into motion, preparing for the wedding. Penelope directed every detail in her usual, careful manner. Cooks and gardeners, maids and stable boys, were sent in every direction with specific duties to fulfill.

Roberto was immersed with the daily business affairs of the ranch as well as constructing our new home. We met at the daily meals and shared the events of the days with one another.

As the end of the month drew near, we received word that Father was boarding the train and would be here within the next seven days. I was so eager to see him and share my happiness with him.

The day before Father was to arrive, Penelope and I sat together in the garden with our needlepoint. Our quiet chatter was interrupted when one of the workers came galloping through the gate, yelling frantic shouts. Penelope dropped her work and stood up immediately.

"Dusky, stay here out of sight until I come for you," she commanded.

Before I could argue, she flew into the house, and I sat frozen. I heard many voices and orders shouted all at once. Finally, through the chaos, I

heard Señor Eduardo's voice become gruff and demanding. He commanded Roberto, Gustavo, and the rider to follow him at once to his study.

The slamming of his office door rang through the house. I sat in stunned
silence. I watched the cooks and girls huddled around a table in the cooking
quarters and several of their family members congregated by the back door.

I strained my ear in the direction of the chaos in Eduardo's study. The
voices carried out through the open window into the garden and were
clearly audible. In my silence, I could hear every word.

"I bring you grave news, Señor."

"Sî, sî tell us at once."

"There has been great violence in the northern countryside, Señor. A
group of unruly bandits have begun to kill innocent people and steal from
their lands and their pockets. I am afraid the last attack has brought a
great and tragic loss."

I could hear the rider's heavy breathing. Everyone else remained silent.

Sweat formed on the palms of my hands, and I wiped them on my
skirt. I felt a sudden rush of panic and started to shake. I struggled to remain still and quiet. I swallowed in order to calm myself, but to no avail.

"They attacked a train, Señor, killing as many as they could, leaving
them for dead and stealing their belongings. In particular, one witness
reported they knew to locate a certain car and passenger. This man was
carrying much money. They never gave him time to plea for his life, I am
told. They dragged him by the hair from the train and executed him in
front of the other passengers. Great turmoil erupted, and the train stood
abandoned and ransacked with bodies strewn along the tracks.

"The police have identified many of the victims. I am very sad to tell
you the man they dragged from the train was your friend, Señor Ricardo,
Senorita Dusky's father."

The world closed in around me, and I cupped my mouth for fear of
the tormented screams that were begging to escape. I became senseless,
and my feet took flight. Bursting through the house, I ran past Penelope
and her staff, oblivious to their voices and their touch.

As I ran, I sobbed, great waves of sorrow crashing through me. The
voices behind me fell flat. I was numb to my surroundings. I ran to the back

gate of the hacienda wall and flung it open in desperation. I flew through the open field toward the river.

I clearly remember falling into the river and climbing the opposite bank, wishing I could keep going, but my chest was on fire. My ribs worked tirelessly for breath as I screamed into the air, "How much more do you want to take from me! How much more! Stop, make it stop!"

Then I fell on my knees and planted my face in the wet ground, my weeping drowning out the screams close by. I couldn't move. My body wouldn't respond.

"Dusky! Dusky!" Roberto's shouting pierced the fog of my grief, and I heard him splash into the water as he fought his way to me. He reached me and fell on the bank next to me.

He picked me up and held me. "I'm here, Dusky. I'm here."

Even though I heard his voice, I was trapped inside the darkness. I couldn't respond. I heard him give an order for his horse to be brought around.

I was lifted up and Roberto cradled me in his arms on the horse. He began the ride back to the hacienda and I drifted away.

I emerged from a groggy, deep sleep in what could have been a day or two. I'm not sure. Cautiously, I opened my eyes to the familiarities of my room. My head ached so terribly. My eyes were swollen.

"Senorita, you are awake," Maria whispered as she came to the side of the bed with a cool cloth for my forehead.

I tried to move my lips, but no sound came out.

"We have been so worried, especially Señor Roberto. May I send for him and let him know you are awake?"

"Not yet, please," I struggled to say. "Please help me to sit up."

Gently Maria lifted my head as I raised myself. She fluffed the pillows behind me, and I took a sip of water.

"Would you mind combing my hair?"

She moved over to the dresser and took the silver brush from the drawer and with gentle strokes began working through my tangles. We spoke not a word to each other.

"There, you look much better."

"Thank you. You may let Roberto know I am awake."

Maria tiptoed to the door and spoke with the valet keeping watch. I wanted more details of Father's death, but I didn't know if I could bear it.

Within moments Roberto strode through the door and approached my bedside. He sat next to me and took my hand.

"How are you, my darling?"

My lips betrayed me and began to tremble as I started to speak. "I don't know. Tell me what you know of Father. I am scared, but I must know."

He leaned over and stroked my face with his hand. The warmth of his touch was healing.

"Father has sent a group of men into town to find out what they can. Tell me what you remember."

Tears sprang from my eyes, and Roberto quickly pulled me to his chest to console me. "Perhaps we need to wait to discuss this. You are too fragile right now."

"No . . . I want to know. Give me a moment, please."

"Of course. Take your time."

Wiping away each tear with a linen handkerchief, I finally found my voice. "I heard the rider explain the train robbery. I remember him saying Father was pulled from the train and . . . shot."

"I am afraid that is all we know at this point. When the men return perhaps they will have more information."

"What about his body, Roberto? Where do we bury him?"

"When we locate his body, we will bury him here in the family cemetery. I am hopeful our men will be successful in gathering information. We will know more in the next couple of days.

"Please, sweetheart, get some more rest." He kissed the top of my forehead and stood. "I'll be close by if you need me."

I nodded my head, and he left the room. I wanted to go with him and walk in the gardens, but I couldn't muster the strength.

Maria returned with a tray of hot tea and rolls. Sliding down my throat, the warm tea brought comfort as I stared out the window pondering how a beautiful day could turn to black so quickly.

Eliza's tears stained the journal page, and the words began to blur. She felt her grandmother's pain . . . and her own. She buckled over and wept. She wept for her own father whom she never knew, the mother she had lost, and the grandmother who now spoke through the words she had written for her. A shared pain of loss knit them together across time.

Standing, she moved about the room, trying to shake off the sting and reflecting on the common turning point in all of humanity . . . shattered hearts. In the midst of the broken pieces it was the scattered mess of her feelings and her life that scared her the most. She could feel it and see it and taste it, and yet, it remained, still waiting to be picked up, cleaned up, straightened up, or swept up. But she didn't know how.

Lord, how does love come in and glue the pieces back together? Perhaps it doesn't. Perhaps love comes in and forms a new heart from what was and from what can be.

Reluctant to stop reading, she wiped the tears from her face and pressed through to finish the story that was already transforming her.

CHAPTER TWENTY-SEVEN

WIPING HER BLURRY EYES, Eliza continued reading.

I must have drifted off after drinking my tea because I woke to a new stream of sun peeking through the window. Determined to get up, I pulled my legs over the side of the bed. With a deep breath and as much resolve as I could muster, I got dressed. Maria entered the room.

"Oh, Senorita, you are up and dressed. How can I help?"

"Perhaps I'll take my coffee in the gardens by the fountain."

"Very good. I will meet you there. Can I let the family know you will join them for the morning meal?"

"Please, I would appreciate that."

I walked outside and took in the fresh air. The morning glories were in full bloom, sunbathing by the fountain. Surrounded by yellows, reds, pinks, and oranges, their royal blue drew my attention. Their vivid color illuminated my heart.

Sitting on the wooden bench in the shade, I watched the birds delight in their morning bath. Whistling and calling to one another, they flittered in and out of the clear water. I, too, wanted to wash off the past and rise clean from its torment.

Maria's coffee brought company—Penelope. "May I join you?"

"Please. Thank you, Maria," I said as she handed me a steaming cup of coffee swirled with hot cream.

"I am glad to see you up today," Penelope said. "We have all been so concerned about you."

"It is a nightmare I can't wake up from. Dreadful thoughts about Father won't let me rest. I knew his trips were dangerous, but I never dreamed of such a tragedy. He always seemed invincible. Sleep has been my only escape, but then I wake up and the horror starts all over again."

"I do not understand why this happened either, my dear. This has brought such sadness and fear to all our hearts. I am so deeply sorry.

"I do not doubt Eduardo will get to the bottom of this. He has sent men not only to Musquiz but also to our northern neighbors for more information. I never imagined something so senseless would fall upon us."

Penelope took a sip of her coffee and continued. "You are home. I hope you know that and feel that. Don't let this deter you and Roberto from starting your life together. Your father would want you to be happy and safe."

My eyes began to burn with unshed tears.

"I am so grateful we received Father's blessing. I know it is what he wanted for me, and as formidable as it may seem, I want to keep walking forward. Being struck with grief before has taught me not to be yoked to it.

"Father worked day after day to ensure his family peace and security. Therefore, I want to honor his life by embracing the future, the hope set before me."

"Your strength is unyielding, Dusky, and it will serve you well. Your youth in years conceals the wisdom of the ages. Although I have felt much like a wilted bloom lately, you have inspired me with your courageous words."

We left our quiet retreat and walked through the courtyard to the family table. The busy servants and familiar smells surrounded me. Everyone's generous hugs and smiles encouraged my heart to keep looking ahead.

Day after day we waited for news from the hacendado's men. Finally, one morning several of the men returned with word. Upon their arrival, we all rushed to the entrance of the house. Señor Eduardo called for order and excused himself with his two eldest sons and the men. Penelope took the crook of my arm and we walked toward the garden.

"We must let Eduardo hear the news they bring first, then he will let us know," she explained.

My anxiety was building, and it seemed like hours before Señor Eduardo called Penelope and me into his study where Roberto and his men waited. Gesturing for us to have a seat, my future father-in-law spoke in a solemn voice.

"The raid of the train took many lives as we suspected. Much was stolen . . . money and jewels alike. Apparently, the bandits took off with young women as well. What has become of them no one knows.

"In all of our nation's history this is the most despicable incident to have ever taken place. These men appeared from the Sierras in the early dawn and surprised the train. The conductor was killed and passengers were forced to get out. Those who didn't were shot in their seats.

"According to one witness there were several people on the train singled out, including your father. He was pulled from the train, robbed, and shot. As always, I am certain he had a large amount of cash on him. When the bandits disappeared back into the mountains, the survivors walked for help. After a long wait through the night, they returned with help. Because of the intense heat, the dead were buried in a mass grave near the railroad tracks. I'm sorry, Dusky.

"However, they did retrieve personal effects they could salvage, and this sack has been identified as your father's. They also recovered his suitcase."

He walked around the desk and sat down beside me and handed me a brown bundle closed with twine and with father's name scribbled on the front. He cleared his throat as tears flowed down my cheeks. Roberto stood behind me, his hand on my shoulder.

"Apparently, this is not the first raid these monsters have carried out, but it is by far the deadliest and most grotesque. For some time they have been raiding villages and robbing banks. Portifiro Díaz has organized troops to put an end to these outlaws.

"This is serious. We have suffered a tragic loss of a dear friend and a beloved father. I have deep concerns for our compadres in the north as well. These raids can easily begin to threaten their way of life.

"We are fortunate enough to be cradled from this senseless violence, but we must stay alert and pray for our neighbors' safety."

Penelope and I sat in stunned silence. The news left a dismal fog hanging in the air. Senor Eduardo plowed through our despair with his booming voice.

"We mustn't live in fear or lose heart. We must pick up and push forward for our future generations yet to come. Roberto and Dusky, your wedding is what is most important to our family right now. We must carry on, especially to honor your father. He is counting on me to see your wedding through, and that is exactly what I intend to do.

"We will honor your father with a service first thing in the morning at the chapel. Then I will ask each of us to continue with the wedding plans and have your wedding two weeks from this Saturday as originally planned."

He stood up and Penelope joined him by his side. "My husband is quite right, Dusky. We would not be serving your father or any of the other victims for that matter if we let evil stamp out what love has grown. It will be bittersweet. We are aware of that, but we cannot let our hearts run dry over such atrocities."

The boldness of her words brought forth a resolve in me and I think to all of us in the room. We left the study sad, but encouraged. Roberto put his arm around my waist while he carried the bundle and suitcase in his opposite hand.

"Mother's right, my darling. I don't want this to ruin our future together. Your strength and grace are feeding us all."

"Don't be amazed by me." I looked up at him, tears still glistening in my eyes. "It is a strength far greater than I that nourishes my soul."

We took the package to my room, and Roberto laid it on the bed. I bid Roberto good-bye and carefully untied the twine. Father's shirts were stacked neatly together along with a bottle of cologne, his shaving kit, and another small, brown package.

I felt its weight. It was heavy like a book. Impatient, I peeled back the paper to reveal our family Bible. I gasped in gratitude and disbelief as I uncovered this beloved treasure. My fingers lingered on every spot of its cover.

"Oh Father," I whispered. "What a gift."

I opened the cover and a sealed letter slipped out. My name was written on the front in Father's handwriting.

My Dearest Dusky,

How blessed my life has been having you for a daughter. Although work took me from home far more often than I truly desired, you never ceased to be the drink of sunshine I needed when I returned. Your warm hugs and effervescent smiles instantly restored my weary soul.

Roberto will be a man of great fortune having you for a bride. Your presence in itself is a gift to others.

I brought you our family Bible to share with your own family someday. I look forward to watching the love you share with Roberto spill over into your children.

May God's Word sustain you and keep your heart always in perfect peace.

With love,

Father

I clutched the letter to my chest and wept.

Dearest man, you have no idea how much you have gifted me today.

It was by the grace of a miracle that our Bible made its way into my hands . . . I had no doubt.

In the morning we quietly filed into the private chapel and lit candles in memory of Father. The padre submitted prayers and supplications. We sang a fitting hymn and closed with a final farewell from Señor Eduardo. He led us out into the open sky and we held a gathering on the veranda with food and flowers.

Eduardo looked at me with gentleness and sincerity. "Roberto told me of your father's precious gift. I am so grateful you received it."

"I am too. Our family Bible means so much to me, and his letter spoke life into my heart. I shall not grow weary for through his words, I am encouraged. There is no doubt in my mind about what he would want me to do."

Roberto joined us, and I took his arm.

"Excuse us, Father. I would like to take a walk with my bride-to-be."

Eduardo bowed. "By all means."

We strolled through the gardens and onto the balcony overlooking the veranda. He brought me to the spot of his proposal. The warmth crept over my cheeks as I remembered his tenderness that divine night.

"Do you remember the night we stood here, surrounded by guests and fanfare? Yet I was determined to offer my heart to you."

I smiled. "I very much remember. You were quite the gentleman, and I was quite taken with you." I stared at his broad chest as he pulled me close.

"Even though you feel your heart is torn, I promise that our love will never fail no matter where life takes us. I love you."

"And I you."

His sweet kiss brought life to every part of my being.

Over the next two weeks, the hacienda busied itself with preparations for the wedding, while I focused each day on allowing God to heal me. I held onto a verse that I had leaned on not long so ago when Mother and Elizabeth died: Be still and know that I am God. *Even at the place of utter despair and loss, He was there. I repeated the verse over and over to calm my weary soul and aching heart. Even when I didn't know what to say, the Lord did. I leaned into God, and He carried me.*

Eliza gasped when she read the words on the page—the same words she had first heard as she sat crumpled on her mother's bathroom floor. She reread the Scripture her grandmother had written and felt a release inside like a wave pushing through stale debris and residue. She felt her body react physically. She knew what she had read was not a coincidence. God was speaking to her directly. She touched her fingers to her ears.

"I hear you. I'm listening. You do see me and know me, but I don't know you. I'm willing to know you. Show me how."

Eliza paused and let the courage her grandmother had shared with her rise to the surface. Once she continued reading, she understood why she would no longer be the same. How could one be infused with a strength greater than mankind could ever configure or contrive and yet stay the same? Impossible.

She wanted to change. She wanted the same strength that had been given to her grandmother in her time of need. Now she understood. Courage, strength, discernment weren't traits she could buy or perfect. Her grandmother's wisdom was a gift from God because she had lived with a heart yielded to Him no matter what transpired.

CHAPTER TWENTY-EIGHT

DREW STAYED CLOSE TO JUAN CARLOS as they crossed the Nueces River and wound through the hills. The dust from the older roads began to kick up and slow down their speed a bit. The drive seemed to take longer than he imagined, but it also offered up several unexpected distractions. He was surprised Eliza had found her way with such ease through the twisting roads and bulging hills. Nothing was as clearly marked as he had anticipated, but the scenery made up for any neglect in directions.

As they passed through Camp Wood and then came to what he guessed was the turnoff, Juan Carlos pulled off the road and signaled for Drew to do the same. Drew put his truck in park and got out. Walking over to Juan Carlos, he saw him reach for a water jug in the back of his pickup.

"The dust will only get worse from here, so I clean my windshield now so I don't have any trouble further up the road. The wipers on this old truck give me trouble sometimes."

Drew nodded and helped him wash the glass. "How much further is the ranch from here?"

"Just under forty minutes," Juan Carlos answered.

"I'm still in shock that out of all the people who could have stopped to help me, it was you. How long have you lived out here?"

"Close to fifty years."

"How did you meet Eliza's grandmother?" Drew stretched his arm to reach the top of the windshield.

"Through family."

Drew wished Juan Carlos would divulge more, but he could tell the man didn't want to give out more information than he already had given. So he decided to change the subject.

"How do you think Eliza is doing?" Drew glanced over at Juan Carlos to see what reaction his question would bring, if any.

His expression didn't change. "I think she is a remarkable young woman much like her grandmother. She is stronger than she yet realizes, but I can see a new light in her eyes now that wasn't there when she arrived."

"I'm glad to hear that. She's pretty extraordinary." Drew caught Juan Carlos' smile across the hood of the car and continued. "I guess the outdoors has a way of doing that to all of us."

"Yes, and so does truth," the older man said.

"What do you mean?"

"The truth always sets you free."

Confused, Drew nodded as if to imply he was following what Juan Carlos was saying, but he couldn't quite make sense of it. Ringing out the rag, he wiped down the remaining wet spots on the glass.

"Señor Drew, I can tell you are a serious man. You think deeply about the things of life and that is good."

"I guess I do. I didn't realize it was that obvious." Drew felt a bit timid about how easily his mannerisms gave him away. Before looking up, he wiped the grime that had settled in the creases of his hands with the damp rag. His eyes squinted in the afternoon sun as he surveyed the landscape around them. He hadn't seen a car pass in the last thirty minutes, and the few houses around them seemed void of any movement. "It's pretty remote out here, isn't it? Not a lot of folks live up here."

"More than you might think, but by the afternoon most are resting. We have a lot of goat ranchers and sheep farmers around here. On a Saturday many, like me, have made their run to town or finished work early, probably fishing the river by now.

"Let's head on up the road. You might want to roll up your windows a little more. My truck will make much dust. Your truck still looks brand-new."

Turning toward his truck, Drew noticed the bright red was dulled by the thin layer of dust. "Probably not a bad idea."

After starting the engine, Drew thumbed through the radio until he heard the faint sound of "Ring of Fire" coming through the static. He adjusted the knob to see if the he could get a better signal. Juan Carlos had already pulled ahead when he finally looked up from the dashboard, so he hit the gas to catch up with him.

As he turned down the backcountry road, regret taunted him. His fingers nervously twitched on the steering wheel, and he entertained second thoughts that his surprise arrival might be a disaster. He ran his fingers through his hair and felt the sweat beading on his forehead. He tried turning up the radio to take his mind off the "what if's," but the relentless twang of Johnny Cash agitated him more. Turning the knob in the opposite direction, he chose silence instead.

Regret. Fear. He never gave in to them, so why was he now? He clenched his teeth determined to strangle any doubt. He had set his sights on loving Eliza for the rest of his life, and he vowed not one whisper of doubt would hold him back. She had run only to survive, and he had pursued her only to let her fall apart in his arms.

The waiting was over. He knew Eliza needed him to steady her, to love her back to freedom and life. He refused to let her wade through the darkness alone. He knew he held the light she needed, and the only way to get it to her was to go after her.

Drew sucked in a deep breath and let it out slowly to calm himself. He had to be there for her. All he could think about was holding her and touching her, letting her sink into him and folding her in his arms. The sweet smell of her skin and the suppleness of her lips upon his were all he desired.

He thought of the last time he had held her. She had seemed so fragile—like a frightened bird, her heart beating wildly, tense in his arms. Despite his best efforts to comfort her, he knew she pulled away in fear of what would happen if she relented and let love have its way. He remembered the weight of his words as he told her he planned to marry her and the confusion that crossed her face. The timing hadn't gone as planned, but he realized he was no longer in control. Either he went after her or he'd lose her.

He hoped God had a plan when he got to the ranch because he didn't. Love was his only hope now. Would it be enough?

CHAPTER TWENTY-NINE

ELIZA WALKED INSIDE and splashed water on her face. She wanted to finish the journals by suppertime even though she felt sleepy. The warmth of the sun and the intensity of her emotional reactions were taking a toll on her. She looked over at her grandmother's bed, but resisted the temptation to lie down.

Pouring some water from the pitcher Carmen had left for her on the dresser, she drank her fill and then walked out onto the balcony again and sat down. With a deep breath, she took a moment to let her mind rest and opened the journal in her lap. She was anxious to read about her grandmother's wedding.

When I awoke that Saturday morning of my wedding, it was to a gorgeous September sky. Wafting through the windows was the fragrant scent of flowers and the smells of meat roasting and desserts baking. I could already hear the clinking of china as the tables were being set.

I slipped my feet into the small velvet flats by the bed and walked to the vanity. Brushing out my hair, I heard faithful Maria open the door and bring in the morning tray.

"Today you will soon be a senorita no more. Instead you will be the gorgeous Senora de la Cruz," Maria announced with gaiety as she set the tray next to the vanity. "Now, take your time to eat, and I will get your things ready for you."

I hardly remember the way the coffee and the pastries tasted. My stomach was flittering, and my mind was full of words and images all at once. The remorse of my family's passing and the sweet joy of marriage to such a dear love swirled inside me as I pressed my hands to my chest to steady my soul.

Picking up the family Bible, I turned the pages and opened to Mother's favorite verse in Colossians. I read the words as it spoke of hearts being knitted together in love. Sensing their blessing of happiness upon me, I closed my eyes and imagined my parents standing before me now, loving me and holding me.

Maria's voice pierced my thoughts. "Senora Penelope has sent you a wedding present. She would like for you to wear it today."

She handed me a gorgeous, red-velvet box tied with a satin ribbon. Carefully, I loosened the ribbon and let it fall into my lap. With steady hands, I opened the box to find a gold necklace with matching earrings worked in soft gold with interlocking scrolls and intricate details of leaves. Each earring dangled from an emerald center, repeating the design from the necklace. I had never seen anything as spectacular as this. I read the note she had slipped inside for me:

Dearest Dusky,

A present for you on your wedding day—a gift I received from my mother-in-law the day I married Eduardo. It is yours to keep until your oldest son marries.

A word of godly wisdom I always remember: Love never fails.

Blessings on your wedding day and always,

Penelope

Slowly, I picked up the necklace and held it to the light. It glistened with each turn of my hand. I placed the necklace back in the box and closed the lid.

"Come, it's time to put up your hair." Maria beckoned and motioned for me to sit in front of her.

She fussed with my hair and finally declared it a masterpiece. Swept up in elegant waves, she carefully wove white gardenias throughout.

"You look like a queen. Now wait until you put on your dress and jewelry," she said, beaming.

After carefully stepping into my dress, Maria buttoned it with swift fingers and turned me toward the mirror. My eyes raced from my head to the floor, soaking in my reflection. It was hard to believe it was me.

"You are so quiet?"

"I . . . I don't seem to have any words right now. I'm a little overwhelmed." I laid my hand on my stomach.

"Here, come sit," Maria said.

"No . . . I'm fine. I promise."

I steadied myself with my fingertips on the edge of the vanity and took a deep breath. The traces of the grief from the past few weeks were still slightly visible, but I could see new life in my eyes. Light had returned to my face and my frame. It was as if the fragments of my life had been repaired—an orphan no more. Rather my image radiated love and courage.

"It's time," Maria whispered over my shoulder.

The dress fit perfectly, and the beading fell flawlessly along each seam. I picked up the cream-and-white bouquet and walked toward the door.

Outside, Señor Eduardo met me dressed in his black topcoat and hat. He extended his arm.

"What an honor for me today, daughter." He leaned in to kiss me, his eyes moist.

Smiling, I slipped my arm through his, feeling the calm of his stature against me. The corners of my eyes sparkled from the instant rush of tears mixed with joy and sadness all at once.

In silence, we walked to the edge of the garden where the small carriage bedecked with flowers and ribbons, waited the short ride to the chapel. A crowd had gathered to wave and blow kisses as we rode past.

When we arrived at the chapel steps, Padre Antonio greeted us, standing alongside Penelope. Immediately, her eyes flooded with tears as she took me in her arms.

"Darling, you are magnificent—the perfect bride for Roberto."

"Thank you."

"Are we ready?" Señor Eduardo nodded his head toward the doors. The bell began to ring, cracking through the air, as Penelope and Padre Antonio led the way.

Señor Eduardo and I paused at the entrance to the chapel. The small gathering of people turned to welcome us. As the doors were swung open wide, I could see Roberto's strong physique, standing at the altar. His smile and posture gave away his affection for me, and my heart fluttered. We locked gazes as I walked down the aisle on his father's arm.

After the wedding, the bell rang over and over to announce our union. Roberto and I ran to the carriage and made a trip around the grounds before the reception amidst a fluttering of flowers and petals scattered by the small crowd.

He took me in his arms as we sat together and waved.

"Stunning would be an understatement to describe how you look today," he said.

"Blessed and free is how I feel. This is a glorious day. I love you, Roberto."

"I love you too, my dear. It will be my pleasure to tell you that every day for the rest of our lives."

He held me close as our lips met in a sweet kiss.

Our life from that moment was a beautiful union. We lived in tranquil harmony with Roberto's family, now my family, too, and everyday life. My husband was a treasure. I never took our life together for granted.

Our first Christmas spent together was so sweet, filled with the aromas of cinnamon, cloves, citrus, and a growing family. We all gathered in the main parlor to share gifts and sweets. Penelope gave me a gorgeous silver brush engraved with a "D" on the back. I still have it to this day. Roberto presented me with a gold pendant, and I gave him a pair of baby shoes. Yes, I was pregnant.

As he pulled the tiny, leather, baby shoes from the box, his eyes twinkled and he grinned. Cupping my hands over my mouth, I could feel the burn of my smile in my cheeks.

"A baby?"

I nodded and rushed to throw my arms around his neck.

The whole family erupted in cheers and congratulations. Roberto beamed with pride and expectation. Our first Christmas was spent celebrating our new life and the one growing inside me.

As the old gave way to the new on that New Year's Eve, 1910 was soon filled with events and transitions.

Gustavo planned to marry Isabella that coming April, and already he spent more time with her family as he would move to Hacendado Nunez' property. With no son, Señor Nunez was dependent on Gustavo to take over his business affairs. We saw him less and less often, but he welcomed the responsibility and challenges his new life held.

He and Roberto planned to align resources once Gustavo took the helm to create an impenetrable bond between the two families. It was quite the talk of northern Mexico. Many hacendados were frustrated with the seeming privilege Señor Eduardo and his sons continued to gain, and bitterness along with envy began to infiltrate the air.

But it wasn't just the elite that felt uneasy in those days. The lower classes were restless too. It was not uncommon to learn of raids and robberies, increasing along trade routes and in towns.

"We must discuss business tonight," Señor Eduardo began over dinner one night in March. "I'm going to increase protection along the walls of the hacienda, especially with the upcoming wedding. I don't like the blistering uneasiness I continue to sense. Even my messengers going back and forth to town continue to get reports of more disgruntlement among the people."

"What does this mean?" Penelope asked quickly, her eyes fixed on Eduardo.

"I'm hopeful this wave of vulgarity will cease. But until it does, we need to be vigilant and post watchmen on the walls day and night." He picked up his fork and continued to eat.

"What do the reports say?" Penelope persisted.

Finishing his bite, he said in a calm voice, "That instead of tensions easing, they seem to be increasing. Whatever has the country stirred up hasn't settled yet, and I'm not willing to take any risks. I want every possible weakness plugged and protected. No more rides alone in the countryside for any of you.

"Some of Dîaz's men are on their way now. He is sending them to ask for aid and assistance I'm sure. They arrive tomorrow. Dîaz is growing fearful and losing control. He needs financial backing, resources, and allegiances no doubt, and he's sending his men to beg for all of it.

"I won't know where we stand until I hear what they have to say. Nevertheless, we can't wait for them to act on our behalf. Once again we need to be independent and handle our affairs on our own. As soon as I get the chance, I will quell this dissension and bring restoration."

By noon the next day the men had arrived and we sat down as a family over an early supper.

"This is preposterous!" Señor Eduardo yelled and slammed his fist on the table. "We've taken care of these native peoples for as long as I can remember, and now their deceived hearts are leading them down a dark path. We must put a stop to this unacceptable behavior immediately."

"We need your contacts, Señor," the general pleaded. "We need to unite Mexico to keep her together. She is bursting at the seams right now. These continued outbursts and violence have everyone on edge."

"I warned Dîaz long ago that he was getting his fingers in too many pots. He should step down."

"Step down? Then Mexico will be wide open politically. Who would take over?"

"What about Madera?" Señor Eduardo said. "He has political prowess and despises that warlord Pancho Villa. Pancho Villa has made a mockery of our government, and he must be stopped. I doubt Dîaz can or will stand up against him." He pushed his chair back from the table. "I'm concerned we are upsetting the women, General. Penelope, Dusky, please excuse us as we retire to the back patio."

Roberto looked at me with concern before he followed his father and the others outside. Penelope and I sat frozen, still within earshot of their discussion.

"Dîaz's cabinet is unraveling. Everybody can see it." Eduardo's voice echoed through the stone colonnade.

"Señor, if you will allow us to use your resources, we could station troops here and throughout the countryside to help keep you safe."

"And paint a target on our backs? Have you lost your mind! No one can be trusted in these times. Tell Dîaz I'll consider his offer, but I want time to think it over."

All this was happening at the peak of my pregnancy. Throughout the next week, Roberto and his father discussed and prepared evacuation plans and routes should the need arise for us to leave.

Even Gustavo's wedding was scaled down to not draw attention from surrounding villagers and bandits. After the ceremony, we traveled quickly home, bidding Gustavo and his new bride farewell. He was committed to her family now. Penelope wept as the carriage pulled out of the courtyard. None of us knew when we would see him again.

To say times were tense was an understatement. We hid provisions in secret compartments all through the hacienda grounds. We slept with guards at our bedroom doors now, and Roberto and I moved back in the main house.

By June, I was ready to give birth any minute, and Mexico felt as if she would erupt as well. A rebellion had broken out after Madera was imprisoned by Dîaz. Many believed it was rigged. Sympathizers for Madera were on the rise, and anger rippled over the land. Madera fled to Texas. Rumors said a party had been sent to hunt him down and kill him.

Amidst the chaos, on June 4th I gave birth to a precious piece of heaven we named Penelope Catarina Victoria de la Cruz. She was the most gorgeous creature I had ever seen. She was the princess of our world.

Even though her birth was a celebration of life, we continued to find ourselves preoccupied with defending ours.

As fall approached, the stress began to take its toll on Señor Eduardo. In mid-September, he called a family meeting.

"Roberto and I are having to make some tough decisions. Every bit of news we receive is disturbing. Several of our family connections have fled to the border and left Mexico for good."

Penelope gasped and began to weep.

"We've gotten word that Madera is retaliating against Diaz and declaring himself provisional president. He has plans to reshape Mexico's political system and possibly push Mexico into a revolution. Our

nation is imploding. As difficult as it is, we can't wait to decide where to stand."

"Are you thinking we need to leave, Darling?" Penelope asked through her tears.

"Yes, I believe you and Dusky and Miguel and the baby need to leave at once. Roberto and I will follow behind. We can't all go together. Since we are prime targets, it will raise too much suspicion. Pancho Villa and his men are ruthless killers who are terrorizing the countryside in the name of freedom.

"My family is my concern now. Fortunately, much of our wealth is securely in Texas, and we can make a new life for all of us on our lands there."

"Eduardo, this is our home. I can't believe you are suggesting we pack and leave it all behind. What will become of it?"

"Penelope, I don't think you realize how dangerous life has become for people of our stature. If we stay, we risk death by a gutless coward like Pancho Villa.

"I want you and Dusky and Miguel to plan to leave in the next couple of weeks with Augustino and his family."

Fright filled my throat, and I locked eyes with Roberto, pleading in silence with him not to make me go without him. He held my gaze, but he never wavered on their decision.

Miguel was stunned. At almost fourteen, he refused to go, but Eduardo gave him no choice.

"I have no one else to send with your mother and Dusky and baby Catarina. You must and you will go."

That was the end of the argument. Miguel's fate along with mine had been sealed.

That night I heard Penelope and Eduardo's voices as they lit up the courtyard with fear and anger. Penelope demanded to stay, and he demanded she go. On and off the conversation went back and forth until the wee hours of the morning. I lay awake with my hand on Roberto's chest, feeling it rise and fall. I knew he was awake as well.

I wanted to scream and demand he go with me and the baby, but I lay silent, paralyzed by the unknown.

Finally, Penelope won. Eduardo consented to her staying with him and Roberto, but Miguel and I made preparations to leave. Trunks were packed and many containers were hidden down by the river in the small caves. We could only take suitcases and what we could carry easily. I packed our family pictures and the silver brush Penelope had given me. I sewed jewelry into pockets under my skirt along with gold coins and the necklace Penelope had given me on our wedding day.

Miguel was prepped to handle any scenario that might happen along the journey. He loaded his jacket with ammo and a pistol and currency. We would travel with Augustino and his family, dressed modestly so we would not give away who we were.

Roberto and I talked and argued and loved until it was time for me to leave. It wasn't what either of us wanted, but we had to focus on the protection of our daughter, and for now that meant splitting apart.

We would flee at dawn. Once we crossed the border, we had decided to change our last name to keep our identities concealed from Pancho Villa and his men who were tracking fleeing families into Texas and slitting their throats. We heard reports of how he hunted down acquaintances of ours and killed them all, women and children included, south of San Antonio.

Before the dawn broke on the day of our departure, we all gathered in the family living room, holding hands and weeping. My heart felt as if it would rip in two. Roberto and I held each other as I buried my face in his chest and wept. He kissed me good-bye and promised to see me before Christmas. He held baby Catarina one last time and kissed her forehead.

Penelope and Eduardo embraced Miguel and clung to one another before the open carriage pulled out of sight just as dawn began to peek over the hills. I looked back the entire time never wanting to forget the hacienda, but more importantly, not wanting to lose sight of Roberto. His figure began to shrink with every turn of the carriage wheel, and when I could no longer see his figure in the distance, I let out the cry I had held back for so long.

Shocked, Miguel spun around and put his arms around me. Augustino's wife took the baby while Miguel held me as my body heaved with my sobs. By noon, I rode listlessly in the carriage without a word to anyone.

We arrived at the train station and boarded quickly, our faces stoic. We all knew this was only the beginning of the perilous journey. We sat in second class and managed to squish into our seats with the dozens of others aboard the train. As the whistle blew and the wheels began to pull forward, I felt as if I would vomit. I held baby Catarina close as she slept peacefully, so wonderfully unaware of her circumstances.

After a long day, night stretched its hand over the sky, and my eyes began to relax. I couldn't have slept more than an hour when the train came to a screeching halt. My eyes jerked open, and I looked at Augustino, sitting across from me, their small son still asleep between him and his wife.

"Calm and quiet," he said sternly, his mustache barely moving while he pressed his finger to his lips. "Stay calm."

Miguel instinctively tensed next to me, and I put my hand on his arm. We could hear shouts and footsteps, coming from outside the other train cars. Gunfire and laughter followed. I felt a sting in my throat and continued to watch Augustino. Armed men stormed through our car, brandishing their weapons, but they seemed unimpressed with its occupants.

After several tense minutes, the train started up again, but we all remained silent. By mid-morning the next day, we were unloaded at the border and made our way through immigration. I scanned the crowd looking for any familiar face—to no avail.

The lines were long, and everyone was restless. We finally made it to the counter, and after a series of questions, we were ushered through immigration. Across the street was the other rail station where we waited to take the train to San Antonio. Augustino went to the telegraph office to send word we had made it across the border.

Our train departed shortly after to begin our journey to San Antonio. Once we arrived, we were met by Timothy Barksdale, Señor Eduardo's conciliatory. He drove us to the Menger Hotel downtown so we could rest for the night before proceeding to the ranch outside Uvalde.

By the next day, everyone had changed clothes and cleaned up for the journey west to the de la Cruz ranch. Ironically, we would be the first ones to ever see the ranch and stay there. Eduardo had Timothy purchased it two years ago to park some of his money in Texas.

Timothy handed me a telegram before we departed.

Dearest Dusky,

I love you and will join you soon. Keep the hope and remember love never fails.

Roberto

My hands trembled, and I began to shake. Augustino came to my side and took my elbow. He helped me into the carriage, and I leaned against the window, my throat dry and longing for another night with Roberto.

"We must go now," he whispered. "We will be there soon."

None of us spoke. There was nothing to say. I think we were all in a state of shock.

I stared at baby Catarina and started to call her Hope from that moment forward. Yes, she was your mother, Eliza. At a mere four months old, she made a hard journey. She was already exhibiting her strong traits of resilience like her grandfather Eduardo. Hope seemed to be the perfect name for her because that is what she meant to me. Hope that Roberto and I would be reunited; hope that she would grow into a strong and regal woman; and hope that whatever circumstances came our way, hope would never be squelched.

Over the next month, we settled into Rancho Perdido and made it our home. Every day I scanned the hills, hoping to see a caravan kicking up dust along the road, hoping to be reunited with Roberto.

"Someone's coming, Senora. I see dust!" Augustino shouted one day from the porch below, and I scurried to my balcony. "Get the others and go to the spring house. I'll come for you if it is safe."

I rushed to gather Miguel and Hope as well as Augustino's wife and their son, Juan Carlos. Running to the spring house, we hid until Augustino appeared in the doorway.

"It is safe. It is Señor Timothy. He has word from Mexico."

I gathered my skirt and fled up the steps, leaving Hope in his wife's arms.

"*Tell us what you know, please,*" *I begged.* "*I pray it is good news.*"

He took a deep breath before answering. "*I wish I could say it was, but sadly it is not so. Gustavo has sent me a telegram. He stated that two weeks ago the hacienda de la Cruz was ambushed in the night, and nothing could hold back the gang of revolutionaries that overtook the walls. They set fire to many of the buildings and executed Hacendado Eduardo, Penelope, and Roberto. I'm so deeply sorry.*"

"*No!*" *I screamed as I ran outside and crumpled on the porch.* "*Dear God, no! Roberto! Oh God, help me! Why him? Why us?*"

We all wept long into the night and for days to come. Miguel and I held on to each other. Along with Hope, we were all the family we had left. My helpless beauty knew nothing of her father's demise.

Gustavo and his bride, Isabella, fled Mexico via boat to France with the rest of her family. He offered for us to come and join him, but neither Miguel nor I had the heart or desire. We had to remake our life now.

I moved the three of us to San Antonio while Augustino, his wife, and their small son, Juan Carlos, remained on the ranch. Timothy was a huge help and a great comfort. Miguel finished his schooling and began to study law. We changed our names to avoid any residual backlash some of the aristocratic refugees were getting as well as to avoid being traced. Revenge was still on the tongue of many as Mexico had finally burst into one of the bloodiest revolutions of her time. We feared for our lives, even in Texas.

I took back my maiden name, and Miguel became Henry Lane.

Now you know who Uncle Henry really is. Yes, he is my darling brother-in-law who has never left my side all these years. He made an oath to his father and Roberto and never broke it once. He stayed beside me all these years—a darling of a man.

Timothy was our business contact, and after several years of doing business together, we married when your mother was almost four years old. She never knew he wasn't her true father. Although a bit older than I, Timothy was a gentleman through and through. I am so grateful for him. He was the soft, tender love I needed, and our life was dear together. He allowed me to be who I needed to be, and he was a blessing beyond words.

If I know you, I'm guessing at this point you may be wondering why I never told your mother. In the beginning we needed to protect our identity. Tensions didn't ease, and Pancho Villa was known to terrorize and hunt down anyone on either side of the border who may have had any allegiance to Diaz. The de la Cruz family was one of the names on his list.

Also, I wanted and needed to move on. I had to let the Lord infuse joy into my heart, but it took years for the bitter roots to die. As the years moved further past our flight into Texas, the harder it became, and we didn't want to bring unnecessary heartache to your mother.

I didn't mean never to tell her. It just happened. The years rolled by and life marched on. To protect my own heart, I let time fill the gap, not wanting to open old wounds. Before I knew it, it seemed too late.

Your mother had heartaches of her own, and I didn't want the past disturbed or uncovered. I knew how to manage my grief, but I wasn't sure I could manage hers as well. It comforted me to relive it in my silence, in my way, or with Henry in quiet moments. You may never understand that, and I don't expect you to. I hardly understand it myself.

There are many mementoes I have kept in the closet for you. Remember the silver brush? That is the one Penelope gave me with the beautiful "D" engraved. I have the jewelry, the necklace as well, kept in the velvet box beside the journals on the second shelf. I want you to have it and wear it on your wedding day, if you so choose. That is what we would all want. That way, we will all be with you. Our love will carry you down the aisle, standing alongside you in spirit.

You've never been an only child with a small family. You have truly been surrounded by a big family this whole time. You just didn't know it until now. You have an extraordinary heritage, and I pray you will pass it along to your own children. Your roots are different and run on both sides of the river. Your grandfather, Roberto, would want you to be proud of who you are on the inside and the out.

I love you dearly, Eliza, and I thank you for taking the time to journey with me. Your heart means everything to me, and I pray this has been a deep comfort to know your true roots.

Yes, there was deep sorrow, loss, and hard times, but I have come to truly know and experience that love is steadfast and patient. I know love protects and trusts. Trusting wasn't easy, but when I gave myself over to love, I allowed myself to find the hope that love brings and the perseverance that follows on hope's heels. Love doesn't fail us. It may stretch us, but love never fails.

I couldn't, and didn't, want to bury all this. Burying only makes the ground around your heart hard. No, I gave all the pain and grief to the Lord piece by piece. You see, grief wanted me to believe that if I let go of the grief, I'd forget Roberto, but that wasn't true. I honored him every day by living.

And grief wanted me to believe I should feel guilty for living, but that wasn't true either.

God gave me His joy, and I took it and walked away from grief to Him. Did I miss Roberto? Terribly. But I allowed the Lord to show me how to love again, how to live again with His strength, His love, His truth.

I didn't want to live trapped in "what ifs" and "what could have been." I needed to be alive in "what was," and the only one who could do that for me was God.

I loved well, Eliza, and I lived by honoring Him and resting in His ways. Knowing I would see Roberto and all my family again in heaven gave me hope to press on and to love well and to be vulnerable and not be afraid to love again. I didn't want my tears to paint a picture of the world. I wanted His picture even though it wasn't what I thought it was going to look like. I let God love me back to life, and He gave me the courage to love those around me and to open my heart without guilt, regret, or fear.

I trusted in the Lord's words. I treasured them in my heart always no matter what happened. No matter what I went through, I knew love never fails. His love never changes. You don't have to be afraid of change, darling, because His love will see you through.

Take heart, sweet girl, and bring your children here to the ranch often. Something beautiful happens when we get out in nature. We hear Him, and our hearts are filled with His peace.

I love you and I know we will be together again.

CHAPTER THIRTY

DRAWING A DEEP BREATH, Eliza let the silence fall around her as tears came faster and faster. She welcomed the freedom to mourn and to wrap herself in her grandmother's testimony. She drew strength from her grandmother's words, from her heart, from all she had endured, and from the woman she chose to be. Her testimony belonged to Eliza now. What God had done in her grandmother, Eliza begged Him to do again, but this time in her own heart.

Standing, she walked inside and paced the room while speaking out loud.

"Take this grief, Lord. Take it as far away from me as you can! It has been filling me with lies and hurt, and I don't want it! I don't want what it is saying! I want your love, Father. I want your sweet, tender love that sees me and loves me right where I am. I need you here with me. Teach me how to live again and not be afraid and silent. Speak your truth."

Be still and know that I am God. . . .

She heard His words again—more clearly this time and with a weightiness she had not felt before. She opened her hands and put her grief, fear, loneliness, isolation, and rejection in her palms.

"I don't want these anymore. What you did for Grandmother, God, do for me . . . right now." She turned her hands over and imagined it all spilling out into the hands of the Lord.

"Now fill me with all that you have for me." With closed eyes, she lifted up her bare hands before Him and felt a rush of warmth pouring over her palms first and then through her body.

I will strengthen you and help you; I will uphold you with My righteous right hand . . .

She pressed her hands against her chest and felt heat filling every part of her being.

"I believe you, Lord. Forgive me for doubting you, for fighting with you. I am still before you now. Thank you for the legacy of hope, love, joy, and trust my grandmother left me. Because of her, I see that my greatest strength is you and your love. Love never belonged to me in the first place; it was always yours to give away and shower upon me. I just never accepted it, knew it, felt it, or wanted it; but here . . . now . . . don't hold back with me. Fill me with more."

For the first time she heard love speak to her. She felt His hand upon her, helping her to her feet, and holding her.

"He is here and I am His and I can let Him love through me and strengthen me. Grief doesn't get to take me. He has me," she whispered over and over.

The room was filled with a softness and peace unlike anything she had ever encountered. She was exhausted, but exhilarated, all in one moment.

"My heart beats for you, Lord. Truly my heart beats with love."

With a flood of joy she heard love's encouragement to dream again, to wrap hope around her, and to fall back into faith.

She thought of Uncle Henry and how much she wanted to know more. She wanted him to hear her heart—her precious, beating heart that was eager and alive all because of the courageous silence of one dear woman who blessed her with one last conversation.

Thoughts of Drew comforted her now. She felt brave enough to love him, brave enough to tell him so, and brave enough to risk.

"If love never fails, then what do I have to lose by loving him?"

She paused and caught her breath before she splashed water on her face and walked back toward the balcony, letting the breeze sweep over her. She closed her eyes and inhaled deeply of the fresh air while resting her hands upon the balcony railing.

Then the sound of a rumbling engine caught her attention, and she opened her eyes. Peering toward the road, she caught sight of the dust being kicked up by a truck, and as she looked closer, she could see another truck behind the first. She knew the older model white truck in the front belonged to Juan Carlos. She strained to see the second.

"Drew!" she gasped out loud and covered her mouth. Her heart could hardly believe what her eyes were telling her. What was he doing here? Without hesitation, she ran toward the stairs and quickly made her way to the front door just as the trucks pulled in.

She stepped onto the front porch and let the screen door slam behind her. She watched as Juan Carlos came over to Drew's door. The two men began to visit before Drew shut his door and turned to look toward the house.

Eliza's heart quickened when their eyes met. She walked down the stone steps as Drew moved to meet her.

"Drew. You're here," Eliza said, walking up to him, smiling broadly. Her eyes glistened with joy. She reached for his strong hands and held them in hers. Before he could speak, she grabbed him and buried her face in his blue shirt. "I'm so glad you're here."

His hands pulled her closer as she stood nestled against him, and he kissed her forehead. She could feel her heart leap into her throat. Love bravely took a stand in her heart.

"I'm so sorry, Drew. I'm so sorry I've held back from you and made us strangers. I was so afraid. I'm done running. It's over."

She pulled back to look at him, wrapping her arms around his waist. "I'm running *toward* love, not away from it anymore. I thought if I ran and pushed everyone away I wouldn't get hurt. But while I ran, I kept tripping over myself and my pain. What my grandmother left me was a testimony of how she never gave up on love, no matter the tragedies of her life. Drew . . ." she paused letting her courage build, "I'm running to you. I'm running straight to you."

Without saying a word, she felt his arms bring her into him as he leaned down to kiss her. The past dissolved. She gave her heart freely and allowed herself to be swept up in the passion and love between them. She was finally free. Free to love, free to dream. With loving nudges and tender words, God had set her free. And now, with Drew, she stood on the edge of a future with hope and purpose. Her heart was settled and no longer wandering and crying out. She felt a sacred silence fall upon her, and she felt love take permanent root deep within.

Breathless, she pulled away and whispered, "I love you. I've always loved you."

She closed her eyes as he traced her lips with his fingers. "I love you, too, sweetheart, and I promise to always love you no matter what, no matter where."

"How did you know to come here?" she asked, feeling his heavy breath upon her face. With their foreheads touching, she laid her hands upon his chest and waited for his response.

"I didn't. I just felt something stirring inside of me to come out here and check on you. I had no idea what you were going through, and I wasn't willing to lose you again."

"I'm so grateful you didn't listen to me. I'm so grateful you drove out here to see me."

"Me too." He stroked her hair.

"I have so much to tell you. I can't wait to show you around." She fondled the buttons on his shirt as they stood face to face, holding one another.

"And I want to hear every detail."

Her head was swimming from his touch and the feeling of his strength next to her.

They held hands as they walked toward the porch.

"How did you meet up with Juan Carlos and follow him here?"

"A flat tire this side of Uvalde," Drew said. "He stopped to help. Out of all the people in the world, he was the one who stopped—which also explains why I've got dirt and grease all over me." He laughed as he recounted the afternoon's events.

"I sort of wondered what happened from the looks of you, but I was too excited to ask." She leaned into him and slipped her arm around his waist.

Pausing at the top of the stairs, Eliza turned to show Drew the view from the porch. His eyes scanned the landscape. "This place is incredible. The water, the hills, the rocks—it would be hard to leave."

"It is amazing, isn't it, and it's been hidden all this time until now."

"Well, it's definitely touched you in an amazing way," Drew said as he looked back at Eliza.

"What do you mean?"

"You look different . . . you look like I hoped you would."

Puzzled, Eliza remained silent, waiting for Drew to continue.

"For one, the troubled creases you carried on your forehead are gone. And your eyes are lit in a way I haven't seen since we spent last summer together splashing in the river and picnicking in the oat field behind the barn at my parent's ranch. I didn't know how to reach you, but I wasn't going to give up. Funny how all along I worried trying to figure out how to fix everything. It was never my job in the first place. God had a plan. I just needed patience and a little more trust."

"Thank you for not giving up on me. It would have been easy."

"I knew I loved you and not being with you wasn't easy. Chasing after you was easier than facing the future without you."

Eliza drank in the warmth of Drew's words and his love. "You must be hungry after the long drive. Let's go inside and sit. There's so much to tell you."

Drew held open the screen door as Eliza passed through and walked into the kitchen.

"Carmen, I'd like you to meet Drew."

Drew extended his hand across the table as Carmen reached for his. "So nice to meet you, Señor Drew. Juan Carlos tells me you met on the road. It is good to hear he was of help to you."

"Very much. I'm not sure I would have had as easy of a time finding the ranch if he hadn't shown me the way."

Eliza poured Drew a glass of ice tea before making him a sandwich.

"Here, let me help." Carmen pulled out a few more items from the icebox and prepared a plate for Drew. "Please go and sit. I'll bring this when I have it ready."

Eliza motioned for Drew to follow her, and they sat close on the small sofa adjacent the rock fireplace.

"I want to tell you what's happened since I last saw you. I never dreamed of all that I've learned about my grandmother. She left quite a story for me to discover." Eliza waited for Drew to speak, but his soft eyes were all the encouragement she needed to continue.

"She lived in Mexico before she ever lived here, and while she was there she fell in love and married."

She watched carefully as Drew's eyes grew wide and slowly shook his head. "Never would have guessed that," He took a bite of the roast beef sandwich Carmen brought him.

"Who would have ever thought? But what is even more startling is that my mother's father was actually Roberto de la Cruz, Grandmother's husband in Mexico."

Drew paused his eating, and his brows furrowed. A surprised look came over his face.

"I know," Eliza continued, sensing his shock. "It really shook me too. He sounded like such an incredible man, and the life she lived there was like a fairy tale. Sadly, the Mexican revolution tore their family apart, and she was forced to flee, along with Henry, who is actually my great-uncle Miguel, as well as my mother who was still an infant."

Drew jumped in. "Wait a minute. Henry is actually your great uncle who fled Mexico with your grandmother and your mother?"

"Yes, that's right, and Juan Carlos was the son of the family that Roberto sent to escort them across the border to the ranch, which actually belongs to Uncle Henry's family." She let her words settle before continuing, realizing she had had days to process this, but Drew only had minutes.

"What else? What about Roberto?"

"She never saw him again. He was executed along with his parents by rebel forces, wanting to destroy the dynasties of Mexico. Sadly, the rebels succeeded in their cruel and murderous ways.

"And even though my grandmother had crossed the border into Texas, the rebels were still hunting down anyone who was left of the wealthy *hacendados*. She and Uncle Henry hid here until the war was over and they no longer feared for their lives.

"That's how she came to know Timothy, who I always thought was my grandfather. He was the conciliatory for Roberto's father and handled his affairs here in the States. After losing Roberto and facing life without him, Grandmother and Timothy developed a sweet and mutual love for one another and married. My mother had no memory of life without him, so she never knew he wasn't her biological father."

"Why didn't your grandmother tell her?" Drew asked before she could continue.

"Preservation. She was scared for a long time. They hid like refugees in these hills, and when they decided to move to San Antonio, she and Henry chose to leave their secrets buried here. I don't think she wanted to relive the tragedy again by disrupting my mother's life. She thought about it many times, but then it was too late, and what good would it have done for my mother other than create a huge loss?"

Eliza knew she was giving him a lot of information to absorb, so she paused in her story.

Drew took Eliza's hand and held it in his lap. "I almost don't know what to say. What she went through is so unreal . . . and the fact that this entire part of her life was hidden all these years." He brought her hand to his lips and gently rested a kiss on her skin.

"She was so courageous, Drew. Just reading her story has already healed my heart in so many ways—ways in which I didn't even realize I was hurting. She had such a beautiful outlook on focusing on the gifts of life rather than on what was stolen. She relied on God to heal her hurts, and He did. He was faithful. It was obvious because even I judged her as not understanding loss and sadness, but the truth is, she knew better than anyone. She didn't want all she had learned and overcome through her struggle to die along with her.

"As I read her journals, I began to change, and my eyes opened to truth about my own life that I had refused to see before. I felt the fear sliding away from me. I began to release what I'd pent up inside: grief . . . fear . . . loneliness . . . rejection. I handed them all over and allowed God to give me something better just like Ada said to do.

"Grandmother gave me such a gift, Drew. She gave me the courage to say yes to love even though I've had to say good-bye to my mother and to her.

"And I know that God stirred your heart to come out here. He led you here. I could hardly believe my eyes when I saw you step out of your truck. I had just finished reading her journals today and had tried to call you several times. I was planning on calling Uncle Henry and having him bring you out here with him. But God was one step ahead of me." She lifted her face toward his, her eyes glowing.

"God was definitely one step ahead of us both," he said. "I still think you calling Henry and having him come out here is a good idea. I mean . . . I'm sure you've still got many questions."

"I do. I wonder if he and Amelia could come out here in the morning. It's too late for them to make the trip now. It's getting so close to suppertime. I think I'll give him a ring and see what he says." Eliza rose and headed for the hallway with the phone table.

"Uncle Henry," she said the moment she heard his voice on the other end.

"Eliza . . . good to hear your voice, dear. How are you?"

"I'm doing really well. Thank you for helping Drew get out here. I'm glad to see him. I finished the journals, and I've got so many questions for you."

There was a long silence before she heard him take a deep breath and clear his throat.

"Will you come here, Uncle Henry? I want to know more. I don't want to leave until we have time to talk here at the ranch. Grandmother said she had several items in the closet. I was hoping you could go through them with me."

"Of course. I'll pack up and leave first thing in the morning. How does that sound?"

"Perfect. I can't wait to see you. Thank you."

"My honor. Love you and see you tomorrow. Bye, dear."

Eliza rounded the corner to tell Drew. "He's driving out in the morning. In the meantime, let's take a walk before supper."

"Sounds perfect." Drew stood and followed her to the door. "Thank you for allowing me to be here with you." Drew looked into Eliza's eyes, and her body responded as they walked hand in hand toward the river down the footpath.

Biting her lip, she said, "I owe you an apology."

"I'm not sure I understand."

"I pulled your heart in a tug-of-war with mine. I wasn't fair to you."

"Eliza, you . . ."

"Please let me finish." She stopped and touched his arm. "I wish my words could tell you how much I appreciate you and respect you. Over and over again you chose me even when I didn't seem to care, even when I've been an unrecognizable mess. You saw me and loved me regardless.

"Sitting upstairs these last few days I realized I had nothing to be afraid of with you. When you told me you loved me, you meant it, but I couldn't trust it until now. Not until I learned what all my grandmother went through. She lived the definition of love. I can't believe I lived with her all those years, and I never saw her pain. That's because she believed God and gave Him the chance to write a new story on her heart. Instead of retreating into her shell, she ran to Him, and He carried her. I want that . . . I want that for myself. If God is willing to do that for her, then I believe He is willing to do it for me.

"Do you remember how I told you I heard the verse 'Be still and know that I am God' when I felt like I was having a breakdown at my mother's house?"

Drew nodded, his eyes transfixed on her.

"That verse, that very same verse, is the one my grandmother tucked in her heart when her mother and sister died. It's the verse she clung to when her father died. God knew that and He knew what she had written and He brought it to me." Eliza's voice trembled with excitement.

"It freed me. I could feel it in my heart and in my body. He freed me, Drew. And then I gave over all the ugly stuff clinging to me and dumped it in His hands. When I turned my hands over, I could feel a warmth come upon me and then I knew . . . I knew that He sees me, loves me, and cares for me. I'm so grateful He didn't give up on me because now my heart gets to love you without all that fear, rejection, and grief. My heart is free!"

Drew swept her up in his arms and caressed her lips with his before placing her gently back on the ground. Standing in his shadow, Eliza's heart settled and she leaned close to him. The crickets around them began to sing as the sun faded quietly behind the hills. The cool of the evening emerged, and they stood touching, listening, allowing their hearts to speak to each other in the silence.

CHAPTER THIRTY-ONE

ELIZA SLEPT PAST HER USUAL MORNING wake-up time and was shocked to see the clock read 10:00. Jumping out of bed, she pulled on a pair of capris, tied an oxford shirt at her waist, and slung a light sweater over her shoulders.

After washing and rubbing cream on her face, she noticed her hair needed attention. A few quick brushstrokes and some bobby pins made her presentable. She dabbed a bit of blush on her cheeks and walked down the stairs.

She couldn't hear much coming from the kitchen and wondered where everyone was. Rounding the corner, she saw Carmen quietly patting out tortillas and humming softly to herself.

"Good morning," Eliza said gently, hating to interrupt her solitude.

"Buenos dîas, Mija. So glad to see you get such good rest. Here . . . I have some hot coffee still waiting for you. Would you like me to make you some eggs? I can heat the griddle quickly?"

"Sounds delicious, thank you. Where is everyone?" Eliza asked as she let the steam from her coffee waft over her face while the heat from the cup warmed her hands.

"Well, Señor Drew was up early so he went with Juan Carlos to look at the ranch and help let out the goats. It's such a pretty day. He wanted to see some of the land while you were still sleeping."

"I can't believe I slept so late," Eliza said, setting her coffee on the table.

"We all were so glad you did. Drew tells me Henry and Amelia are coming, yes?"

Eliza nodded. "Yes. I finished the journals yesterday, and I still have a lot of questions I want to ask him. This has been a beautiful, amazing surprise. My heart is really full in a sweet way with all that my grandmother shared. She was even more exceptional than I ever realized."

"Yes, she was. I'm so happy you have heard her love through all of this. It was not easy for her to share her past. She prayed very hard that you would take all that she had and let it heal you and help you grow you. I think I see that her prayers have been answered." Carmen blew a kiss toward heaven.

"Her prayers and mine have truly been answered." Eliza turned when she heard footsteps mounting the back stairs. Drew opened the screen door followed by Juan Carlos.

"Good morning, sunshine." Drew leaned in and kissed Eliza on the cheek. "It's good to see this fresh air helped you sleep so well."

"I was a little shocked when I woke up and realized what time it was. I hadn't planned on sleeping so late. And if I know Uncle Henry, he probably packed the car yesterday and left at the first sign of daylight. They'll be here any minute."

"Wonderful," Carmen said. "Perfect timing for lunch. Go enjoy the rest of the morning while I work in here. I'll have a nice big lunch ready for everyone by noon."

Standing up, Eliza nodded and pushed in her chair. "Great idea, and thank you for all you do, Carmen." She turned to Drew. "Do you want to walk a little along the road before they get here?"

"Sounds perfect." Drew smiled and reached for Eliza's hand.

Right before they set out on their walk, Eliza heard the grinding of a car's wheels as it crushed the dirt road underneath its treads.

"I think they're here already." She strained to look past the trees. As soon as she did, she spotted the hood of Henry's Wagoneer rounding the corner. "That's them!" Eliza flung her arm in the air and started waving as her feet flew down the steps.

When Henry stepped out of the car, she threw her arms around him. Embracing one another, joy and tears overflowed. Both overcome with emotion, they held each other while Eliza wept.

"I hardly know what to say, Uncle Henry. It's been so emotional and unbelievable these past few days." She looked up at her uncle and noticed tears brimming in his eyes.

"And I'm looking forward to hearing all you have to say." He hugged her once more before they walked toward the house.

"Drew, good to see you." Henry patted Drew on the arm as he stepped onto the porch.

"Good to see you, too, sir."

"I take it your surprise arrival went well?"

"So far, so good." He grinned.

Eliza held the door open for Amelia. "Maybe we could sit in here before lunch and visit?" Eliza's voice was soft but laced with excitement.

Henry led Amelia to the armchair by the fireplace before settling into the chair next to her. Eliza patted the cushion next to her on the sofa for Drew. She rubbed her hands together waiting for everyone to get settled.

A sea of questions swirled in her mind. She found it hard to focus on just one. Leaning her arms forward on her knees, she rattled off several inquiries, never pausing until Henry gently put up his hand to signal for her to take a breath.

"It's a lot of new information to process, Eliza, and your grandmother did a wonderful job."

"She did." She smiled and took a deep breath. She felt Drew's hand upon her back, rubbing her gently as she reached to wipe away the few quick tears forming. "Please tell me what you remember."

"We could be here the rest of the week," Uncle Henry replied as he folded his hands in front of him, looking away before continuing.

As Henry seemed to relax into his chair, Eliza scooted closer to Drew who placed his arm around her shoulders. She listened as Henry's words began to paint the memories.

"The only thing I know about the massacre is what Dusky wrote. We received word close to Christmas that a night raid had taken place. My parents and Roberto were executed in front of everyone. We had no way of knowing more than that. We tried to connect with other workers at the hacienda, but we had no luck. It was painful to keep trying; it was nothing but dead ends."

"What ever happened to the hacienda?"

Amelia and Henry exchanged looks, and Amelia reached for his hand across the arm of the chair.

"We went back," he began, "about seventeen years ago to see what had become of the land and my family home. To say it was difficult would be an understatement. We followed the same roads that led out to the hacienda and could see its walls in the distance. As we got closer we could see the extensive damage time and neglect had brought. Parts of the original facade remained while others had crumbled into a heap of rock. Vines and shrubbery had overgrown much of what was left. We entered through the main entrance and could see some farmers with their families still living among the ruins. None of us could stop the tears.

"I feared for Dusky, but she was strong, determined to find what had been hidden and bring it back with us. We made our way to what was left of the main house and knocked on the door. A housekeeper cautiously answered, and we explained the reason for our visit. She agreed to let us in, and we walked through the overgrown gardens. We could see parts of the old fountain still standing, and the large courtyard that once hosted dances and parties was cracked and lifeless. It was haunting really. It was in complete disrepair, but somehow that seemed to make it easier to accept in a strange way.

"We had the driver take us down to the river. Dusky and I searched through the overgrowth for the small caves where we knew Father and Roberto had hidden several cases of personal items. The river had changed course. It wasn't easy, but we did find the caves. Inside we found all the old crates and asked the driver to carry them out to the car. Some were filled with old, rotted business papers, and others with linens, silver, and jewelry. We repacked what we could salvage and left the rest.

"As we drove past the hacienda, we said our final good-byes and rode in silence. It was similar to visiting a graveyard—nothing was pleasant about it, but we didn't expect it to be. We both wanted to see what had become of our home and find what had been left in the caves.

"Mexico had changed much after we left. Our hearts broke over her battled land that was torn apart and the many who lost loved ones."

"What about Gustavo? Did you ever see him again?" Eliza softly interjected as she watched Henry's gaze on clasped hands.

"Sadly, no I did not see him again, but we wrote letters back and forth frequently. He made a new life for himself in France with Isabella and did quite well. He wanted to come to Texas to visit but never quite made it. He died about fifteen years before Dusky passed. He did have several children, and I hope to keep contact with them and perhaps visit them one day."

Eliza tilted her head to one side. "How come after going back you all felt like you still couldn't share your story?"

Clearing his throat he answered, "Too much time had passed. Obviously, we were no longer in physical danger, but there was a danger of losing our hearts again. Dusky feared Hope would be angry with her or it would cause her pain, and besides, there was something sacred about our silence. We became protective of what we had all been through. It seemed easier to make a new life rather than try to remake the one that was lost.

"Time allowed your grandmother to love again, and she wasn't willing dampen her love with Timothy by recreating the past. It was not an easy decision to stay silent. In the beginning, we were forced to stay silent simply out of the need for preservation, but after a decade we chose it.

"Just like love, it, too, will always be a choice, Eliza. No matter where you are or what you are doing, the choice to love is there. It comes at a cost, no doubt. But to live and not love is a much higher price to pay than to love and love well."

"You're so right. I didn't see it, but now I do." She turned and smiled at Drew.

Henry stood and reached for Amelia. "It smells like lunch is almost ready. Shall we freshen up before we eat?"

"Of course," Eliza said, jumping up off the sofa. "I'm so sorry the minute you all got here all I could think of was talking."

"I understand. We were just as eager to talk to you." Uncle Henry winked. "Excuse us while we freshen up. We'll be back down in time for lunch."

Eliza hugged Amelia as Drew moved to help Henry with his bag. Henry put up his hand before Drew could carry it up the stairs. "Please, you and Eliza visit. We've got the bags. There's not much to carry."

"Yes sir." Drew released his grip on the leather handle and set the bag on the floor. "Eliza, you want to finish our walk we started earlier?"

"Great idea." Eliza wove her way through the living room furniture and walked toward the front door. "Let's go down to the heart rock garden Carmen was telling me about. Want to?"

Drew nodded, holding the door for her.

Arm in arm they took the path that led away from the front of the house toward the east side. The trees and shrubbery had grown over the little gravel path, but Eliza knew she was going the right way. Finally, the brush cleared and a small garden nestled along a slow trickle of water opened up before them with a tiny bench situated on the edge.

"How sweet! Look at all the rocks stacked over here. They're all in the shape of hearts." Eliza picked one up. As she rose to show him, Drew placed his hand over hers.

"I've got something to show you first."

Eliza's eyes locked on his as he pulled a small velvet box from his pocket. Steadying the box in his palm, he opened its cover before her and knelt to the ground.

"Eliza Cullen, will you marry me?"

She gasped and covered her mouth with her hand. His eyes shone with love, and it seemed as if they breathed as one. Trembling, her legs grew weak beneath her. She bent down to him and cupped his face in her hands.

"Yes . . . yes, I'll marry you and love you for the rest of our lives." She held her breath as Drew placed the ring on her left finger and kissed her hand.

"This ring belonged to your grandmother. Henry gave it to me before I drove out here. I wanted his permission to marry you, and he asked if I would like to propose with this ring that I believe was your grandmother's wedding ring . . . from Roberto."

"Oh, Drew! It's stunning . . . so gorgeous." She caressed his face almost tumbling into him. He caught her as she fell on top of him. Laughing, they held each other as they lay on the ground. "I love you."

"I love you too, Eliza."

What grief had tried to separate, love had woven together. Her heart was home. Change happens, but a heart filled with love is steadfast because love never fails.

Connect with the Author at:
www.ashleekinsel.com